Break out of the Darkness

Dave & Lynn
Two Special
& wonderful People's
Best Wishes
Linda &
Thomas Mittner
"2001

Break out of
the Darkness

Linda Thomas Mittner

Writers Club Press
San Jose New York Lincoln Shanghai

Break out of the Darkness

Writers Club Press
an imprint of iUniverse.com, Inc.

For information address:
iUniverse.com, Inc.
5220 S 16th, Ste. 200
Lincoln, NE 68512
www.iuniverse.com

ISBN: 0-595-18702-1

Printed in the United States of America

DEDICATION

First I would love to thank God, and my spiritual guides and angels, for their never-ending inspirational guidance, and everlasting spiritual love!

With All My Love, Dedication, And Gratitude, To My Wonderful Husband And Kids

Tom

Nichole

Melissa

Tommy

And Taylor Lynn

With Love To…Leo, Sophie, Kathy, and Robert…Our Parents

FOREWORD

Why does abuse happen? One cannot provide a singular explanation for the burning rage that lives deep within an abuser's soul. Katie Connor, a sweet, caring teenage girl, would soon learn of the rage firsthand. The safe and loving world created by her family would soon collapse.

Her trouble starts when Katie, just sweet sixteen, begins dating Danny Jenkins, a boy she met at school. At first he was the perfect gentleman, but his true nature soon surfaced. The relationship turns to sheer horror for Katie as she experiences the unspeakable side of Danny's obsessive rage. Threats against her family, among other reasons, coerce her into staying with him. Katie becomes his target, caught in a web of violence. Feeling like a trapped animal trying desperately to escape Danny vows he will kill her first if she ever decides to leave him.

Eventually, this pattern leads to an abusive marriage. After years of desperation, hope arrives in the form a kind, handsome young man named Eric Sommers. An explosive love affair with him changes her life forever!

Will Katie get out of Danny's stronghold grip, finally breaking free? Will she risk her life for her one true love? Perhaps Danny will stop Katie dead in her tracks, or vice versa! Only a twist of fate will decide it all, in this intriguing novel of courage and strength, and the "journey of life" our paths can lead us through called, the "Human Spirit."

PREFACE

---

*Every 9 seconds, a woman is being physically or verbally abused

About 1 in 4 women is likely to be abused by a partner in her lifetime! But because battering is not usually reported until it reaches life-threatening proportions, the actual number of families affected could be estimated that one of every two women, will be abused at some point in their lifetime.

ACKNOWLEDGEMENTS

A Special Thank You To:

Jeanne Diehl
Christian LoGrasso (front and back cover)
Barb Gill
Trae Roberts
Keith Kozlowski and Jenny Desiderio

PROLOGUE

While walking silently down the hall, the plush rug pressing softly against my bare feet, I squinted my eyes to see the light ahead, the distance doubling with every step I took. My heart thudded faster as I heard the thundering steps approaching me from behind. Tears welled up in my eyes as I raced down the hall, my breathing reduced to rapid starts and stops. Steps echoed behind me, as I turned to see a vicious smile across the face of the beast that lunged toward me as I ran. He knocked me down and forcefully got on top. The drool slid from the beast's mouth as it dripped onto my face.

I could smell the dry odor permeating from the demon's hot, decaying breath. Its eyes glowed like the embers from a dying fire. A hand gripped my throat as I tried to scream. The beast's other hand was raised far above his head and landed on me with a force that rattled my teeth. Tears burst from my now bloodshot eyes while his fist was, once again, brought forcefully down onto my stomach. I gagged, as the beast howled with glee.

I suddenly awoke in a pool of sweat, shivering, as the image of the nightmare faded, too slowly. Quietly, I slid to the edge of the bed and put on my slippers. The cool evening air chilled my perspired face. Walking toward the bathroom I looked back where I just came from, where he lay next to the place I had just been moments before. Again I shuddered. A loud snorting noise carried throughout the hall as the demon, my husband, peacefully slept.

I walked silently into the bathroom fumbling for the light switch. The light glared so brightly I had to squint. Partially shielding my eyes with my arm, I stared at the twenty-three year old in the mirror, examining the darkening bruise under my left eye.

My body was throbbing uncontrollably as I reached for the knob in the shower. As the water streamed out of the nozzle, I slowly began removing my clothes, revealing the bruises on my stomach, a reminder of the horror from the night before. I pulled the towel from the rack and placed it on the floor next to the shower. Stepping into the warm pulsation of water, it immediately soothed me as the water massaged my back. A stream of salty tears began to slide down my face. I was careful not to cry too loud, for I couldn't risk waking him again. My life depended on it! Staying in the shower until my hands and feet became wilted, I reached for the towel. The soft cotton caused me to wince as I tried to blot my throbbing face. My legs could no longer hold the weight of my body as I collapsed into the space between the toilet and the shower. I once again cautiously cried, pulling my legs up toward my chest. A silent fear came over me as I heard my husband roll over in bed. I quietly and quickly put on my sweat-soaked nightgown and tip toed out of the bathroom, turning off the light.

The hallway seemed even colder than the room. Since we lived in a rickety older apartment, I treaded carefully, reaching around for the railing of the stairs. Finally locating it, I began to creep down the steps. A creak ricocheted throughout the house as I placed my entire weight on the fourth step from the top. I immediately froze, my eyes widening, as if I was a deer caught in the blinding light of an oncoming car. Standing still transfixed in fear, waiting until silence again prevailed, I continued my journey downstairs, where I hoped it would be safer. I reached the kitchen and turned on the light. The brightness stunned my eyes, but not as bad as they had in the upstairs bathroom. Walking over to the pantry, I reached inside for a tea bag and placed it gently on the counter. On the cupboard across the room I spotted an inappropriate gift from his mother, a black mug that read "World's Best Husband." Sneering, I retrieved a new more colorful one instead. Careful to remove the boiling water before the whistling started, I poured my tea, sat at the kitchen table and began adding the cream and sugar. Stirring the tea, my mind began to wander. —Back to a time when this all began, and how my days could have slipped away from me, turning my whole life into a living nightmare!

CHAPTER I

It was an eventful day, my sixteenth birthday, and the day our school team; the bears, was playing our rival basketball team, the Warriors. Everyone who attended was on the edge of their seats, because it was such a close game. The word "defense" was echoing off the walls of the auditorium as we jumped to cheer for our team. Following a brief time-out, the players scurried back onto the court for the jump ball.

The referee tossed the ball, and it sailed up into the blinding lights of the gym springing two players into action. A battle took place in mid-air, elbows swinging, causing a Warrior to fall. One of the Bears snatched the ball up and headed toward the basket, firing the shot with three seconds left. Silence filled the stands as the ball sailed through the air. Even the cheerleaders ceased their screams of encouragement at this moment. I dropped my pompons to watch the ball soar right through the basket, causing a loud clanging sound throughout the gym. The player who shot the ball dropped to his knees. Our team had won! We snatched up our pompons and began to perform a victory dance.

A group of us decided to go to the local hangout to celebrate. My friend Karen and I packed up our equipment and walked with the crowd toward the pizza place. As we walked in, the smell of pizza filled the air causing our stomachs to rumble. The pizzeria was filled with kids playing arcade games and popular songs on the jukebox. This place produced so many fond memories for me, yet little did I know how soon, and how completely, they would be overshadowed.

A guy that I've seen around in school, but didn't really meet yet, approached me near the dance floor. He was cute, seemed very nice, and had all the right words to say. I found out from one of my friends that this boy had liked me for a while, and was coming to a lot of our games to watch me cheer. His name was Danny Jenkins. The only thing that my friends were concerned about was the gang of guys he was always hanging out with; they seemed like a very rough crowd. After talking to him I realized he seemed so different and somehow a bit mysterious. Unfortunately, so many girls are drawn to this type of guy.

It started getting late and I had to make sure I was home by curfew. As I was saying goodbye to my friends, Danny asked me very sweetly, if he could walk me home. I hesitated at first, but Karen was giving me this huge smile and the thumbs up sign behind Danny's back. I managed to say yes through our giggles.

As we strolled down the street, Danny asked me where I lived and I told him that I lived on Parkhurst.

"Really," Danny said, "I only live four streets away from you on Hampton Street."

"That's funny" I said, "I've never seen you around here before."

Danny said, "That is probably because I hang around my friends' houses, and they live anywhere but here!"

"What do you mean?" I asked

His only response was that there wasn't enough "action" in this neighborhood, whatever that meant.

I kept silent on the rest of our walk home. Danny broke the silence with a very strange comment. He stopped me, took my hands, and asked me if I hated him. He said, "I mean I never did anything to hurt you, have I?"

At first I was stunned, thinking to myself, "Why would this guy who I hardly even knew ask me such a question?" Quietly, I told him I didn't hate him. "Hate is such a strong emotion and besides I don't hate anyone," shyly adding with my head down, "I really just don't know you yet."

Danny said, "Well, I hope I can change that for you. I really like you Katie, and I think that you are very pretty."

We approached my driveway and Danny walked me up to my back porch, asking if he could please call me. I hesitated, but he assured me he had nothing in mind except to get to know me better. Before I could answer him, he gently placed my face in his hands and gave it a very soft kiss. "I really do like you Katie. Can I call you tomorrow?"

I told him, "Sure, I'll probably see you in school tomorrow."

He kissed my hand, waved goodbye, and walked down the driveway. I smiled and waved back.

The next day in school as I got to my locker, I spotted Danny standing beside it. He had his hands behind his back and a smile a mile wide. "Good morning Katie," he said to me as he offered me, as a sign of his good intentions, a bouquet of red roses.

I was speechless. "Thank you Danny, they're beautiful."

"Not half as beautiful as you are Katie," he said. "Would it be okay if I came to watch you cheer at the game tonight?"

I said, "Sure." He seemed so sweet and so sincere.

Danny, along with a group of his friends showed up at the game. They sat near the cheerleaders. My best friend Heidi and I had been practicing all summer long for a very difficult routine, and of all nights, our coach picked this one to show it off. I was so nervous because Danny was watching my every move. Thankfully, we completed the lift successfully. Danny and his friends stood up, clapped, and cheered us on! It made Heidi and I feel so important.

After the game was over we strolled over to the local hangout. Again, Danny sporting a huge smile, surprised me with yet another dozen red roses. I told him thank you for the flowers, and it was that day that Danny professed his love for me. At this point I was quite smitten by him, and could not find any reason why I shouldn't give this guy a chance. After all, he has been so nice to me. That night, my life changed forever! I would soon find out, it wasn't going to be for the better. My path would lead to a long chain of events, taking me into a destructive and dangerous life style!

As the months passed by, Danny and I became inseparable. His friends would allude to him being henpecked. Those at school who knew of Danny's tough guy reputation said he seemed almost reformed.

One day, Danny decided it was time for me to meet his mother. He was having a party at his house and begged me to come. He said, "I told my mother all about you, and I explained you to her right down to those big beautiful blue eyes and your fragrant long blond hair."

I shyly answered with a yes. How could I resist that?

The night of the party arrived. I was very nervous about meeting his mom, replaying in my head an earlier warning from Steve, one of the guys on the football team. He had told me to be careful of Danny's family. "They are a strange group of people," he warned me.

I wondered to myself how Steve could say such a thing.

When I asked him to elaborate, he explained that his friend Molly was involved with Danny's brother Tim for a while, and it was a horrible experience. "Danny's family isn't normal, she told us, they're very strange."

Politely I interrupted Steve to defend Danny, going on to tell him how sweet he is to me, and that this girl was probably bitter because she got dropped by Tim.

Steve tried to make me listen, but all I said was that I appreciated his concern but this was about Danny, not his brother. Our conversation ended there and I walked away. I just didn't want to hear anything bad about my boyfriend. We have been going around for months now, and we've been getting along great!

Since I only lived a couple of streets away, I walked over to Danny's house. He met me halfway, greeting me with a warm embrace and kiss.

We walked hand in hand to his house, where you could already hear the sounds of a party in progress.

We entered the back door following a couple of unfamiliar, dark haired girls. Naturally I was a bit puzzled when Danny's mother greeted them with a smile, inquiring if one of them was Katie. I wondered, if Danny had explained me to his mother, then why was she asking them if they were me; I have very blond hair. As we approached her holding hands, I smiled and introduced myself. It seemed by her actions, that she took an instant dislike to me. His mother looked down at our clenched hands, then back up; she mumbled hello and walked away. I was mortified! Danny explained to me that his mother was just tired. His reassurance didn't help. I suddenly felt very uncomfortable and uninvited. Then Danny said, "Never mind about my mother" and led me downstairs to where everyone else was.

The room was so filled with smoke that I could barely breathe. I thought it was strange that beer and marijuana were allowed at his house, especially with a parent at home.

As the night dragged on, Danny, who I had never seen drink alcohol, was getting intoxicated. I didn't drink, and I was feeling very uncomfortable. Wanting to leave, I approached Danny to tell him. He had a strange look on his face, especially his eyes; they had this cold, dead glare in them. He insisted that I stay.

I told him that I was leaving and started up the steps.

Danny came after me. He grabbed me by my hair, pulled me back down the stairs, and told me I wasn't going anywhere. I couldn't believe this was happening to me! I completely backed down out of fear and stayed.

The smell of pot was getting stronger and the alcohol was flowing faster. It startled me when someone smashed a beer bottle against the wall. I wondered how Danny's mother could allow this kind of party to go on in her house.

I had enough and was leaving. As I made my way toward the stairs, Danny grabbed me a second time, violently pushing me against a pole. He grabbed my face very tightly in his hand and barked, "Didn't you understand the first time Katie? You are staying here."

I screamed. Never in my whole life have I been so scared! Many questions were flowing through my head. Why didn't his friends stop him? Why didn't his mother hear my screams and come to help me? I felt so trapped and alone. Out of sheer terror I managed to choke out, "Okay," and retreated quietly to the corner, wishing repeatedly that this was only a bad dream. My curfew was eleven o'clock on weekends, so I just sat there and watched the clock. The rest of the night seemed to drag on.

The guests, including Danny, were getting so drunk they began to pass out. I seized the opportunity to get out of there, fast. On my way out I noticed his mother passed out on the couch, a bottle in one hand and a cigarette in the other. No wonder Danny's house was the big hangout. I hesitated, only for a moment, and kept on walking until I reached the safety of my home.

The next morning was Saturday and Danny showed up at my house early, as if nothing happened. Since I was very quiet he asked me what was wrong.

I asked him if he remembered anything from the night before.

He said "No, not too much; I must of passed out."

When I told him what he had done to me, he seemed shocked.

He got down on his knees and apologized countless times, swearing he would never do anything to hurt me, begging for my forgiveness.

I forgave him, believing in his sincerity. That's where my biggest mistake started!

Danny kept his promise for many months and was so sweet and considerate. This was an exciting year, our senior year! I continued cheerleading, with Danny and his friends attending all of my games. They were my own cheerleading section!

The most glorious autumn arrived; how I love the fall. It is such a beautiful time of the year. During this time our friends would all get together at the nearby park. We had a lot of fun walking along the nature trails, jumping into the creek, just acting crazy.

Then one day our outings started to include a new activity. One of the guys brought something called hard cider for us to drink. They mixed it up with kool aid and passed the bottle around. When my turn approached, Danny told me to go ahead and take a swig, it tastes just like apple cider. I was so naive, having no idea it was hard liquor. Every time it came around, I took a sip. Feeling light-headed and sick to my stomach, I realized I was drunk! How I got home that night or how I got into my house without my parents suspecting something is a mystery to me. I do remember the next day having the worst headache and feeling really sick. I asked my mom if I could stay home from school. Of course I told her that maybe I had the flu.

A couple of days passed and we decided to return to the park to meet our friends Karen and Kevin. We always had a lot of fun with them. Danny, once again tried to get me to drink the hard cider. When my turn came I would pretend to drink it, never wanting to have the experience of a hangover again.

Suddenly, Karen and Kevin walked over to the next shelter, apparently fighting. Danny told me to ignore them. Then I saw Kevin push Karen to the ground, and that I just couldn't ignore. Kevin picked her up and they went on to yell obscenities at each other. Then to my surprise, Kevin whacked Karen across the face and threw her over the picnic table. I ran over to help yelling at Kevin to stop! Danny ran after me as drunk as he was, grabbed me and ordered me to stop.

I turned towards him and said "I can't, I've got to help her."

He got that cold glassy look in his eyes, like another evil person took over his body. He grabbed me by my hair with one hand, made a fist with his other, and hit me so hard in the face that I fell to the ground.

I cried. "What did I do to deserve this except to help a friend?"

He said that I didn't follow his orders.

I started to cry, holding my cheek. I looked over toward Kevin and Karen. As fast as their fight had begun, they were making up even faster lavishing in an embrace. They were kissing and hugging as if nothing happened.

Danny decided not to stop with one whack at me. He pulled me by my legs over toward the edge of the rocks overlooking the waterfalls. I was screaming for him to stop, as the gravel was tearing at my skin while he dragged me closer and closer to the edge of the falls! He scooped me up and held my face down over the cliff's edge, telling me that is where I'd end up some day if I ever decided to disobey him. He wouldn't stop until he knew I was frightened enough to believe him.

I cried as I again gave in and told him what he wanted to hear. As if nothing happened, we walked back to the shelter. He put his arm around me and said "I love you Katie and no one will ever split us up."

I just couldn't understand this kind of controlling love. His interpretation of love is not what I was raised to believe and yes, I was stupid for staying with him, but I was just a teenager who was just plain scared!

CHAPTER 2

Looking back on my childhood, I recall both of my parents working. We came from a big family, five girls and twin boys. Every week we would all go to church, my parents walking down the aisle proudly followed by a procession of their seven prides and joys. My dad was very active in the church, doing Gospel readings and playing the organ for the church choir.

Our Christmases were, and still are, so festive and memorable. We would all gather around the organ and sing, as my dad played countless Christmas tunes. We just couldn't get enough of the carols. My life was wonderfully enriched with a lot of love, good values and respect.

My mom worked as a nurse and my sister Cindy and I would volunteer for whatever was needed. We would also visit with the elderly who for whatever reason, had no one left in the whole world to visit them. All these things are what love is all about. But it was also my downfall in my crusade to help others that Danny took advantage of my good nature to fuel his evil!

Winter arrived and I looked forward to the holidays, my favorite time of year. Even during this festive time, Danny's mother still kept her distance from me. Tim told me that their mother was jealous of mine and Danny's relationship. It was quite obvious that Danny was definitely a mama's boy, as some of our future fights were a direct result of her.

When I met Danny's father for the first time, it was quite unsettling. Although he seemed charming and pleasant, there was definitely a chill in the room that surrounded the family as we sat there in silence. Later I found out from Tim that although his parents slept in the same bed and lived in the same house, they never uttered as much as a word to each other.

His dad seemed to like me though, that Christmas day back in 1979. It was the first Christmas they can remember that he ever opened gifts with them right on Christmas day. Usually it was sometime in February that he'd get around to his. His sister Debbie told me I was the cause for this. All I did was hand him my gift and he went on to open the rest of the family's gifts too! Unfortunately it was the one and only Christmas he did this; and it wasn't long afterwards, that Danny's father ditched all of them for another woman.

For our first Christmas together, Danny gave me a huge stuffed giraffe, which reached all the way up to my neck. Around its neck was an adorable birthstone necklace. I got Danny a new leather coat, knowing he thought they were really cool.

I felt I had finally tamed the beast! Even thought he was thought of in school by some of his peers as the cool tough guy, in my own mind I thought that I changed that a little bit. But unbeknownst to me, it would end up being disastrous and hopeless.

CHAPTER 3

My birthday was in March and I was about to celebrate my eighteenth birthday.

Danny decided to fix me a fancy dinner. He was a fantastic cook, a result of his part-time job in a high-class restaurant. I decided to try a baked Alaska recipe, which I learned how to prepare in Home Economics Class. The whole dinner turned out great! I was really pleased with it. For my birthday Danny bought me a really pretty birthstone ring, which he placed on my finger, and afterwards, we just stayed in and watched television. Again, Danny was so sweet and caring to me that night.

The following day, Sunday, we decided to go to the park with a group of our friends. It was fun sledding down the hills, peaked with new fallen snow. There was a touch of warmth in the air; you knew spring was imminent.

Of course the guys brought the hard cider to keep them warm, so they said. All I knew was I did not want any. Danny kept trying to persuade me to drink it. "Come on have some" he said, his voice changing to a more harsher tone.

I told him no, that I didn't like it and to stop asking me.

He got so mad at me for disobeying him he yanked my hair back really hard, which jolted my head backward. He started to pour the gallon of cider over my face, laughing at me while saying, "You're such a pussy Katie."

The cider stung my eyes and I begged him to stop. It seemed that the more I pleaded with Danny, the more he enjoyed torturing me. I finally pushed his hands up and away from my face, and he knocked me off the bench. Afterwards, he started to kick me repeatedly. I begged him to stop, as tears streamed down my face. The finale was one swift hard kick to my back. I felt like a punching bag, lying there defenseless until our friends returned from their walk.

Two of the guys grabbed Danny and sat him down at a picnic bench, asking him what his problem was. Their voices went in one ear and out the other. He was so drunk that his head just bobbed around. Eventually, he fell asleep in that spot.

I could hardly get up, my whole body hurt. My two friends came over to help me. Heather asked me if I was all right and said, "Katie, I think you should get rid of Danny before he kills you!" They just hugged me because I couldn't even talk; I was shaking and I just wanted to go home. I had to compose myself to do some soul searching. Heather offered to give me a ride, but I told her I needed to walk. The park was about an hour from my house. I said goodbye to my friends and left Danny asleep at the table.

About halfway into my journey home, a car slowly pulled up behind me, sending a cold, eerie chill up my spine. When I heard the constant blowing of the horn, I knew it was Danny.

He pulled up right next to me and shouted, "Get your ass in this car Katie."

I kept on walking, trying not to acknowledge him. He quickly pulled the car a few yards ahead of me and got out in a seething rage.

I started to run pleading with him to leave me alone.

He grabbed me by my coat, dragged me to the car, and pushed me in. While his hands clawed at my throat, he pulled my face right up to his and devilishly whispered, "You will never tell me to leave you alone, never!"

I gagged, as he squeezed my throat tighter demanding an answer. I was scared, just barely catching my breath, but I managed to nod my head.

He released the grip of his hands from my throat. "What was that Katie? I only heard those marbles shaking around in your head."

Coughing, I said "Yes."

"Yes what Katie," he asked again.

"Yes, I will listen to whatever you tell me Danny."

I was silent for most of the way home. Danny had a sickening content smile on his face, which made me cower with fear. Staring out the window, I silently wept. He dropped me off at my house. Like a zombie, I got out of the car, not even acknowledging his good-byes. I went into the front door without looking back and heard the engine race as the car squealed away.

When I finally got into bed, Danny continually called me on the phone. The sound of his voice stirred a sickness inside me. By midnight I took the phone off the hook so my family wouldn't know what was happening.

The next morning I had to force myself out of bed to face another day. I decided to walk to school with all my friends for added protection. About halfway to school, Danny pulled up next to us, laying on the horn demanding I get in. Managing to hold my ground, I was silently thinking he wouldn't do anything with my friends around. I was right; he sped away leaving skid marks all the way down the street. When my friends questioned his behavior and called him a jerk, I shrugged my shoulders and kept on walking.

Just as I suspected, Danny was waiting for me at the school entrance, firing questions about why the phone was off the hook and how dare I ignore him.

I shouted that I took the phone off the hook and I wanted him to leave me alone for good; it was over! I turned to walk away and he pleaded with me to stay, as he repeatedly said he was sorry. I just turned around and ran to my class.

That day I received over 20 letters of apology, describing ways he wanted to make it up to me and how it would never happen again. I threw all of them into the garbage, having no desire to be with Danny anymore. I had to tell him that it was over for good.

After school the next day he hunted me down, again begging me to reconsider my decision. I coldly let him know I thought we should go our separate ways, and left him standing there with that cold look in his eyes that I was so familiar with.

It was a fairly quiet evening. My parents were at a school meeting with a teacher. Just as I was beginning to relax, the ring of the phone startled me. It was Danny. Telling him there was nothing else to discuss, and that it was over, I hung up on him. I went on to do some homework, although I couldn't concentrate. I fell asleep not wanting to have to think about the situation that I was in.

Around 6:30 p.m., my sister Cindy woke me up, saying that there was someone in the driveway laying on the horn. My body immediately froze.

I peered out the window to see Danny and another guy in the car. He was shouting, "Katie, get your ass out here right now!"

My sister begged me not to go, but Danny was now at the door pounding on it, telling me to get outside. Even thought I was terrified I obeyed, feeling like I could get this settled so that he would leave me alone for good. As I stepped outside my sister followed; Danny told her that we needed to talk alone.

Cindy glaring at Danny said, "If you hurt my sister you're going to regret it." She turned and walked back into the house.

Danny again said the same things he had been saying since I first told him it was over. I stared at him blankly and tried to tune out his voice, as he told me how much he loved me, and how he couldn't live without me, and how he needed another chance.

I told him that there would be no more chances, and that we both needed to get on with our lives! That cold glare gazed over his eyes as he asked me if I knew who was in the car with him.

I looked over, not recognizing the face.

"Ricky Ravin," Danny said.

I surely knew the name, and it was one that sent a chill down my spine. He was in and out of jail for many offenses, his most recent for assaulting a police officer.

Danny snickered and said, "He's here to help you change your mind."

"What do you mean?" I asked.

Danny told me that if I didn't go back with him, Ricky would come out of the car and stab my sister while I watched. He then sneered, adding that all it would cost him would be a couple bags of weed. He then told me I had ten seconds to decide, and began counting down.

As I observed my sisters looking out the window, I hung on to my decision to break it off. Cindy told me to come inside, as Danny motioned to Ricky to come out of the car. Ricky opened the car door and started walking toward us. I noticed the silver gleam of the knife in his left hand, and looked at my sister Cindy standing on the porch. I yelled, "Fine Danny, you win. I'll go back with you!" While Cindy kept begging me to come in, my sister Chrissy called the police.

Danny ordered Ricky back into the car, the same demonic smile appearing on his face. He knew he had won again. Danny gave me a kiss and uttered, "I knew that you really loved me Katie." He hopped back in the car and left.

By the time the police arrived, Danny and Ricky were gone. I had nothing much to say to the police except that I had a misunderstanding with my boyfriend. I was so scared fearing if I said anything else, Danny would have someone I loved hurt. I can't believe Danny got even dirtier, in his game plan to keep me under his control.

My sister Cindy was a lot stronger than I was. Since she heard the conversation between Danny and me, she told me that I need to get out of the relationship, and that I should have told the police what really happened.

I found myself making excuses for Danny's behavior, explaining to Cindy how most of his family are abusive alcoholics, and how Danny has become just like them. He was capable of doing anything because he feels he has nothing to lose. As for my decision to stand my ground that night and dump Danny, we undoubtedly would have been purchasing a coffin that evening. I guess I just couldn't chance it!

I made everyone promise not to tell our parents about the circumstances of that night. I couldn't even imagine what my parents would have done; but now I realize whatever it was could have only benefited me.

That night preparing for bed, I stayed in the bathroom scrubbing my lips until they bled, wiping Danny's dirty lingering kiss off of me. Disgusted and degraded, I was wishing the water could wash him off me completely.

The next day a florist truck pulled up to our house and a guy came to the door, delivering a dozen red roses for a Katie Conner. After taking them in, I opened the little card that read "Forever yours, sorry about our little misunderstanding, Love Danny." I threw the card and the roses in the garbage. I started to hate the beautiful flower, the red rose, the same one I always used to admire.

Danny called that afternoon to tell me he was stopping over. He asked me if I liked the roses.

I just told him, "Yes, thank you."

He continued to say that he'd be over soon.

My good friend Marilyn was over at my house and I confided to her everything that was going on.

She told me she was scared for me, and that I had to do something about Danny.

I explained it was easier said than done, no one seemed to under-stand how my hands are tied. I just felt so helplessly alone.

After Marilyn left, Danny arrived and couldn't have been more apologetic. I led him downstairs into my basement because I didn't want anyone to hear us. He cried, telling me how he didn't know why he does those things to me, and how he can't imagine his life without me.

Danny asked me out to dinner and a movie, if I felt up to it. Cautiously, I accepted his invitation. Afterwards, we decided to take a ride to the beach. It was a beautiful night and we strolled hand in hand along the sand. We stopped for a moment and he pulled me down with him in the sand. The mood was set right and I was very nervous. What did he expect of me? I knew that I wasn't ready for sex yet. My feelings for Danny were all mixed up. I knew in my heart I could never really be in love with him.

While we were lying in the sand, with the full moon beaming brightly overhead, he started to kiss me. I wanted to turn my head, for it was starting to be obvious to me that I didn't want Danny near me. Hating his touch next to my skin, his breath near my face, the way his whole essence just turned my stomach. He continued anyway, kissing me harder. Slowly, he ran his hands up and down my body, surprisingly gentle, telling me how much he loved me.

As he started to pull my skirt off, I froze. I just couldn't do it because I wasn't ready yet. I grabbed my skirt and pulled it back up to my waist.

He told me, "Don't do that, it will be okay."

I told him that if he really loved me he would wait until I was ready. To my surprise he agreed, so we just sat there looking up at the stars.

CHAPTER 4

After a couple of weeks went by, I thought that the bad days were behind us. I was doing great in school, and Heidi my cheerleading sister and I were having so much fun. We had learned so many new cheers for our homecoming game.

Heidi didn't like Danny. She knew some of what was going on between us, and said that I could do better than a jerk who treats me bad.

Heidi was dating one of the top jocks of the football team, Mike Patterson, and she wanted to set me up with his friend Greg, who also played football. They were the two most popular, most handsome guys in school. Heidi told me that Greg already liked me.

I responded that "I'm already in a relationship with Danny."

Heidi said, "Why would you choose that creep Danny, over a chance to be with a great guy like Greg?"

I rationalized saying, "No one understands him like I do. He had a really rough life growing up with alcoholic parents and an abusive father." Danny told me the whole story one night, as he broke down and cried.

"Danny's father, John Jenkins, was truly a sick man. His father liked to torture Danny's mother. Early into their marriage he'd beat her, and if that weren't enough, he'd beat on the kids too. They have three kids, two boys and one girl. When they were little, Danny's father would punish them in strange ways. He would make them light matches, not allowing them to blow them out, until it burnt their little fingers. He'd repeatedly make them sleep in the bathtub with no pillows, blankets, or towels. They would get beat with belt buckles and numerous other objects, causing Danny to have a chipped front tooth from one of these episodes.

Danny's mother just turned to the bottle for comfort, and overlooked all the abuse their father made them endure. If a mood set him off, he would put a bar of soap in their mouths and tape them up with duct tape, sometimes for an hour at a time. He was heartless and cruel.

As if that wasn't enough, Danny was particularly ashamed that his father sexually molested their sister Debbie, and not just once, but countless times. Danny said that once, he and his brother Tim witnessed one of the episodes. One day they were playing hide and seek in the basement, and decided to hide, when they heard Danny's father and Debbie come down the stairs. The basement door slammed shut as he was pushing Debbie down the steps, telling her to shut her mouth. He threw her little body onto the couch and started to unzip his pants, ordering Debbie to take off her skirt and underwear. Then he just rammed his body on top of hers and proceeded to rape her. She wept so silently, they barely heard her plead for him to stop. He slapped her across the face and told her to shut up when he would hear her whimpering. Her tears seemed to form huge puddles, almost as big as her whole body, as she did what she was told to do.

Danny and Tim watched on with anger and fear, wanting to kill their father. Since they were only nine and ten years old at the time, all they could do was just watch in horror. Tim and Danny were scared, wishing to help Debbie, and Timmy started to whimper himself.

When his father was finished, he walked right over to where they were hiding, and with a big grin on his face he said, "I know that you two boys were watching us. I hope you enjoyed it. I know your sister did, all girls do. Maybe you learned something today boys, but just make sure you keep this little episode to yourselves, if you know what's good for you. Understand!"

They were both so scared they just nodded their heads.

He tucked his shirt back into his pants and walked slowly up the stairs. He then paused for another moment, looked back and said to them, "That's the only free show you get." Smugly smiling, he continued back up the steps.

When they knew the coast was clear, the boys hurried over to Debbie. She was lying on the couch lifeless, with a blank stare on her face. They helped her get dressed as they all hugged each other, and broke down and cried. It was on that day that Danny said aloud, "I am gonna kill him someday!"

Debbie became impregnated with her own father's child at the age of fifteen. It was a little baby girl, who was quickly given up for adoption. Keeping his own dirty secret, Danny's father was the first to tell everyone that it was his daughter's punishment for being a tramp. He referred to her as a bad seed."

Heidi interrupted me, "What was Danny's mother doing when all of this was going on?" I told her that she was usually passed out cold, after she'd had one too many drinks. Danny refers to his mom as a victim too.

Heidi replied, "I think that she was selfish and a failure to her own kids for turning to the bottle, instead of her obligation to her own children! It can happen to you too Katie, if you don't get out of this relationship. I feel really bad for how they were raised, no child should have to withstand such abuse, but Katie wake up, Danny is just like his father!"

Now Heidi was even more intent on making me break it off with Danny. She was afraid that the history of Danny's family would repeat itself. Again, I somehow felt sorry for Danny, and tried to make Heidi understand that I thought I could really help him.

CHAPTER 5

That week we were invited to a friend's party. I remember walking into a smoke filled room, with the strong smell of pot permeating the air. I felt so out of place, not wanting to try it. Danny kept on insisting, "It will relax you." Obviously he didn't get relaxed enough, because he started shouting at me, "You jerk, just take a puff," as he practically shoved the pot down my throat. I cried and begged for him to stop, but pleading wouldn't help. When I stood my ground, he grabbed me by my arms and through the crowd of doped up bodies, dragged me upstairs to a room with black lights and the smell of incense burning. He pinned me down and raped me that night. It was all such a blur. Nobody responded to any of my screams. The loud music is forever etched in my mind. Years later, I still get flashbacks listening to one of those songs.

I remember scratching his face with my nails, pleading for him to stop. He completely overpowered me, slapping my face to quiet me. He ripped off my clothes and forced himself on me. All I can remember is that it hurt so badly, I couldn't wait until it was over. How can someone who tells you they love you violate you so cruelly? When he was finished, he ordered me to get dressed and go home, then proceeded back downstairs. He had ripped my shirt and broke the zipper on my jeans. How could I go home and explain this?

As I came back downstairs, my friend Karen saw me. She already had been having sex with her boyfriend Kevin, so one look at my ripped clothes and running eye makeup and she knew what had happened. She came over to me and hugged me as I cried on her shoulder. She, who was always fighting with her boyfriend, told me that she felt sorry for me, but that it won't hurt as much the next time. I stopped crying and said, "There will never be a next time!"

Just as I uttered those words, someone whacked me on the back. The force of it told me it was Danny. He pulled me by my shirt and said that we were going.

Karen gave me a kiss on the cheek and said goodbye.

I was very quiet in the car. Danny had overheard my conversation and demanded, "What do you mean there won't be a next time? You know you loved it! All girls do they just can't admit it."

I was so afraid to say a word, and became increasingly sick to my stomach just thinking about him touching me again.

Later on that night the telephone started ringing, and it was Danny. I instinctively hung up on him. This continued into the night until I took the phone off the hook. I was awakened at 2:30 a.m. by a car revving its engine in front of our driveway.

Danny shouted, "Katie, get out here now." When I didn't respond, he peeled out of the driveway only to return every ten minutes and do the same thing all over again. I don't know why nobody heard him, especially after he smashed into a parked car across the street. Afterwards, he took off and didn't come back.

Later on the next day, one of my brother's friends Billy told him that he saw the scene that Danny made, but wouldn't say anything out of fear thinking Danny was crazy, and would come after him.

After a terribly restless night, I woke up feeling exhausted, and asked my mom if I could stay home from school. I told her I didn't feel very well.

She checked me out thoroughly and noticed a couple of bruises on my back and arms. Quite concerned, she asked me what happened.

I glanced at roller skates sitting in the corner of my room, and proceeded to make up a story about how I took a bad fall while roller-skating. My mom, accepting my excuse, asked me to be more careful.

How I wished I could just blurt out everything to my mom about what was happening, but I was so afraid for them. My parents are the sweetest, most forgiving people I know, and very dedicated to the teachings of the Catholic religion. I know that they would go crazy if they knew how Danny was treating me. Coming from a very religious family, I think I based many of my decisions on my beliefs. Especially as a teenager, the choices you make can be dead wrong, if you are guided by religion only, instead of common sense.

The next day I went to Heidi's house and Danny was the topic of our conversation. Heidi stated that what Danny went through was unbelievable and cruel. But as an adult, he can now choose to change how he treats others. She told me if he didn't like the abuse as a kid, especially witnessing his mom getting beaten and his sister getting raped, then why is he repeating history and hurting me! Moreover, why do I take it and stay with him?

I really didn't have an answer for her because I really didn't know why I stayed, except I knew I was scared. Abruptly, I changed the subject.

The next day at school I was extremely exhausted. Danny was waiting at my locker and asked me to go to a football game with him. I was excited because I had never been to a Professional football game before. Our friends Karen and Kevin were going with us.

The day of the game arrived. The weather was quite cool and I made sure I dressed accordingly. The game progressed, and I was having fun cheering our home team on, when I noticed Danny smoking a joint with Karen's boyfriend. Besides smoking pot, they were also drinking vodka from bottles in paper bags, their way of keeping warm. I could always tell by Danny's eyes when he was getting intoxicated. I hated that look; it turned my blood cold.

I tried to ignore his obnoxious behavior at first, but then as always, he tried to force me to drink. When I refused, he shoved me into Karen scaring us both. He splashed the vodka into my face, and instantly my eyes began burning and tearing, causing my mascara to run down my face.

I started to cry and headed toward the bathroom, but Danny decided that it wasn't enough to humiliate me. He ran up behind me and grabbed me by my hair, just before I made it inside.

A security guard came running over to ask me if I was okay. He grabbed Danny by the shirt and asked, "Is this guy bothering you miss, do you know this guy?" He could see how shook up I was.

Afraid and not knowing what to say, I just told him that Danny was my boyfriend and that we were having a little fight.

The guard proceeded to tell me that I could have him arrested for harassment, but I refused. The guard appeared puzzled by how I was reacting to the situation he saw me in. Realizing he couldn't change my mind he said, "Make sure that he doesn't drive home," and walked away.

I told Danny to go back to the stands, and I went into the bathroom and sat in there for what seemed like hours. Karen came in to see how I was doing. We just sat on the floor and hugged each other, wondering why we both take this abuse. People were starting to stare, but to us we didn't care, it was like they were in a different world!

Karen was in the same abusive situation as I was. She told me that she really loved Kevin, and couldn't imagine her life without him. "When we are not fighting," she said, "Kevin can be so loving and understanding." It was then that I realized Karen could never help me; she was as blinded and afraid as I was. We finished crying, washed off our faces and went back to our seats.

It was already the third quarter and Danny was out of it. He just sat there in his seat looking dead drunk. I heard Kevin ask Karen if we were with other guys, because we were gone for so long. They got into a fight and he called her a tramp. She tried explaining things to him, but in his condition he seemed oblivious.

The game ended and our team had won! At least something good happened. We had to practically carry the guys back to the car. Neither of them was feeling any pain.

I told Heidi about what happened the next day in school. She said she was going to have me committed if I didn't break it off with Danny.

I did a lot of soul searching in school that day, not having Danny around to distract me, since he was absent nursing a hangover. I thought to myself, how did I let this relationship go this far? I could have had a lot of chances to date nice guys that wouldn't abuse me.

At the end of the day, Danny made it to the school to pick me up. Of course he was very sweet, and told me he was so sorry for what happened at the football game. He said he just didn't know what came over him and wouldn't ever hurt me again.

While thinking that I've heard this for the hundredth time now, I told Danny to take me to the park, and that I wanted to talk to him. I was very quiet and somber on the way over, but in my mind I was rehearsing how I was going to tell him that it was over, and how we should go our separate ways for good.

As we pulled into a parking space, a favorite song of Danny's came on the radio; it was one I did not like. Danny waited until it was over and then came around to my side, opening the door for me. He grabbed my hand and helped me out. We walked hand in hand to one of the shelters and sat on the bench.

I told him how I felt, that I really liked him, and how we have had some good times together, but that we can't keep going on the way we were. Continuing I said to him, "I hate it when you drink, because it causes you to get so violent. Even without alcohol, you have a relentless rage inside of you; any little thing can set you off. My own parents don't even treat me that way." He grabbed onto me and held me tightly for dear life! He started crying and apologizing, telling me that I couldn't leave him, that he loves me more than his own life. He begged me to please give him another chance saying, "I can't live without you Katie."

I've never seen a guy break down like that before. I said, "Danny, I can't do this again, please understand, we'd both be better off apart."

The tears stopped like a faucet turning off. He said, "I'm taking you home now."

It was 6:30 p.m. when I said my final farewell to Danny, as I walked cautiously away from the car. An eerie feeling came over me about how well he took this, but at the same time I was relieved he didn't get into a violent rage. I walked up my driveway and waved goodbye.

He looked at me, glaring at me for a second, then revved the engine and squealed out of the driveway. He must have hit ninety miles per hour in the short distance from my driveway to the end of the street.

I was a little bit shaken when I got into my house. My Mom and Dad were out at a doctor's appointment, thank God. My brothers and sisters were home and wanted to know what happened. I never knew what to say and was always covering up for Danny.

I got all of my homework done and called Heidi. I had to tell her what happened. She was happy for me, but said I should still be very cautious of Danny. I told her he pulled away mad but I think it'll be okay. Maybe he finally realizes we're better off apart. We talked about the prom and our homecoming. It felt good to be hopeful about my future, without the fear of saying something wrong to my boyfriend and getting slapped around.

Around 9:30 p.m. I was reading up in my room. The phone rang and it was Danny calling for me. He was obviously drunk and he kept repeating to me that he would never let me go. He said to me over and over, "You tramp! Do you have another guy you're letting screw you." He was so mean that I just hung up on him. He called back again and again. I finally took the phone off the hook upstairs so my family wouldn't catch on.

Around 12:30 a.m. Danny drove up in front of my house. He was yelling out my name, "Katie, Katie. Come out here now!" Then he started honking the horn. I was so scared I didn't know what to do. My bedroom was on the street side so I opened the window and told him to quiet down.

My dad heard the commotion and called me downstairs to ask me what was going on. I forced myself to tell him that we had a fight and broke up. My dad went out the front door to try to talk to Danny, but when Danny saw my dad, he quickly departed.

I apologized to my family for his behavior, knowing I could never tell them about the abuse. I felt so ashamed.

The next day was Saturday. Heidi called me up and told me we had to practice our cheerleading routine for our homecoming.

I walked over to her house, which was about a quarter of a mile away. While approaching her house, I saw Danny's car come up from behind. He rolled down the window and told me to get in.

I told him to go away and leave me alone! When he stopped the car, I ran as fast as I could to Heidi's house; my legs felt like rubber!

He screamed at the top of his lungs, "Get out here Katie I want to talk to you!" Heidi's mom wasn't home because she had gone grocery shopping. Heidi told me to lay low and not to go outside.

He persisted by pounding on her screen door. I realized right then that if I didn't go outside he'd pound down her door.

Heidi kept on grabbing my arm and telling me, "No Katie, you are not going out there! He'll hurt you!"

I told Heidi that I would be all right but I had to go out there and calm him down. As soon as I went outside he pulled me over to the car, which was three houses down. I could smell liquor on him. After pushing me into the car, he sped away toward his house. He dragged me into the empty house, as his family wasn't home. Danny announced, "I'm gonna rape you right here, right now!"

I had to get out of there or change his mind somehow. I told him, "Please, can we talk about this, Danny please!" I ran out the back door. He chased me and pushed me to the ground crying, "I love you Katie, I won't ever let you go!"

I managed to get up and he grabbed me again. He told me that if I left him he would kill himself. My eyes were so filled up with tears I could hardly see him. He dragged me over to his back porch, where there was a beer bottle on one of the steps. Picking up the bottle, he smashed it on the steps and started slicing his arm with the cut glass.

While screaming for him to stop, I was thinking how responsible I would feel if he bled to death. I kept on yelling, " Stop it Danny; please stop!" But he continued to slice through his arm crying, "Katie take me back or I'll die!" There was so much blood running down his hand, I had to get him to stop, so I screamed "O.K. O.K. Danny stop, I'll go back with you!" I managed to get the glass from him, and we went back into the house where I wrapped his wounds tightly in towels. Danny's brother Tim arrived and, without hesitation, we rushed him to the hospital.

Tim and I sat in the waiting room while Danny was getting stitched up. Danny told the hospital staff that he accidentally put his arm through a glass door when he tripped. We brought him back home and put him to bed. Tim told me I could go and that he'd take care of Danny.

We talked about everything that happened. Tim really liked me as a friend. He probably didn't understand my point of view, because his family was used to all this abuse. I cried and told him that I didn't understand Danny's mood swings; he goes from calm to angry in an instant. He's like a Jeckyle and Hyde!

All Tim could say as he gave me a hug was, " Katie, he's just like my old man."

I asked him if he could talk to Danny about letting me go.

Tim replied, "Look Katie, I'm having a party at my apartment tonight, and there will be a lot of our friends there, so why don't you come by and I'll see what I can do. At best, I'll be there to protect you!"

Danny picked me up from my house around 7:30 p.m., bearing a dozen red roses with a beautiful vase. We got to Tim's apartment and Tim winked and smiled at me. I felt a little at ease, knowing Tim was watching out for me. He told his guests to help themselves to the food and drinks.

Everyone wanted to know what happened to Danny, and his story about his arm stayed the same. He told their friends the same story he told at the hospital. Everyone made a fuss about his arm; I think he liked being the center of attention. I asked him not to drink, especially since he was on pain medication, and had been drinking earlier that day.

As the night progressed even Tim started drinking, which meant I'd probably be on my own. Danny had sneaked away from me enough times that I knew he had started drinking, but he wasn't quite drunk yet. Tim decided to talk to Danny about his behavior toward me. Danny had blown everything out of proportion, and accused Tim and me of sleeping together, just because Tim seemed to care. They got into a fight, and a couple more guys joined in. I was screaming for them to stop! Danny turned to me glaring right into my eyes and yelled, "I'll kill you, you little tramp!" With one swift move he grabbed a handful of my hair and tried pulling me towards him. Six guys intervened to stop the attack.

Tim took me by the arm and told me that I'd better leave, because he didn't know what Danny would do.

I told Tim I didn't know what I did wrong. I was just talking to his brother, family.

Tim told me that Danny gets insanely jealous. Tim said, "Danny thinks that if you even talk to a guy, you want to hop in bed with him." As he walked me to the door, Tim told me he would calm Danny down. As I began walking down the street, I could still hear him yelling and shouting. On my way home a cop car passed me by, headed in the direction of Tim's house. I felt so sick inside. Again, I feared that I would never get away from Danny.

The next day Danny came over to my house looking like a truck ran him over. He apologized for everything that happened. Then he asked me how I felt about our relationship.

I told him that I'd try a little harder not to make him so angry. A dinner invitation followed and I accepted. He said that he had to leave, but he'd be back later to pick me up.

On my way upstairs my sister Cindy stopped me. She said she heard through the grapevine that Danny's been beating up on me.

At first I laughed and told her, "That's silly."

She could see right through me being older and wiser, and already out of high school for two years. Also, she really knew me well and begged me for the truth.

I asked her if I could trust her with the truth.

"Of course, Katie" she assured me.

We went upstairs to our room and sat on the bed. I started to tell Cindy about everything, right from the beginning.

Cindy blew up, she grabbed me and demanded, "Why? Katie, why are you staying with Danny? Him and his family they're all screwed up, and he's gonna screw up your life too!" Then we sat there and started to cry. She pulled me to her, hugged me and said "Don't worry Katie, it'll be okay. I'm going to protect you, you know, but I need to know, do you really love Danny, or are you just afraid of him?"

It didn't take me long to realize I didn't know anything about relationships and love, but one thing I did know was that I didn't want to be in this relationship anymore. "You know Cindy, I really don't like him, so I guess I definitely don't love him."

Cindy said, "Break it off with him, and this time don't take him back no matter how much he apologizes or cries. Just don't give in Katie."

I felt so much better after talking to someone. I had always blamed myself.

Later that day when Danny arrived, I told him I needed to talk to him before we went out. We went downstairs to my basement. He looked at me with a hesitant glare, and I could already tell that he knew what I wanted to say. Feeling a little safer in my own house, I planned to just blurt it out, hoping that he would immediately leave. I said, " I don't want to stay in a relationship where I am constantly in fear of getting beat up and abused. Danny, you constantly verbally and physically knock me down."

He didn't utter one word, coldly he just turned around, walked upstairs and left. I had practiced everything I wanted to say which included so much more, but he never gave me a chance.

I went upstairs and replayed the conversation for my sister, telling her how scared I was.

Cindy told me not to worry; maybe for a change, Danny is scared. I still couldn't believe that it was done knowing how violent he usually is; his calmness frightened me.

Nighttime arrived. My parents had gone out to a school board meeting leaving just me, two of my older sisters, and my two younger brothers home. At 7:15 p.m. a car slowly pulled up in front of our house laying on the horn loud and long. I rushed to the window and saw Danny's car. After a couple of minutes, he came out of the car yelling for me to come out. I could tell by his staggering walk that he was drunk.

"Katie, get your friggen ass out here now!" he bellowed. I was so scared. Cindy pulled me back in and told me no, you're not going out there. Then Cindy went to the door and told Danny to go home and sleep it off. He ignored her and just kept yelling. She ran outside to quiet him down and he pushed her to the ground. I came running out, fearing he would really hurt her. He grabbed me by my arm with one hand, my hair with the other and pulled me over to the side of the house. He said if I didn't change my mind, he'd kill Cindy and me right now. I told him to just leave us both alone. As he grabbed my face, Cindy got up and ran over to us. She grabbed him by the shirt, and whacked him with a big stick. "Leave my sister alone," she ordered.

He just laughed and said, " Ooh, I do like them feisty!" He brought up his fist to hit her, but I grabbed it in mid air.

"Please Cindy," I begged, "Go inside."

She said, "I'm going in to call the cops and you're going to jail."

When Cindy ran off he grabbed my face and squeezed it again. "Make the right choice Katie or"….. He slowly flipped out a knife, saying, "I bet this will slice through the both of you like butter," he bragged. "Katie, you're mine and you might not live to regret it, or better yet, maybe your sister won't live either, and Katie, it would be all your fault."

Just then, the police pulled into the driveway. Danny squeezed my hand so tight that he dug his nails into them. As the officers approached us I knew what I wanted to tell them but didn't have the courage to say. The police officer asked what the problem was.

My sister Cindy came flying out the front door to try and tell them what had been happening: how Danny's been beating me up, and how he threatened to have her stabbed. The police asked Danny if this was true.

He just smiled this insidious smile and told them in his most noble tone, "We all just had a little misunderstanding, and now everything is under control."

The officer looked at me for my response. Danny squeezed my hand so tightly that he was cutting off my circulation. As my head went down in shame, I told him that we had a fight, but everything was all right now. The look on the officer's face told me that he knew I was lying and scared.

Cindy screamed, "What's wrong with you Katie? I want to press charges." Then Danny said, "I want to press charges on her, she tried to assault me with a stick!"

The officers assessed the whole situation; they couldn't do anything by just Cindy's allegations alone, since it was her word against Danny's. One officer did add very sternly though while looking directly at Danny, "I sure hope nothing is wrong, because I love to put away guys who hurt girls, so I won't have to be coming back to this type of call again, right young man?"

Danny smugly smiled and answered, "No sir, and there was no reason for you to have wasted your time here tonight either."

One of the policemen responded, "You're a real wise guy, aren't you?"

"No sir," was all Danny said.

They turned around and walked away after giving Danny a final warning they would be keeping an eye on him.

I asked Cindy to go inside, telling her that I would be all right with Danny. She had such a disappointed look on her face.

Danny of course looked smug, he knew he had won again. He put his arms around my neck. Slowly he pulled me over to him whispering to me, "You are mine Katie forever, and don't you ever forget that!"

A tear ran down my cheek, as I felt once again, that my battle was lost. He retreated to his car and took off.

Cindy confronted me as I walked in, asking me why I didn't tell the police the truth. All I wanted to do was cry. I ran upstairs to be alone. Cindy couldn't leave it alone and followed me, asking me repeatedly, "Why, why Katie did you do that?"

I told her that my life was over. "No matter what I do, break up or stay with Danny, he'll kill me or you."

"I'm telling Mom and Dad," Cindy threatened.

I told her, "No, please you can't, he'll probably kill them too!"

"We've got to do something." she said.

"I'll handle it Cindy, I promise, I will make sure he knows not to treat me this way anymore. Danny needs to feel secure, and he needs to know I care about him, that is the only way he will stop hurting me. I know he will change for me." I was lying right through my teeth!

Cindy said, "You tell him I will get him if he does anything else to you."

"I will, I promise" I said. It was a promise I just couldn't keep. I felt so trapped and all alone. I got myself into this situation, and I just decided not to confide in anyone anymore.

CHAPTER 6

The days seemed to be so long. I know that it's said that the best year of your life should be your last year of high school, but I went into a real depression. Even my friends noticed. Before I started going out with Danny I was so happy and energetic, but now my future seemed anything but happy, only bleak.

One evening Danny called me up, and said he'd pick me up in a few minutes to go to a local tavern called Skeeters. The bar had a huge pool table in it. I loved the game and excelled at it, having grown up playing pool at my Uncle's tavern.

Some of our friends met us there and we got a great pool game going. We started playing one on one, no teams. I made it to the finals, but Danny was eliminated on the second game. He headed straight for the bar and immediately started doing shots, which got him very drunk.

All the players were eliminated except me and Joe, who was a really nice guy. As the game progressed it was getting quite exciting. I thought I was going to win the jackpot, which was up to thirty dollars! As I was hoping to win the match by calling eight ball to the corner pocket, Danny came running over to me and pulled me by my shirt screaming, "You tramp," and dragged me to the front of the bar. He said, "I saw you and Joe rubbing up against each other. You want to hop in bed with him don't you, you slut. You don't want to do it with me but yet you want him—don't you, you bitch."

"I didn't do anything with Joe, Danny, please. His sleeve may have touched my arm while we were playing, but that was all. He's our friend." It was like he never heard a word I said; he was drowning it out with his loud, slurring screaming.

Joe and the other kids came running over to try to stop him from hurting me. He fought them all, until one of our other friends John decked him. They tried to help me escape but Danny got up and grabbed me again. He picked up a beer bottle, smashed it on the bar, and put it up to my throat, telling everyone to back off. The bar owner, thank God, reasoned with him and Danny handed the bottle over the bar.

Danny sat down and pulled me into the chair next to him. I had tears streaming down my face. Everyone was so worried about me, but I told my friends I would be all right. They didn't believe it, so they went into the other room and kept watching me. Danny was very intoxicated; he just about fell asleep in his beer. Wishing he'd never come around, I kept silent until he picked up his head and told me to stop crying. He called me a baby, and said that he was the best thing that ever happened to me. Wanting to vomit, I knew not to say a word, so I kept silent. The next moment, he slapped me across the face telling me to answer him.

Joe came running over towards me, grabbed Danny by his shirt, and decked him. "There Danny, how does it feel being hit back? You say you're so tough. If hitting a woman makes you feel strong and tough, it only makes you look like a total asshole! You're a big joke, and if you ever hit Katie again, your mother will be going to your funeral!" Joe handed me the thirty dollars and said, "Here Katie, this would have been yours if you would have been able to finish the game."

I was reluctant but he put it into my pocket. I looked at Joe wanting to hug him, but I just smiled and said, "Thanks." He went back into the other part of the bar with our friends.

Danny knew he had an audience and tried something new. He took my class ring that I unwillingly gave to him off his finger, and dropped it into his beer glass. I watched it descend to the bottom of the glass.

I thought back to how he ended up with my ring in the first place. My parents couldn't afford my high school ring, so my sister Cindy gave me hers so I wouldn't feel left out. It was one of the most sincere gifts of love I ever received, and it came to me from Cindy's heart. I really did cherish it, but when Danny gave me his school ring to wear, he wanted me to give him mine. I told him the ring was a special gift to me from my sister and I couldn't give it to him. I told him to keep his ring instead. Not caring what it meant to me, he took my hand and forcefully yanked the ring off my finger saying, "There now, it's mine to wear." Again, Danny won.

Mortified by this scene, I told him I wanted my ring back and he could have his.

Pausing for a moment, he snickered, "So you really want this back Katie?" A second time but in a loud ambiguous voice, he said it again. He then took my head and pushed it to the tip of the glass and shouted, "Take it, go ahead and take it!" He kept shaking the back of my neck with his hand as he kept repeating himself.

While crying for him to stop, I tried to reach my hand towards the glass to pull the ring out. He pulled my head back by my hair and grabbed the ring after smashing the glass with his fist.

Joe and the guys came running towards us, while the bartender told him he was way out of line and too drunk to be in the bar. That only aggravated Danny, adding more fuel to his fire. He grabbed my ring and ran to the front door. "Kiss your stupid ring goodbye," he muttered, and with all his strength, he threw the ring out the door. I surmised my ring probably ended up at the gas station across the street.

Joe didn't make it in time to stop Danny from throwing it, but he did tackle him down to the ground. Danny was so drunk that I could have probably beat him to a pulp myself. Slowly, Danny got up and grabbed my arm to pull me out of there. Joe and a couple of other guys grabbed him and told me they'd drop him off at his house. One of my other friends took me home.

When I got home, I had to explain to Cindy how Danny threw the ring across the street from the bar. At first, she was concerned about me, then said, "Don't worry Katie, we will go over and look tomorrow." She asked me if he hurt me, and all I could say was no, not physically.

In the morning, we went to the gas station across from the bar and spent two hours looking for the ring, to no avail. We gave the station's owner our telephone number, in case anyone finds it. I was so devastated I started to cry. Cindy tried to convince me that it was okay, as long as I was all right, but I couldn't help but think to myself, why does life seem so incredibly unfair?

Chapter 7

Before I knew it, graduation day was fast approaching. My parents had planned a party for me after the event. I got a job at a drive through photo booth in order to save enough money for my dream to become a hairdresser, as I loved working with hair.

Danny still had his job as a cook at a restaurant, right around the corner from the photo booth that I worked at. One night my friend Rachel and I decided to go out for awhile after I got out of work, about 8:00 p.m.

I was in the process of getting the night deposit ready, a little earlier than usual. While putting the deposit bag on the floor by my feet, I proceeded to put the fifty-dollar change fund for the next shift in the booth drawer. A man approached the window and I told him that we were closed. He nervously told me to keep putting the money in the bag and that I shouldn't make him mad or unfortunately, he would have to shoot me.

Thinking it was curtains for me, I felt a surge of adrenaline from the tip of my toes to the top of my head shoot up my body, like a flame of fire. After getting the money together, he inquired if there was any more?

"No," I told him, as my foot was still on the night deposit.

He told me to slowly turn towards him and give it to him through the window. While doing as he said, he ordered me to put my head down and count backward from 100. Otherwise, he would have to shoot me.

As I placed my head down on the table, I prayed and wondered if the bullet to my head would hurt or burn.

Rachel arrived, pounding on the window while saying, " Katie, Katie." I realized at that moment, that I was still alive and that the robber was gone; I started to cry.

She said, "Did you and Danny get into a fight again Katie?"

I told her that I was just robbed! Rachael was frantic, but immediately went to a nearby store and got a security guard to call for help. The police arrived in an instant. They asked me so many questions about the gunman's description, but I was so shook up I couldn't remember much.

Somehow, Danny heard about the robbery and came running over. I was talking to one of the police officers who was joking around with me, to make me feel a little more at ease. Danny misinterpreted it as flirting. He told the cop, "Well, it must be nice to stand around socializing when you should be out looking for the thief."

The policeman replied, "Hold on young man, who are you and what is your problem?"

Sarcastically he answered, "I'm the victim's boyfriend, you know, the girl you've been flirting with."

The cops told him that he'd better leave before they book him for interference. Of course, he refused and another cop had to escort him away.

I was so shook up that I just wanted to go home. My parents were very upset about this incident, and my dad told me that he wanted me to quit. The next day I called the photo place and told them that I wouldn't be back because it was not safe. My boss told me that they would have more police cars patrolling, but my reply was still no, which turned out to be the wisest decision. The booth was robbed again within the next two weeks.

As time went on, Danny had to work a lot more nights. This was great for me because I didn't have to see him as much. He always managed to call me though at least three times during the night. Knowing he was checking up on me, I wouldn't go anywhere.

One day my friend Mary came in from college, and asked me if I wanted to go out with her and her friends to a country western bar. I was anxious to get out and said, "Yes!" I asked my sister to tell Danny, if he called, that I was asleep and didn't feel well. He would have flipped out if he knew that I was out with friends.

I wasn't into country western at the time but I thought that it would be fun anyway. There were so many people there. I learned a couple of the line dances. What was nice about dancing at one of these bars was that you could dance with anyone and be anonymous. I had a great time!

As the evening progressed, we sat down and started to catch up with one another. Mary's friends were named Lisa and Laurie; they seemed so nice. Lisa wanted to become a doctor and Laurie wanted to pursue an engineering career. Mary had her sights set on being a teacher. I almost felt out of place since I wasn't in college, but they were all great and really made me feel like part of their world.

It was so nice to go out and be with friends. I was having a wonderful time! I really loved being without Danny. Mary knew about a lot of things that had happened, and asked if I was still with Danny. I told her that I was, but not by my choice.

Mary talked about Christmas break from school. She and a bunch of girls were going down to Florida for a vacation. She invited me along to get away for awhile, especially from Danny. "Who knows?" she said, "You may finally meet a nice guy."

It sounded great, but I told her that I needed to think about it and that I would let her know.

It was getting late; we all decided to head back home. We hopped in Lisa's car and were on our way, listening to some great tunes on the radio. After a stoplight turned green, Lisa put her foot on the gas and in a split second, a car ran a red light and slammed into Lisa's car on the passenger side. I will never forget the sounds of the glass breaking, metal crunching, shrieking screams, and the sound of the car crashing into the door. Lisa hit her head on the windshield and I bumped my shoulder against the front seat. When I looked up to see how Mary was, all I saw was blood and glass. Mary's side of the car took the hardest impact. Laurie was hurt too.

Thank God, another car stopped to help. He saw the whole accident. Mary seemed so lifeless. We were all crying to her, "Mary, Mary," but she was unconscious. Just then, a police car and an ambulance pulled up. They got all of us out except for Mary. None of us wanted to go to the hospital until we knew Mary was all right. They worked on trying to get her out, so they wouldn't hurt her any more than she already was. I asked one of the paramedics if she would be all right, but he wasn't sure yet.

The driver of the other car was intoxicated and only sustained minor injuries. He was so drunk that he couldn't even stand up straight. The guy that saw the accident gave his statement and we thanked him for his help. We all stood together, holding on to each other, crying and praying. One of the policemen approached us and asked for Mary's next of kin's address and phone number. I felt my heart drop to the ground. "Does this mean…"

"No," he stopped me, "She is in critical condition but we need to get in touch with her family, so they can meet us at the hospital."

We all had to go to the hospital to get checked out too. What a nightmare this was! We had such a wonderful night; how could it have ended so tragically? I felt cursed! "Please God, help my friend Mary. She is so sweet and she needs your help."

All of our families met us at the hospital, except Lisa's. Since her parents didn't live in this state, they had to fly in. My mom worked as a nurse at the hospital, so we asked her to find out about Mary's condition. Laurie and I were treated and released, but Lisa had sustained some head injuries.

Mary's mom was crying on her husband's shoulder. We felt so bad for them. My mom came over and told us that Mary was in pretty bad shape. She had internal bleeding, head injuries, and a possible lacerated liver. They would know more after surgery.

The hours seem to drag as Mary was in surgery. After six hours, the surgeon came out to inform us that Mary would be all right. "She's still listed as serious, but she should pull through."

"Thank you God," I cried out. It was 6:15 in the morning when my mom and I finally got home. After a long and hectic night I still couldn't fall asleep, since I was constantly thinking about Mary.

Later on that day Danny stopped by. He had found out what happened. You would think that he'd be concerned about Mary and the rest of us, but all he said was, "Well Katie, see what happens when you sneak out on me. You get punished. Just remember that next time."

I thought about how I get more hurt when I'm with him. He was so cruel. It was like he was relishing in the fact that we were hurt.

He told me that we were going out to dinner that night, but I wanted to go to the hospital to see Mary. Danny told me, "I have something important to tell you and you have to go with me."

I compromised and went to see Mary earlier. Since Mary's mom had told the hospital staff I was family, I was able to spend ten minutes with her. She looked so helpless, hooked up to a lot of machines, barely speaking. I felt so bad for her. I told Mary I was so sorry about her condition. She didn't recall too much of what happened. I told her that when she gets better, we would go line dancing. She smiled, squeezed my hand, and then closed her eyes.

I left the hospital and went home to get ready to go out to dinner with Danny. He picked me up at 7:00 and our reservations were for 7:30. I was glad he wanted to talk to me alone at dinner.

I wanted to tell him that at the end of the summer I was thinking of moving down to Florida with my cousin Roseanne. This was a way of getting away from Danny and this lifestyle. Feeling bad about leaving my family, I hoped I would return in a couple of years when Danny finds himself another victim to torture. I knew that this was a drastic measure but I have no other choice. Danny would never follow me down there, because he'd never leave his mother. He would be tied to her apron strings forever.

We arrived at the restaurant and ordered dinner. It seemed like a nice night out so far. When he was sober, he always tried to act different in front of other people. I started to believe he really does have a split personality. After dinner Danny got up from his seat, knelt down on one knee pulling a ring out of his pocket, and asked me to marry him.

I was shocked! I kept telling him to get up; I needed to tell him something very important.

He insisted on a yes answer first.

A couple at the next table kept looking over and smiling. The girl looked fooled by this romantic gesture. Little did she know, it would be a death sentence for me to say yes. I finally got Danny to sit back down in his seat. He was angry, I could tell by the look in his eyes that he wasn't going to like what I had to say, but I just had to say it. "Danny look, you and I do not get along very well. We are always fighting and in the end, you always beat me up."

He interrupted me to say, "Katie, it won't be like that when you marry me. I promise I won't hit you anymore."

I responded, "I've already heard that line over a hundred times Danny,"

He said, "But it will be different once you marry me, because then I know that you will really be mine."

At that moment I stopped him, "I don't want anyone to own me Danny. I want to do things on my own, for me first. To know I can do it." Then I just blurted it out that I'm moving to Florida with my cousin. She already has friends down there, and we can all room together and get jobs. I need to do this for me right now, please understand."

He was very quiet for about two minutes and then he lost it. He slammed his hands down on the table, came over to me grabbing me by my sleeve and said, "Now you understand one thing Katie, you're not moving anywhere away from me."

As he started to pull me out the door, the waiter stopped him and said, "First sir, you did not pay your bill and second you are causing a scene. Would you let the young lady's arm go."

He pushed the waiter to the side, threw a couple of twenties at him and said, "Here, this should cover our dinner, and your tip is to stay out of my business." I could tell everyone in the restaurant could see the fear in my face. At that moment, it looked like everything was moving in slow motion. I didn't know what my fate would be!

We got out to his car and he pushed me into the seat. I just barely got my foot in the door before he slammed it. He got in and took off very fast. He retrieved some hard liquor from under his seat, opened the cap and started pouring it down his throat.

My first thought was to jump out, but I was still recovering from the car accident. I started to cry, "Danny, please slow down!"

He said, "I'd just as soon slam this car into a pole and let both of us die, than to let you ever leave me." As he poured down the vodka, wiping his mouth with his sleeve he warned me, "And if you insist on leaving me, you definitely won't have any family to come back to, and you'd better believe it Katie."

We stopped at a light. As he turned to me I said to him wiping the tears from my eyes, "What do you mean by that?"

He stared at me with that callous cold look in his eyes and said, "I mean exactly what I say. I will kill your whole family without a trace of evidence, and I wouldn't even flinch an eye. Your family could have an accidental fire, when they're fast asleep. Or how about carbon monoxide poisoning, or maybe the brakes could fail in their cars. So Katie, did I persuade you enough to marry me, or do you need physical proof?" Tears were pouring down my face, when at that moment we were startled by a horn. As the light turned green the guy behind us wanted us to go. Danny was so mad at the other driver for this transgression; he got out of the car and started swearing at the guy while staggering over to his car, holding the bottle of vodka in his hand. The guy just rolled up his window and took off as fast as he could.

Then Danny returned to the car and put it into gear, telling me not to say another word. We drove for what seemed like hours before he stopped at the park, where we all used to hang out. He pulled me over to him and started to kiss me. He grabbed my face with his hands and said, "I told you you're mine and you will marry me won't you Katie?"

As he squeezed my face harder, I dared one more time to say I really need to do this; I want to move to Florida for just a little while.

After letting go of me for one minute, he hauled off and punched me in the stomach. As I doubled over in pain, he told me, "Go ahead and do it Katie, just try and leave me. You know I will definitely do what I told you I would do, and if I get caught, so what It'll be three square meals a day for me in the slammer. So, which person should I kill first?"

I stopped him and said, "Okay Danny, you win, I'll marry you."

He smugly sat back for a moment and said, "I knew you loved me Katie."

I felt like vomiting, as I thought to myself, this would be my own death sentence.

He made me put on the ring and said, "There, now it's official. Let's go and tell everyone the good news."

I knew from my gut instinct that he probably would have killed either someone in my family or me for sure. Especially when he drinks, he doesn't care what happens, or who he hurts! I told him it was late and that we should do this in the morning. I felt so sick to my stomach and so empty inside. How could I let this happen and how can I get out of this one without someone I love getting hurt.

He took me home, kissed me again, and told me how much he loves me. I walked into the house and went right up to my room. I cried myself to sleep thinking, how could this be happening. I no longer had any goals and dreams to look forward to. You start to wonder if you'd be better off dead! The strength of my loving family kept me going, but I just couldn't tell them about Danny. I knew that he would do something to them, and that was a chance I was not willing to take.

The next morning he came over bright and early with flowers in hand, red roses. He asked to see my parents and all my sisters and brothers. When they came into the room, he just blurted it out, "Katie and I are getting married and we would like to have everyone's blessings." There was silence around the whole room for a moment. They knew we argued, but they didn't have a clue about any of the abuse. They looked at me as I forced myself to smile. I couldn't stop a couple of tears from rolling down my face. Maybe they thought it was tears of joy.

My dad took my hands gently into his and said, "Is this what you really want Katie?"

Danny stepped next to me and grabbed one of my hands from my dads, squeezing it until I finally said, "Yes dad, we will be planning for a February wedding," which was just eight months off.

CHAPTER 8

I asked my four sisters and my friends Heidi and Karen to stand up for me.

Since Heidi and Karen knew what was going on, they tried to talk me out of it. Heidi told me, "Katie, go to the police. We will all testify for you." They both kept on saying, "You just can't marry Danny."

I tearfully told them that I was not worried about myself, but for my family. "You know he will hurt any one of them just to prove that he could, and I can't take that chance. Danny told me when we get married things will be different, maybe they will be if he feels more secure.

Heidi interrupted me, "Katie you've heard this for years, and has he changed? And what if you have kids with him, did you ever think about that?"

I had enough of this, my mind was made up. I told them I had to do it, and that they just cannot understand what point I'm at. I begged them, " Will you please stand up for me at my wedding?"

"You know we will Katie, we love you." Then Heidi told me to bring some of our cheerleading pictures out to change our mood, and we spent the rest of that night reminiscing about the good old days, before I met Danny. How simple and wonderful life seemed then.

The next day I was surprised when Danny admitted to me that he needed to curb his rage. One of his friends suggested that he join a gym, and do some weight training to see if that would help. He told me he went ahead and signed up at a local gym.

As I spent the next few weeks planning the wedding, Danny did seem to be improving. I thought that maybe working out was reducing his anger.

After about four months, Danny wanted me to start coming to the gym to watch him work out. Sitting through his hot sweaty routine, I could tell he was starting to get obsessive about it. Afterwards, he'd look into the mirror and start posing and flexing his muscles. Some of the poses looked apelike to me at first, until I knew more about bodybuilding. I spent all my spare time watching his routine while pumping up his already high ego. For now, this seemed to calm him down; I figured it was better then getting beat up.

With the wedding day fast approaching, we found our first apartment. It was very small and quaint. I really liked it. The landlords, who were very sweet people, lived in the other half of the house, Mr. and Mrs. Willis, or June and Al as they wanted us to call them. I got close with June as time went on, after I got married to Danny.

The big day was a few days away and everything seemed to be going smooth. My mom's neighbor Jesse made a beautiful cake. The last dress fitting went great!

My bridesmaid's threw me a stagette party and the guys gave Danny a stag, both on the same night. Of course, they had a stripper for Danny. Danny had given up social drinking since he was so much into his bodybuilding, but on this particular night, he got falling down drunk. He supposedly couldn't remember the stripper being all over him, or that he took off his clothes and danced with the girl. Afterwards, he took her in the back room and had sex with her right on top of the kitchen counter.

One of my good friends told me about the incident, hearing about it from her husband. They got into a fight when he found out that she told me about it, as he had asked her not too. I also heard about the incident from one of my other friends.

The next day, Danny and I went over to the apartment to paint. "How was the stag?" I asked him.

He said that it was all right.

"Did you drink?" I asked him.

"Yeah, I had a couple of beers." He said.

"I heard you drank until you got drunk, and did a striptease act with the stripper. Then I heard you had sex with her on the counter in the back kitchen. Is that true Danny?"

There was a dead silence. While up on the ladder painting, he threw down his paintbrush and said, "Who the hell told you that?"

"I have my sources," I said. "I'm asking you if you did it with the stripper?"

He got this enraged look on his face. Jumping down off the ladder he grabbed me and put me up against the wall saying, "Yeah, maybe I did have sex with her. It's more than I get from you. You want to wait until we're married. Well I needed it sooner!"

I asked, "How many other girls have you been with Danny since we've been going around?"

He slammed his hand against the wall next to my head and said, "It's none of your fucking business how many girls I screw. You're marrying me anyway."

I screamed, "No Danny, it is my business. I can call off this wedding, and you can go and marry one of those other girls that you've screwed!"

"That's it!" he yelled. He ripped off my clothes and I started to scream. He took the duct tape that was next to the paint cans and taped it over my mouth. As I fought him with all my might, he threw me down to the floor and raped me. I hated it so much. It was violent and it hurt. When he was done, he stood up and pulled up his zipper. He smugly smiled and said, "There, now I'm marrying one of the girls I just screwed!" He went back up the ladder and continued painting like nothing happened.

I got up and pulled the duct tape from my mouth. I went into the bathroom putting on the shower as hot as it would go, and wept. The water seemed to scald me, but it also seemed to cleanse me from Danny's violent attack. Now again, I was faced with the agony of being reduced to "life in imprisonment." I barely got out of the shower when Danny started pounding on the bathroom door, telling me to get out and help him paint. I didn't feel like painting anymore, much less looking at his face; but I got dressed and came out anyway.

"Now don't you look pretty. Maybe you should get screwed more often, " Danny said.

Ignoring him, I resumed painting.

I thought about him while driving home. He just seems like such a cold-hearted and calculating person. His heart, if any, is made of ice, and his soul, if he has one, is empty. He doesn't have any feelings towards anyone, and I think he really enjoys hurting people; it gives him a sense of power.

When I got home I was exhausted. My friend Jenny was at my home that night visiting. She was married less than a year ago to her high school sweetheart. She could tell right away that something was wrong. I went upstairs and Jenny excused herself, and followed behind me. She sat on the bed next to me and put her arm around me, asking what was wrong.

I was so ashamed; I didn't want to tell her.

"What did Danny do this time," she inquired.

My eyes flowing with tears, I told her that at the apartment Danny raped me and covered my mouth with duct tape. Through my tears I said, "Jenny, it was so horrible and it hurt so bad, I hate sex!"

Jenny stopped me and said, "Katie, with the right person that you love, sex is wonderful and doesn't hurt. What Danny did to you today was an act of violence. Katie, do you still want to marry him? Do you love him?"

"No, I don't love him," I immediately blurted out.

"Then why are you marrying him? Call the police and tell them what happened, and maybe they'll throw him in jail for raping you!"

"I can't. If I do, he'll get out and he will get me. I know he will."

"Please Katie, let me tell your mom and dad."

"You can't Jenny, please. I can handle him. Besides, he's not hitting me anymore." I had to lie to her.

She just shook her head and hugged me. She picked up my head and gently placed her hand on my face and said, "It 's your decision, but please promise me Katie, if he ever lays a hand on you again, especially after you are married, you'll tell me. I want to help you but I can't if you insist on staying with him and still marrying him."

"Thanks Jenny " I said, "I'll be okay."

I just grabbed my panda bear and curled up in a ball on my bed, and went to sleep.

There were only a couple of days left before the wedding. Danny informed me that we would be making a pit stop at a local barbell company around the Poconos, where we would be staying on our honeymoon. He told me that a lot of the wedding money would be used for barbell equipment, some super size cans of protein drinks, and anything else he thought he would need.

I asked him how much he figured this would cost.

He said, "Look Katie, I don't care if it costs us our whole wedding, I am doing this!" Again, he spoke and I had to be quiet. He is really getting involved in this bodybuilding. I thought it wouldn't be so bad. Maybe he wouldn't be so violent, since he wouldn't be drinking any more. As time went on, it would only get worse.

Chapter 9

The big day arrived and I was so nervous. I got ready at my mom and dad's house. My mom, my sisters, and friends made the morning so much fun. My sister Leslie drew me a bubble bath with a little glass of wine to relax me. My mom pampered me with an elegant breakfast fit for a queen! I could hardly eat though, having such butterflies in my stomach. My sister Chrissy fixed my hair while Carrie helped me with my makeup. Leslie and Cindy helped me get dressed. They made sure that I had something old, something new, something borrowed and something blue.

Just as I was finished getting dressed, the photographer arrived. I remember feeling numb. I also remember looking in my mom and dad's bedroom mirror, just staring at myself, thinking about what will happen to my life after today. I didn't want time to go any further. I just wanted to stay in my parents' room forever. It was such a safe and loving space to be in. These were not the dreams for a typical bride. Just then, my sister Cindy came in and said, "Oh Katie, you look so beautiful." I started to cry. Cindy said, "I'm sorry Katie I didn't mean to make you cry." "It's not you Cindy," I said, "I'm just a little nervous."

Just then, my mom and dad came in to bring me out for pictures. It's amazing how you can change your personality to suit many different people.

We took some of the traditional pictures at the house before the wedding. It took a lot of energy just to get through it. I had to smile, when instead I just wanted to cry.

My parents drove me to the church. Danny and the guys were already waiting there for us. The mass seemed to take a lifetime, but I got through it. We then said our vows. Danny had made sure the priest didn't forget the obey part. It had to be a part of our vows just for him. The priest, who turned out to be Danny's uncle, gave us his blessings.

He had arranged for his uncle to be the priest. There was a few times that I wanted to go to his uncle and tell him everything. I thought some higher power might be able to get through to him, but if I were wrong, then it would be worse. At this point, it didn't matter anymore, because he now pronounced us man and wife.

Everyone in the church began to clap, but my thoughts tuned out the sounds. I was thinking, "Oh God, what did I do?" I couldn't help how I felt. Just then, I was snapped out of it by a jerk of my hand. Danny grabbed my hand as we walked down the aisle together.

After we finished greeting the guests and the pictures were taken, the wedding party headed for the limousines, already stocked with champagne and wine. We proceeded to the Botanical Gardens to take more pictures. It was too cold and gloomy to go outside for any pictures, a perfect setting for my doomed marriage!

The reception was held at a local fire hall, which is all we could afford. We arrived around 6:00 p.m. The whole wedding seemed just like a movie in slow motion.

By the time the dinner was done, Danny was already starting to get very intoxicated and loud. All I could think of was that anything could happen now. I got along with Danny's brother Tim. I think Tim even felt sorry for me most of the time, knowing how Danny was towards me. He's even tried to break up many of our fights. Tim stood up with my sister Cindy. He was Danny's best man and Cindy was my Matron of Honor.

Our first dance of the night went well and when it was time for the second dance, all of the wedding party joined in. Halfway through it, Danny's brother Tim cut in to ask me to dance. Danny gave him a funny look and stepped back for a moment. Tim grabbed my hand and we enjoyed the rest of the dance. He told me not to worry and promised to take care of me. "I won't let Danny hurt you anymore he whispered, you are too sweet for him to do this to you." Tim was like a big brother to me and I was like a little sister to him.

When the dance was almost finished, Danny came over to us and pushed his brother aside. He told him to get his friggen hands off his woman. My stomach started to get tight as I feared Danny was going to start a fight. I grabbed Danny's hand and told him to finish the dance with me.

He pulled me in very tight, put his mouth up to my ear and said, "What did you two talk about? Did he turn you on? Did you rub up close next to him? Did you want to screw him?"

I pushed him away and said, "Stop it Danny. He's your brother."

At that point, the photographer called us over to cut the cake. We agreed before the wedding not to smash the cake in each other's faces. He had me go first, and I did it just as planned, fearing the kind of mood he was in. When it was Danny's turn he totally humiliated me, by getting it all over my face and down the front of my dress. The photographer told Danny that was enough, and that he needed more shots of us elsewhere.

My sister took me to the bathroom to help clean me up. Cindy told me, "What's with Danny now?"

"I don't know, I think he's drunk." I said.

"I thought he stopped drinking." She asked.

"Yeah, he is a selective drinker now."

My other sisters, Chrissy, Leslie, and Carrie came in and helped me out. They asked why he messed me up so much, when I didn't even get any cake on him!

"I don't know," I said. I put on some more makeup and went back out.

I went over to the photographer and he said to me, "I've done a lot of weddings, but I've never seen the bride get so covered with cake. Are you okay?"

"Yeah, I'm used to this kind of stuff."

He looked puzzled, and I quickly changed the subject. "Where do you want to take the next photo?" He pointed over to a picturesque wall.

I quickly found Danny, off flirting with one of our friends Sherry. His one hand was up on the wall over her head and he had his other hand on her shoulder, moving it very slowly down her arm with his finger. Tim went over to get him. I think Tim said something to Danny, because he had this weird look on his face. He left Sherry and came over to us.

At this point, I tried even harder not to be conspicuous. I already think some of the guests felt a little uncomfortable. I couldn't wait for this day to be over. As the night went on Danny started drinking even more. When I asked him to cut back a little, he looked at me slurring his speech and said, "Look bitch, you're my wife now, so you don't tell me what to do, I tell you what to do."

I wanted to get the main events done, like throwing the bouquet but Danny came over and said, "Wait a minute, we have to get the garter off first." I just wanted to get this over with. It turned out to be an embarrassing moment for me, with some of his intoxicated friends cheering him on for more. It was now time for him to throw the garter, and it just so happened his brother Tim caught it. One of my friends Brandy caught the bouquet.

By the end of the night Danny was obviously drunk. The photographer wanted to take a few more pictures, but Danny couldn't even stand up anymore. His eyes were glassy and his tuxedo was falling apart. He promised me he wouldn't ever drink another drop of alcohol, but I knew his promises meant nothing. Tim came over to my rescue. He told the photographer one more shot of the bride and groom leaving, and that should wrap it up. Danny was getting a bit loud, flinging his arms all over the place telling his brother to leave him alone; that he can stand up himself for this last photo. Slurring his words, Danny pulled me next to him, telling the photographer that on the count of three, he could snap the last shot. He counted one, two, and before he reached three, he turned towards me and threw up all over the front of my dress! He laughed and said to me, "Boy Katie, you really look like a mess." Thank God my mom and dad, and the majority of my relatives had already left. I stood there mortified, while starting to cry.

Cindy grabbed me! "Katie, he looked like he did this on purpose," one of my friends blurted out. I could have died! My sister had some extra clothes in her car, and since this wedding was officially over, I put them on. The dress was totally ruined and Danny thought it was so funny.

Tim came over to the bathroom door and started to apologize for Danny's actions. He told me Danny was passed out cold, and that he put him into the car. He asked me where he should take him. I told him that we reserved a honeymoon suite at a hotel, but instead, just take him to our apartment. What I really wanted to say was to drop him off the nearest bridge!

My sister drove me to my apartment; it seemed to take forever. As we drove Cindy said, "Katie look, I want to know if Danny is still hitting you. I don't know if you realize this Katie, but mental abuse is just as destructive as physical abuse!"

I looked at her somberly with my mascara running down my face from crying. Looking like a raccoon and smelling like a sewer, all I wanted to do was go home and get into a hot shower. Cindy began her questions again, and I interrupted her. "No, it's all right Cindy, I am just really exhausted." The conversation stopped there about Danny. When we got back to the apartment Tim helped Danny into the house and put him to bed. We all sat at the table for a few minutes talking. I offered some coffee or tea. Tim told me to let him know how Danny does.

I said to them both, "Thank God we don't have a plane to catch in the morning, we probably wouldn't make it." We were driving to our honeymoon destination; it would take us about seven hours. They both hugged me and said good-bye.

CHAPTER 10

I had the cards, gifts, and envelopes from our guests in my wedding bag, which I put on the top of our bedroom dresser, figuring we would go through them in the morning. I took a shower and laid on the couch, since I couldn't even stomach lying next to Danny. The rest of the night seemed to go very slowly. I thought about what kind of a future I would have, not a very promising one. I knew that I got myself into this. "Should I have called Danny's bluff? Would he have really hurt anyone in my family?" My gut instinct told me yes, he would have!

I soon drifted off into a peaceful lull, until I was startled by the sound of breaking glass! I realized that it was morning. Danny got up and threw down one of the gifts we received. He broke a beautiful dish someone brought us. "Cheapskates," he said, "I wanted money." He already had gone through all of the envelopes and gifts. He came over to me pulling me off the couch by my hair and said, "What's the matter, did you sleep with some other guy last night? Why didn't you come to bed with me?" He grabbed me by my nightshirt, and smacked me with the back of his hand across my face with all of his might. I put my fists up to protect another blow and he pushed me down and laughed. I held my hand to the side of my face to rub it. It hurt so badly. As tears welled up in my eyes, I asked, "What did I do?"

"I went through all those gifts and envelopes and I think you took some of the money. We should have gotten more!"

"I didn't touch any of it Danny! I just showered and went to sleep. I didn't come to bed because I didn't want to disturb you."

" Just go get ready, we have to leave, and go wash your face up, you look like hell! The way you look, no one else would want you anyway."

When I got into the bathroom, my face was already swollen; I knew that I would have a huge bruise on it. I washed up again and patted cold water on my face. It was very hard to cover the redness with makeup.

He shouted from the kitchen," Katie, move your ass, let's go!"

I already had everything packed, so I was ready to go. We got into the car and took off. As we drove I kept very silent. My face was throbbing.

We were driving for an hour when Danny finally said something. "Hey Katie, 'ya know I'm really sorry about this morning. I don't know what got into me. I'll try not to do that again."

Words, just words I've heard for so many years. I have come to realize that statement meant it was just for the moment.

He grabbed me by my shoulder and said in a softer tone, "Come here Katie, sit right next to me." I really wanted to stay right where I was sitting. The silence was quite relaxing. He kept it up, "Katie, come over here now!" I moved slowly over to him. He put his arm around me and said, "There now, isn't that much better." He started stroking my shoulder moving his hand down to the side of my breast. I felt so awkward and nervous, as he was driving at 55 miles per hour.

"Danny don't!"

"Katie, do not tell me don't. You are my wife now and you do what I tell you to do!"

He unzipped his pants, pulled out his genitals, pushing my head down to it. He told me to blow him. A truck driver was passing by and slowed down to watch, while giving the thumbs up sign and blowing his horn. I was so humiliated I jumped into the back seat. I couldn't do what Danny wanted me to do, I'd rather eat worms! He was shouting, "You bitch, get back up here and finish me!"

I totally ignored him and I wouldn't even answer him. There was silence for a while, and then I heard him moaning. I peered through the space between the seats, and noticed he was finishing himself off! I realized that he is even sicker than I thought.

I stayed in the back seat until we arrived at the honeymoon lodge. He stopped the car, got out and checked us in at the front desk. Returning to the car still ignoring me, he started taking our things out of the trunk. I got out of the car, grabbed some things and headed up to our room. When we were finished, he jumped on the big round bed and put his hands over his head laughing, "So Katie, did you like watching me in the car? Did that turn you on?"

"Danny you're sick, I said, you can't even wait until you get somewhere private. What other perverted things will I find out about you?"

"Come here Katie," he said. I stood there for a moment while he continued, "Let me show you how a real man can make love to you."

I wanted to ask him who he had in mind, but my body just froze. I would have done anything to get out of this situation. I said, "Look, it's getting late, so lets go down and eat dinner before they stop serving." They only serve up until a certain time here.

Surprisingly, he agreed. I ordered a chicken entree and Danny decided on steak. He also took the liberty of ordering a big bottle of wine, followed by a bottle of champagne, compliments of the resort. I'm not a drinker, but I must have drunk half of both bottles. I figured, it would be easier to deal with what I'd have to endure later with Danny. I know that most people look forward to their honeymoon, but that's not how it was for me. I felt helpless, knowing I made a decision I have to live with, by just going through the motions without emotions. As the saying goes, "You've made your bed, now lie in it."

By the time we were done with dinner, I was feeling no pain; Danny was getting pretty loaded himself. He already ordered one more bottle of wine. I couldn't drink another sip though, since I was starting to feel nauseous. He poured me a little more and said, "Come on Katie, drink up!"

I told him I couldn't and that I felt really sick.

"Katie, you're such a pussy. Just have one more glass." He came over to me, put the glass up to my mouth and said, "Drink it Katie." I tried to refuse, but then he threatened to shove the rest of the bottle down my throat if I didn't. The waiter could tell this scene was getting a little out of hand, so he approached our table and asked if there was anything he could do. Danny said, "Yeah, mind your own business." The waiter looked at me with disbelief, but I just put my head down. I thought to myself that we have to be here a whole week, and I'd better not get Danny started. The waiter just walked away. Danny grabbed me by my hand and said, "Come on Katie, we are going up to our room, and in his other hand he grabbed the liquor bottle.

We got up to the room and I was starting to feel even sicker to my stomach. I told Danny that I was going to throw up. He started laughing as I ran for the bathroom and threw up our entire meal. As I knelt on the floor hugging the toilet seat, Danny came in and asked me how I felt. I said, "Better."

He put the bottle in front of my face and told me to take another sip. "It'll make you feel even better Katie, come on and take a sip."

"I don't want anymore Danny, please." But as always, Danny wins; he put it up to my mouth and I took another sip. Still a little tipsy, Danny pulled me by the hand onto the bed, proceeding to rip off my clothes. We had sex that night and I hated every minute of it. All I can remember was from that night on, anytime we had sex I had to pretend I was with someone else just to make it bearable. It's amazing how fantasizing can get you through just about anything.

The next morning I felt like a truck had run me over. At breakfast, all I could stomach was a cup of tea and a dry piece of toast. Danny just laughed at me, mocking me for feeling so sick, and bragging how much he could drink and wake up still feeling great. I wanted to tell him that's a good sign of an alcoholic, but I knew better.

We had an itinerary of events that were handed to us when we first arrived at the resort. I loved horses, so I really wanted to try some horse-back riding first. Surprisingly, Danny agreed. After breakfast, we headed out towards the stables. A handsome well-built guy, that was grooming the horses, came over to ask us if we were experienced in horseback riding. He said his name was Derrick, and he wanted to know if he could be of any assistance. I told him that I've only ridden a horse a few times and Danny even less. He brought over a couple of horses, and told me mine was very gentle. Derrick proceeded to do his job, helping me onto the horse. Danny came running over to us, yelling rather loudly, "Get your hands off of my wife."

Derrick, looking startled replied, "Sir, I am just helping the young lady onto her horse. I assist everyone."

"Well then go assist some other girl, this one's mine."

I was so humiliated; I can't even imagine how Derrick must have felt. I looked over at Derrick and he bowed his head to me and backed off.

Before Danny helped me onto my horse I said to him, "Why do you keep embarrassing me? Do you enjoy tormenting me?"

He answered, "You can't even begin to know how I could really torment you Katie. I saw the way you were looking at that queer; I suppose that you wanted to sleep with him, didn't you?"

It seemed senseless to argue with him. I just jumped up on my horse and took off. Danny jumped up on his and started chasing me. Scared, and hoping my horse was gentle, I turned to see where Danny was. He was grabbing at a tree branch and snapping it off. When he got closer to me, he whipped it at my head and the edge of it nicked me right across my face. I could feel the blood running down my cheek. Upset and angry, I stopped the horse and jumped off it. Danny followed suit, jumping off his horse right next to me. "Are you crazy," I shouted.

He grabbed me by my shirt, twisting it so it would tighten up towards my throat. He shouted at me, "Don't you ever run away from me again." Then he made me promise not to as much as look at, much less talk to another guy again.

Feeling like I was choking, I said "I can't promise you that Danny, I work with girls and guys."

He said, "Well then this will be an incentive for you." He made a fist and punched me in the side. I fell down to my knees crying for him to stop! He took his foot and started kicking me in my side. I felt like a trapped animal that was about to die. Before he could get in one more kick, Derrick and another guy heard my screams, noticed what was happening, and started yelling for Danny to stop. Danny just looked at them smugly and told them to mind their own business.

The other guy went over to try to calm Danny down restraining him, and Derrick came over to me, to see how he could help me. He said, "Judging from what I've seen and your husband's attitude, this isn't the first time that this has happened to you is it?" I must have looked a mess. I could tell that my face was still bleeding. Derrick reached into his pocket and pulled out a towel, trying gently to blot my face. He knelt down beside me and quietly asked me my name.

I said, "Katie Jenkins."

"Well hi Katie, you look pretty hurt. I'm going to see if I can stand you up."

A few yards away, Danny was still ranting and raving to the other guy who was trying to keep him away from me. I could hardly stand; Derrick picked me up and carried me back to the stables. The other guy radioed to have security come quickly to the scene that Danny created. As Derrick carried me through the trail, he asked me, "Katie, why do you let your husband do this to you? Have you ever had him arrested?"

"No," I promptly answered, "He would only come after me worse when he would get out."

As we got back to the stables, Derrick called for an ambulance to take me to their local hospital. He suspected I might have broken a rib by the way I'd wince at the slightest touch. He looked at me, and asked if it was all right to look at my side. He lifted the side of my shirt to reveal a bruised and swollen area. Danny wasn't there yet, and Derrick didn't want him to find out where they were taking me. He asked me if I would consider pressing charges. "I'm sure, judging by your reaction, that this guy has beaten you up before." I was too embarrassed to even answer him, but just then, Derrick said, "Well Katie, your transportation has arrived." He helped me into the ambulance and told me he had to fill out a report. He made it clear to me that he had to write down the truth as he had seen it, and that it wasn't a fall from a horse that I was injured from.

When I got to the hospital, they took x-rays. I waited in my room for awhile by myself, thinking about what a memorable honeymoon this would be. After sitting on the bed contemplating how much worse this could have been, the doctor came into the room and reported, that in addition to all the bruises and contusions, I also had two broken ribs. He proceeded to ask me what had happened and I didn't know what to say or do.

Just then, I heard Danny's voice outside my room demanding to see his wife. In fact, everyone in the hall probably heard him. They asked him to settle down and said that they would take him to see me. When he walked into the room, he came over to hug me. He brought my head to his chest and pretended to be so concerned for me. "Oh Katie, honey are you okay?" he asked.

Again the doctor asked, "Can somebody please tell me what happened."

Of course, Danny jumped in with his version, of it being a horrible accident. "She fell against a rock after she tripped over a twig on the ground. She's really clumsy you know, one of those accident prone people."

The doctor looked disgusted as he filled out a report. One of the interns looked at me with disbelief and obviously knew that Danny was lying. He looked directly at me and asked me if it was true.

"Why wouldn't it be?" Danny boldly attacked. Then he said "Tell them Katie, that everything I said was true?"

I just put my head down and agreed with him. You could tell these guys weren't buying Danny's line, but he had to write down the story as he was told. The doctors told me to take it easy, the ribs will heal on their own, and he gave me a prescription for some pain medication.

After that disaster, we went back to the honeymoon resort. Danny flagged down a taxi and was pissed about how much it cost him for this trip to the hospital. But at least he left me alone for the rest of our honeymoon.

He did, however, make me partake in his morning workouts, acting as weights by lying on his back or shoulders doing his pushups. I was so sore; every time that he went up and down, it put pressure on me. His focus in life now was getting obsessed with bodybuilding again.

The rest of our honeymoon seemed to drag since I couldn't do much; I couldn't wait until it was over. The highlight of my week was soaking in the resort's hot tub and steam room, while Danny would spend hours down at the resort's gym.

On one of our last days there, Danny went down to the gym. I slowly strolled down to the inside pool area. Entering the water, I stayed on the second step of the pool, where the water level was just over my shoulders. While relaxing, I heard a familiar voice ask me how I was doing. It was Derrick, the guy from the horseback stables.

I told him I was doing fine.

He said, "I heard through the grapevine that your husband broke a couple of your ribs?" I didn't know what to say. He knelt down by me, put his hand gently on my shoulder, and asked me if I reported it as it really happened. I looked up at him and just shook my head no. Derrick asked me why I was doing this to myself.

Still silent, I had to fight back the tears that flooded my eyes. I managed to choke out a few words, "You just don't understand Derrick."

"Yes I do Katie, I understand that a beautiful, nice girl is being treated like an animal. I'm going to give you the number of someone that you can call, and they'll be able to help you out Katie, but you have to be willing to talk about it. Your husband is not going to stop abusing you if you stay. Do you want to stay with him Katie?" I put my head down, I couldn't give Derrick an answer.

While slowly getting out of the pool, Derrick grabbed a towel and wrapped it around my body very gently. I told him I just wanted to go back to my room.

Derrick told me that he'd walk back to my room with me, if it were all right.

I think I was playing Russian Roulette with my life, fearing what Danny might do if he saw us walking together. Thankfully, I knew he'd still be in the gym for hours yet. As we approached my suite, I stopped and thanked Derrick for what he's tried to do.

He took both of my hands, gave me a soft kiss on my cheek and said to me, "Please Katie, for your own good, get rid of this guy before he kills you! All guys are not abusers that want to hurt girls, especially sweet girls like you Katie." He reached into his pocket and pulled out one of his cards with his name and number on it, and the number for the crisis center for abused and battered wives. "Here take this." He said.

I thanked him and clutched the card in the palm of my hand, while telling him that I had to go. I was afraid if I didn't leave that second, I'd never go back home. As I opened the door, Derrick put his hand over mine, and said to me that if I ever needed someone to talk to, just call him and reverse the charges.

"Thank you again Derrick, you really helped me out, I don't know how I can ever repay you." He said, " Leave your husband Katie, and don't ever look back!" He leaned over and gave me a kiss on my lips! His lips were so warm and soft, and I wanted to kiss him back but I said, "I really do have to go back in my room now."

"I understand." He said.

I waved goodbye, smiled and closed the door. I stood against the closed door, put my head up against it, as I broke down and sobbed. I thought about what a great guy Derrick is, and how I have to be stuck with Danny. Soon I composed myself and started packing, as we would be leaving the next morning.

On our way back home, we had to stop at the Barbell Company that Danny had been talking about since before we left for our honeymoon. He was like a child in a toy store. He purchased weight benches, leg extension machines, and all sorts of weights. Before arriving at the store, he said that he was just buying a few things. He used what was left of our wedding money and told me to give him my credit card. He couldn't get one himself because of bad debts he accrued, so I had one in my name alone.

I said, "Danny, don't you think that you should have a limit?"

His response was "What for? You'll be paying the charges off, so if there's not enough money, get a second job."

I told Danny that I didn't feel well and I needed to lie down in the back seat. As we proceeded towards home, I knew it would be a long ride. I think that maybe Danny was feeling a bit guilty for breaking my ribs. He tried to keep striking up a conversation with me, but I wasn't in the mood to listen to him, much less talk to him.

I had the card that Derrick gave me clenched tightly in my hand and it gave me peace and solace, even though there was only a couple of numbers on it. I felt a connection to Derrick. It was a wonderful feeling to have a nice guy treating me with respect. I also knew that if Danny ever found it, or knew of me calling Derrick, he'd go ballistic. So as we drove back on the big, beautiful open roads, I slightly opened my window in the back seat and let my memory of Derrick, and possible help, blow right out the window. Turning to watch the paper take flight into the wind, I wiped the tears as they ran down my cheek. Closing my eyes for the rest of the way home, I replayed Derrick's kiss over and over again in my dreams.

We got home in six hours. Danny unpacked the car while I went into the house. I was still quite sore. The makeup I put on to disguise my facial bruises and cuts had already started wearing off. Our landlady, Mrs. Willis, noticed I was hurt and asked me what had happened.

Danny, as usual, jumped in with his far-fetched version of the truth. He told them that I fell from a horse on our last day at the resort, adding that I was checked out and will be fine. Mrs. Willis looked at me in disbelief, as she watched me put my head down.

"Katie, are you really all right honey?" she asked.

"I'm fine Mrs. Willis," I responded.

Mrs. Willis then told me that when I was up to it, she would help me get started on that afghan I wanted to learn how to knit.

My reply was short and sweet, "I can't wait, but right now, I'm going to go lie down. The pain pills the hospital gave me made me very sleepy." I excused myself and passed out cold in bed. Before I knew it, daylight was peeking through my bedroom window. It was the next day already, and you know what they say about a good night's sleep, "Things will be better in the morning." As long as I wake up to Danny every morning, I know in my heart, I will never wake up to a better, "next day."

Chapter 11

The days and weeks seemed to go rather quickly, especially with Danny being on his best behavior once again. He was content for now to keep busy with his bodybuilding and work.

Now it was time for Danny's mother to start her long and everlasting interference in our lives. It wasn't enough that Danny and I had problems of our own to deal with, but now his mother's constant interfering would take me to a new level of a living nightmare. She was a very small woman, but she had a very big and powerful hold on both of her sons. It just didn't seem normal to me that a decent mother would go out with her sons, and encourage them to drink, and then get as drunk as they got!

I remembered back to a time when Danny and I had one of our many fights, before we were married. My friend Marilyn and I had gone out. We had a great time, and it just happened to be such a beautiful, warm summer night. You could actually see all the stars shining so brightly in the sky. Marilyn and I had gone to her uncle's house; they were having a huge birthday party for their daughter Sherry, who just turned sweet sixteen. Many of our friends were there, and as the party got under way the band arrived. It felt so good not having Danny right by my side, no worries, and no complaints. It was quite relaxing. Sherry's Dad did not allow any alcohol at this party, it's amazing how much fun people could have if they just stayed sober. At least you can remember the fun you had the next day!

As the night started winding down, Marilyn asked me if I wanted to leave. I said, "Sure, you're driving."

She asked me if I was hungry.

I laughed and said that I was still stuffed.

Marilyn said that she ate earlier when we first got there, and that she didn't snack on anything throughout the rest of the night, so she was a bit hungry. She said, "I feel like a cheeseburger. Do you want to go with me to get one?"

I said "Sure, but I don't want anything to eat."

We stopped at a burger joint near our house. As Marilyn pulled into the restaurant's lot, she noticed Danny's brother's car in the parking lot. She pulled two cars away from Tim's car and parked. She said, "Wait here Katie, I'll go in and be back in a flash."

I fiddled with the radio to see if I could tune in a song that I liked. As Marilyn came out of the restaurant, I noticed her glancing over at Tim's car. She paused for a moment, stopped and continued back to her car. She got in and said to me, "You are not going to believe who is in that car with Tim; It's Suzie Sinclairey."

I couldn't believe it. "You mean he's cheating on his girlfriend Michelle for Suzie?"

"Yeah, but you got to remember that Suzie will sleep with anyone!" Marilyn got silent all of a sudden.

"What Marilyn, what's wrong?" I asked.

"It's Danny. He's in the back seat of the car, and I think he has his arm around another girl."

I was shocked! How can he have the nerve to beat on me and then cheat on me too? I was so mad; I told her that I am going out there to see who it was, thinking I could use this to totally break off this night-mare relationship.

Marilyn grabbed me by my arm and said, "No Katie. You don't know what he'll do, especially if he is drunk. Besides, it was dark maybe I was wrong. It could have been that Danny was alone."

"Nice try Marilyn." I said, and boldly got out of the car and walked over to Tim's car. I abruptly approached the car and Tim looked right at me and said, "Hi Katie." He seemed a little embarrassed by my unexpected intrusion, but Marilyn was right; in the front seat, all cozied up next to Tim, was Suzie. My eyes then shifted towards the back seat where I was not only shocked, but also sickened. Danny too, was all snuggled up with—his mother!

She was obviously as drunk as her sons were, if not more. Danny had his arm around his mother and she had her head on his shoulder. As he tried to acknowledge a familiar sounding voice, Danny, a bit wobbly with his head, looked as though he had just gotten off a spinning ride at an amusement park. His eyes just about rolled up into the top of his head. He was so wasted that he didn't even recognize me! His mother, on the other hand, seemed to recognize me and even spoke a little to me, but with a slur. She always whined when she talked and that night it was even worse. She said, "Hiii Katieee, weee went out tonight and my Dannyyy here was my date. We danced and played pool and had such a wonderfullll timeee."

I just gave her a disgusted look, turned around, and ran back to Marilyn's car. When I got back into the car, she asked me what was wrong. I just told her "Let's get out of here and fast!"

Marilyn asked me who Danny was with. I told her that she was not going to believe it! "Guess," I said.

She replied, "Carol Walker?"

I said no, with a puzzled look.

"What about Denise Bukley?" She asked.

I again said no, and asked her why she would think that it was any one of those girls.

Marilyn's voice changed, as she dropped her head slightly and said, "Katie, I gotta tell you something. Danny has been seen around with those other girls and there are a few others."

"What do you mean that he has been seen with them?"

Marilyn replied, that Carl Rictor and Ricky Romma said that Danny's been screwing around on you for a long time already. He even brags about how many notches he puts in his headboard every time he scores.

I was dumbfounded and responded, "While he's been with me?"

Marilyn nodded adding, "Even Denise Bukley who has been with him said that he got so rough with her during sex, that she never wanted to go out with him again!"

"Why am I hearing this for the first time Marilyn. How long have you known?"

"Only a month, but I really didn't think that you would believe me Katie, honest, besides I was trying to wait for the perfect moment, so you could see for yourself. I'm really sorry Katie. So who was Danny with?" Marilyn asked.

"You'll never believe it, it was his mother!"

"His mother? Are you sure Katie?"

"Yes, I tried to talk to her, but she was incoherent. Both her and Danny were totally intoxicated."

Marilyn asked, "Are you saying he is sleeping with his mother?" I said, "All I know is I wouldn't be surprised if they were!" We both shivered, as the thought ran through our minds. We left the conversation at that and decided to call it a night.

The next day Danny stopped over at my house and we decided to go for a walk. He obviously didn't have any recollection of the night before. He once again, acted like nothing was wrong. I was so upset about what Marilyn told me that I just blurted out to him, "So Danny, I heard through the grapevine that you've been sleeping around on me."

Still half-drunk, he just looked at me and laughed, "Who the hell told you that Katie, one of your little friends? Oh, wait, you don't have any friends!"

"I'm tired of you putting me down Danny and I want you to tell me the truth about Denise and Carol."

"Who?" He asked.

I repeated it for him, this time screaming it in his face, "Denise and Carol!"

All of a sudden, he backslapped my face. I started to cry as I held onto my face with both hands as he began shouting, "Don't you ever question me on who I sleep with. I do what I want to do, and with who I want, and I don't have to answer to you!"

"So you are sleeping with other girls," I wept. Then what am I to you? Just let me go, and you can sleep with a hundred girls!

He continued laughing and ignorantly added, "I can't Katie, you'll always be my spare!"

Later that day at Danny's house, I told him that his family was strange and I accused him of sleeping with his mother too. Talk about the worst fright night show you could ever imagine! The look in Danny's eyes and on his face said it all. Before I could say another word, he grabbed me by my shirt and walloped me in the head so hard, that I fell against the kitchen cupboards. He bent down and slowly pulled me up. While shaking me like a ragdoll, he lifted me up into the air and shouted in my face, "You lousy slut. You think that I sleep with my mother!" Spit was spewing out of his mouth while he was screaming. He removed one hand from my shirt, and used it to punch his fist into my stomach. Gasping for air, I fell down to the floor and curled up in a ball holding onto my stomach.

I cried, "Stop it Danny, please stop, please."

In his sarcastic tone, he mimicked me and began kicking me on the floor, repeating over and over again, that I was a bitch. While raising his fist to swing again, it was stopped in mid air. Tim was home! He had come in through the front door. I didn't know how much more I could have taken.

"What the hell do you think you are doing Danny?" Tim yelled.

Danny started to cry and said, "She deserves it Tim, she accused me of sleeping with mom." There was a long pause of dead silence in the room, Tim looked slowly at me, and tears started running down his cheeks.

"How do you know this Katie?" He asked.

Danny yelled, "Shut up Tim, just shut up."

Tim helped me up and said in a whisper, "Some secrets are better kept within the family, okay Katie. Just forget this happened."

I never really got an answer to my question. I do know in my heart, by the way they both acted that day, that the memories of their sister's rape, at the hands of their father still haunting them, and all the abuse they have endured, this family's secrets, already ruined a lot of lives. I laid it to rest that day.

CHAPTER 12

Being married to Danny will be quite challenging, but I was really looking forward to resuming a somewhat normal life. I got a job as a salesperson at a fancy clothing store. It wasn't long before I was promoted to head cashier, my move from a cashier position. I really loved all the people that worked there; it was like being in one big happy family because everyone got along so well. I didn't think that you were supposed to love going to work so much, but I did. My boss, Joan Archer, who was about ten years older than the rest of us, was like a mother to us. Most of the people were around the same age, early to mid twenties. There was a specialty coffee shop attached to our store, where we would all meet for breaks and lunches.

One day a handsome, young and charming regional manager named Eric Sommers relocated to our store. All of the girls went nuts over him. We all got to know him really well. He seemed like a great guy, for a boss that is. His method for high productivity was to treat his employees with respect and dignity.

After Mr. Sommers was on board for a few weeks, my friend Sue who worked the service desk told me there were rumors that Mr. Sommers really liked me. We did spend a lot of time together on our breaks and lunches, which he would often pay for. I told Sue that Mr. Sommers was a friend to everyone and liked all of us.

Sue said, "No Katie, I mean he likes you, you know, guy and girl stuff. Do you understand what I am saying?"

My face must have turned every shade of red! I replied, "He knows that I am married."

Sue said, "Katie, we know it's a marriage on paper, no love no happiness. It's about time that you get rid of Danny. How long are you going to continue to let him beat on you. It's about time you started living a normal life." Surprisingly, I told Sue that I secretly dream about being with Mr, Sommers! Sue said, The way he looks at you Katie, so adoringly, I'm sure you can turn that dream into a reality!

I thought to myself about what Danny would do if I told him that I wanted to leave, or if he knew someone else liked me.

A couple more months passed by and the holidays were quickly approaching. Our store's Christmas party was going to be at an elegant restaurant this year. It was going to be tough to get out of the house at night without Danny. I knew he would forbid me to go. I bought a brand new dress anyway, and left it along with everything else I would need for that night, at Sue's house. The party was going to be on a Friday and luckily, Danny had been scheduled to work until 11:30 p.m. The Christmas Party was starting at 7:00 p.m., which adds up to four hours to go out and finally have some fun. I was really excited! Although I was planning to take my own car in order to arrive home before Danny, the plan was for me to get ready at Sue's house.

The day of the party arrived. Danny finally left for work around 4:00 p.m. I took a relaxing bubble bath while listening to my favorite radio station and drinking a cup of tea. It's amazing how a simple pleasure like a warm bubble bath can make you feel so good. I slowly drank my cup of tea and closed my eyes.

My thoughts began to drift far away from here. I imagined myself being with my store manager Eric Sommers tonight at our Christmas party. He is so handsome and so kind. Just remembering the sweet smell of his fragrant cologne made me feel like he was really here with me. I thought about talking with him, and dancing slowly next to him with our arms wrapped tightly around each other. I envisioned him kissing me so softly on my lips, making it last through the night!

All of a sudden, I was back to reality by the sound of the phone ringing. I jumped out of the tub and threw a towel over myself to go answer the phone. It was Sue asking me if I could be at her house by 6:30 p.m. Still slightly in a trance, I told her that I would be there with bells on!

I had to sneak around a lot, just to get ready for this party. Danny is such a snoop. It's terrible to have a husband that ravages through all of your possessions. He would go through my phone book, wallet and purse. When I would find money missing and confront him, he would just say, "What he made was his and what I made was his, and that was that." The new dress I purchased for the party, had I told him, would have provoked a 20-question quiz.

Springing into action, I had to hurry up and gather up everything I needed to take over to Sue's house, so I could finish getting ready. Her house was always so festive! Sue lived at home with her mom, and her mom loved to decorate, even more so for the holidays. When Sue came to the door she was already dressed and looked dynamic! She rushed me up to her bedroom and told me to get dressed there. "Hurry up Katie." she hollered. "I want to help you with your hair." She put my hair up and it looked great. Sue and I complimented each other and gave our egos a great big boost! "Well, off to the ball Cinderella." Sue announced.

I followed her in my car. When we arrived at the restaurant the party was already underway. Most of the employees were a group of loud and fun-loving partyers, very upbeat. I enjoyed being around them so much. Everyone was there including the store managers, district regional managers, and of course Mr. Sommers. We knew immediately where he was, right smack in the middle of all the available girls! I almost felt guilty for day dreaming about him.

Sue and I went over to the bar. She ordered a Slo Gin Fizz and I ordered a glass of red wine. As we went to find a table we heard a "yoo-hoo" from behind us. It was Joan Archer, our boss and friend saying, "Come over here and sit girls. I saved your seats." Joan really liked Sue and I a lot. We were like sisters, Joan being the older and wiser one. She also could talk to us for hours about her physic abilities. Some of her stories could make your hair stand on edge. I think we all have the ability to be physic, and as time goes on, I realize that intuition and dreams can play a really big part in all of our lives. You either learn how to use your intuition, or you can choose to ignore it, but usually, it's right!

Joan was really excited about this evening. Sue and I just couldn't believe that we were sitting at the boss's head table. Sue told me that Joan thinks the world of me and wants desperately for me to get away from Danny. She also said that Joan wanted to get Mr. Sommers and me together somehow. Joan thought we would make a cute couple!

I said to Sue, "Sure, like that would even be a possibility, especially for someone like me in my present situation, having a maniac for a husband!

Sue just looked at me and sighed. As I sat down I noticed Joan had this huge smile across her face. My seat of course, was next to Mr. Sommers. All of a sudden, I was overcome with feelings of nervousness and anxiety. The party was just staring to kick into high gear and everyone seemed to be going with the flow. Sue and Joan kept on nudging me to go up to Mr. Sommers and ask him to dance.

We all got up and started walking to the bar to get a drink, and as we were standing around laughing and talking, I noticed from the corner of my eye that Mr. Sommers was staring at me. We made perfect eye contact and he winked and smiled at me, showing off his beautiful dimples. Joan noticed this happening and nudged me while quietly saying, "I do believe Mr. Sommers is flirting with you Katie." I shyly smiled, I felt just like a schoolgirl, and secretly wished to myself that he would come over to talk to me, or ask me to dance. Mr. Sommers had jet black, slightly wavy hair, with big brown eyes and a smile that would warm your heart. While bringing myself back to reality, we decided to take our drinks back to the table.

I found myself drinking that glass of wine very fast, which gave me a slight rush. I was starting to feel a bit warm, and told the girls that I would have one more drink before leaving. But, I wasn't going up for just the drink, I was hoping to see Mr. Sommers. As I stood there waiting for my glass of wine, I felt a tap on my shoulder and heard the words "my treat." I froze for a moment, knowing exactly who it was. As I turned around, my heart was pounding and there he was, standing right in front of me! I quickly came back with a joke and we both laughed because the drinks were on the house all night. I asked him if that was his best pickup line, and he came back with, "That line never seems to work." I could feel my face turning red, and my whole body turning to rubber. My heart was doing double beats. For one of the first times in my life I was speechless! My thoughts were drifting, wondering if Sue was right about Mr. Sommers liking me, or if he was just kidding around. He asked me if I wanted to go for a walk.

I didn't even hesitate, and answered, "Sure."

The restaurant was huge and it had countless banquet rooms and a beautiful courtyard. A Mercedes Benz was revolving on a pedestal with brightly shining lights all around it. Mr. Sommers told me that he is really into cars, especially the older ones. He told me that before he was fifteen years old, even before he got his driver's license, he already owned a few cars. I said, "What kind of cars did you own?" He said "I owned a '71 Nova, '70 Dodge Challenger, and a '40's coupe." They, of course, were all apart and rusted, but he said that he liked to restore old cars back to new again. Mr. Sommers mentioned that he was trying to get a car ready for an upcoming car show, a cherry red 1969 Chevelle!

I told him that I loved Chevelles, especially red ones.

He smiled and said, "Ahhh, a girl after my own heart!" We strolled along the halls; the decorations were phenomenal! Everywhere was mirrors with lights; it was a wonderland of pure beauty. I felt a bit uncomfortable at first, but the scenery was too beautiful, and the company was too pleasurable to resist. Whenever we would pass by a ceiling fan, I couldn't help but smell the wonderful aroma of Mr. Sommer's cologne. He asked me if I was ready for the holiday season.

I said, "The holidays are always so hectic. I come from a very large family and Christmas time is very special to me." I discovered it was the same for his family. The more we talked the more nervous I got; I didn't know why I felt like this, since we always talked in the coffee shop at work. Since he already had an idea about my abusive relationship with Danny, he asked me how things were going between us. I said, "It was all right." He turned towards me and said, "Katie, is it really all right?" I couldn't look him straight in the face and tell him that it was. He gently picked up my chin with his hand and said, "Look at me, please Katie, we all care about you…I really care about you."

I looked up at him. He wiped a tear from my cheek, as he pulled me in close to him and embraced me. I hugged him back. For one of the first times in my life since I met Danny, I felt a surge of warmth and security. At first I didn't say a word; I dreamed about this, and I wanted the moment to last. I took a step back, looked up into his big brown eyes and said, "Mr. Sommers I…"

"Katie," He said, "Please call me Eric."

I smiled and said, "Okay, but only when no one is around."

Then he just blurted out, "Katie, are you in love with Danny?"

I couldn't believe that I did this; but I looked straight into his trusting gorgeous eyes and said, "No, and I don't think that I ever really was!"

We were standing in front of the most beautifully decorated inside garden, which had huge gold fish swimming around by the fountain. It was at this beautiful garden that Eric brought me close to him and kissed me. I hesitated for just a moment, but then our lips joined again. It felt so wonderful, so right. I never felt like this with anyone! After our long and passionate kiss, Eric held me in his arms and told me that he really liked me a lot. All I could think about was his kiss. When reality hit me I looked at Eric and said, "I really like you too Eric, and I know that every other girl who works for you likes you. I mean you are a young, handsome, and wonderful guy!"

He laughed and said, "Katie, your innocence is so refreshing. I'm sure that you know from our kiss that I like you in a different way, and I think that you feel it too."

I was so confused, I wanted to tell him that he makes me feel so alive and special, but all I could choke out was, "Eric, I'm married, and to a very vicious guy. Nothing could ever go any further than this." I could have bit my lip off saying it.

Eric replied, "But Katie, you don't even have a good marriage, why don't you want to leave him?"

"I would love to leave him, but no one knows Danny's temper more than me. He would kill you or me or anyone else who would get in his way. I just don't want to drag you into my screwed up life Eric, you're too wonderful of a person for that."

He tried to convince me that his uncle was a lawyer and both his brothers were cops, and that they could help me, but it didn't work. I was too scared.

I looked at Eric and said to him, "You could know the Pope and the President, and even they wouldn't be able to stop Danny. Once he is on a rampage, nothing stops him. He just doesn't care."

At that moment Sue came by looking for us and said that it was time to eat. Sue had a smile on her face a mile wide and her eyes were twinkling with curiosity. Eric threw me a wink and we all headed back up to the party.

The food was delicious and we all had a lot of fun at the table. After we were finished eating, Sue got up from the table and headed out to mingle with everyone. There was no one left except Eric and me. He kept trying to talk to me, but the music was so loud that he finally leaned in closer. He moved my hair gently away from my face with his hand and whispered in my ear, "Katie, you look beautiful, and you smell really good, would you do me the honors and dance with me?"

I thought to myself there's nothing more that I'd rather do, but I said, "Maybe later." I could have slapped myself. Eric stood up and pushed out his chair. He then pulled out mine and slowly raised me up by my hands as we both entered the dance floor. The band was playing a beautiful song, one I still remember to this day. I never wanted it to end. Eric was such a good dancer; each step was perfect rhythm. I felt like I was floating on air. He pulled me in close and asked me out after the party, but I explained that Danny didn't even know that I was here, and that I would have to leave early to get home before Danny did.

"Katie," he said, "Let me help you."

I interrupted him and said, "It's the way it has to be. Right now, I just want to enjoy this dance with you." We finished the rest of the dance in silence. He held me even more tightly next to his body, and I knew at that point that I had fallen in love with Eric.

After the slow song, the band changed the music to a Country song that you could line dance to. I looked at my watch and realized that it was already 10:30 p.m. I told Eric that I had to go! An endless group of girls wanted to pull Eric back onto the dance floor. He was reluctant to go but they dragged him over to do a line dance. He just looked at me with concern, and I just smiled back at him.

Sue was sitting at our table talking with someone. I told her frantically, "I have to leave. If Danny gets home before I do he's gonna kill me!"

Sue and Joan got up and came over to hug me. "Whatever you do Katie, don't drive home fast, and do not let Danny hurt you." Sue said.

I hugged them both back and told them to tell everyone that I had to go, and to especially tell Eric that I'm sorry that I had to leave so suddenly.

Sue and Joan looked at each other puzzled at first, and then looked back at me smiling saying, "Oh, you called him Eric now!" I laughed and started to leave as Sue yelled to me, "Hey Cinderella, you owe me a good story tomorrow!" While driving home, all I thought about was the wonderful kiss that Eric and I shared. I could still feel his warmth on my lips.

I knew I'd have a few minutes after I got home before Danny would be there. He usually got out at around 11:20 p.m. I couldn't believe it; as I approached our apartment, I saw Danny's car there already! All I could think of is he must have had a slow night and got out early. Panicking, I pulled over a couple of doors away and changed my clothes in the car, while trying to think up a story to tell Danny. After I pulled into the driveway I slowly got out of the car, leaving my clothes in the back seat. I closed the door behind me when suddenly I felt a hard tug on my coat.

"So Katie, where in the hell have you been!" Danny barked. He must have been sitting outside waiting for me.

" I…. I…"

He interrupted me, grabbed me by my throat and said, "You have been a naughty girl Katie and now you have to pay the price."

I just blurted it out, "I went to my store's Christmas party Danny, and I didn't tell you because you probably wouldn't have let me go."

"Your dammed right about that you little slut," he shouted. "Did you screw anyone there?"

"No!" I shouted back. "I was just there with my friends."

He laughed hysterically saying, "You don't have any friends Katie, you are a loser," while pulling me into the house and slamming the door behind us. "You have no business going out!"

I hesitated and said to him, "Look Danny, if you had a Christmas party I wouldn't tell you that you couldn't go."

"You bet your ass you wouldn't," he said. "You don't ever tell me what to do." At that moment, he took off the belt from his pants and said, "Now little girl, I'm gonna have to teach you how to listen." He doubled the belt over, snapping it at me a couple of times. Then he grabbed me by my hair, pushing me down to the floor. He took the buckled part of the belt and hit it on the middle part of my back countless times.

I screamed for him to stop yelling, "Stop it Danny, please stop it hurts." His blows to me were stopped by a very loud knock on the door. It was our landlords!

Danny told me to shut up and be quiet. He got up, composed himself, and went over to open the door. I heard concern in Mr. Willis' voice as he asked Danny, "What seems to be the problem here, we thought we heard Katie screaming?"

Danny made sure he opened the door, but only slightly, keeping his foot against it. He answered in a stern voice that nothing was wrong.

Mrs. Willis asked him if she could please see Katie.

Danny put her off by saying, "No, you can't, she's sleeping."

They asked him what all the noise was and Mrs. Willis timidly, but directly, asked Danny if he was hitting me or pushing me around.

Danny's voice changed to a softer tone, "Oh no, I would never hurt that wonderful wife of mine. It was probably the TV you heard. I had it on very loud but be assured, I'll make sure from now on I keep it down."

I kept silent on the floor, lightly sobbing. I knew what Danny was capable of and I didn't want to get the Willis' involved. Danny said goodnight to the Willis' while he closed the door on them. After a few minutes passed, Danny came over to me swiftly kicking me in the legs while saying, "Get your ass up Katie, in the morning, we are looking for a new apartment. These people are way too nosy."

I thought to myself about how much I love it here and how I don't want to move. Instead, I went upstairs and got ready for bed. As I was changing, he burst into the room and once again yanked me down to the floor. He unzipped his pants and forced himself into me. It really hurt, so I just turned my head and bore the pain. Feeling so ashamed of myself, and wishing Danny would just die, thoughts of just killing him strongly entered into my mind!

When he finished, he just got up and went to bed. I always felt like I was repeatedly being raped, no love or compassion. I hated it, and I hated him! The only feelings I ever experienced with Danny now were those of contempt!

I didn't see what the big deal was, when everyone talks about how great love and sex are, until my kiss with Eric tonight! I had never felt such warmth and closeness before. His lips were so soft and his breath, so sweetly warm. I felt so wonderful and kind of fuzzy inside. I lay in bed and dreamed about Eric for the entire night. I didn't want the morning to ever come.

CHAPTER 13

The next day I went to work feeling very sore. Danny got a couple of huge welts on my back last night. Thank God, the Willis' arrival stopped him from hurting me even more.

Sue came over grinning from ear to ear. When I checked in she caught up to me and said, "Come on, spill it girl, what happened when you and Mr. Sommers, oh I mean Eric, went on your walk?"

I told her that nothing happened, and that we had a nice time talking.

"That's it!", she blurted out.

Then I added, "Oh yeah, he's a really great guy, and a wonderful kisser! Sue screamed, "I knew it! Oh Katie, you got to get rid of Danny now!"

Sue also told me that Eric seemed so disappointed that I left so early. Then she said, "Oh Katie by the way, the sweater and dress that you ordered came in this morning. You can try them on before we start work." Sue brought me my outfit and I tried it on in the dressing room. I carefully pulled my shirt off over my head, the welts on my back really hurt. As I bent down for a moment to step into the dress, Sue ran in with the matching scarf that went with the dress. She stood there for a moment staring at the bruises and welts on my back. Her eyes seemed as big as golf balls as she dropped the scarf and cried out, "Katie, what happened! Wait, that maniac did this to you, didn't he."

I just looked at her and said, "It was kind of my fault Sue, I shouldn't have gone to the party. Danny got home early and…"

Sue just grabbed me and hugged me gently as we both just cried.

She said "Katie, it's not your fault. He's a sick psychopathic asshole! Why can't you see that?"

I said, "I do see that Sue, I'm not stupid, but I can't do anything at this point. Danny would surely kill someone in my family or me! I know he's not right, but he also will NEVER let me leave him either."

"I'm going to take care of this for you Katie, I am going to kill him myself." Sue was so upset for me that she was shaking.

I calmed her down and told her everything will be all right. It was time to start our shift and we agreed to meet in the coffee shop for lunch and talk more, but I made her promise not to tell Eric about what Danny did to me! "Promise me Sue please, swear on your family's lives that you won't tell anyone." Sue nodded her head yes, while putting her head down into her hands.

The day seemed to drag. Eric was working the later shift and had not yet come in. Finally, lunchtime arrived and I met Sue in the coffee shop. We were both exhausted from the party the night before. Sue always managed to make me feel so much better about myself, and she was as good for my self-esteem as Danny was bad for it. We both ordered our food, and I also got some tea. Just as I took the first sip, I looked up to find Eric standing over us. I could smell his cologne. My stomach felt like it had butterflies in it; what a great feeling it is to feel so alive!

Eric's shift was about to begin. He gallantly said, "Good afternoon ladies, how did you enjoy the party?" winking at me.

Sue and I still had a few minutes left in our lunch hour, but she decided she had to go and make a couple of important phone calls. She grabbed what was left of her lunch and smiled at me saying, "I'll see you guys later."

Eric asked me if I minded if he sat down with me for a moment.

I was afraid to say yes in fear I would never want him to leave. I said, "Sure Mr. Sommers."

He sat down right next to me as he leaned over and sweetly said, "You can call me Eric Katie, remember?"

"Oh yes, I remember," my mind in a trance, was wandering back to our kiss again.

Eric asked me if I would like to escort him to a meeting that was being held the next day. He said it would be during my work hours so I would be paid.

I said, "Yes, I would love to."

He said that we could both go in his car if that was all right.

The number of butterflies in my stomach doubled, as I told him "That would be great!"

Eric then proceeded to ask me how I was doing, he said, "I had an incredible time last night. Katie, you are a great person to be around." A tear rolled down my cheek as I tried so hard not to cry uncontrollably. Eric reached over to wipe my tear away, asking if he had said something wrong.

I quickly spoke, "Oh no Eric, I loved last night. You made me feel so warm and wonderful, I've never felt like that before. You were such a gentleman. It's just me, I feel so happy when I'm near you." Looking at the clock, I knew it was time to get back to work. I told Eric I would see him later.

He took his hands, placed them over mine and said, "Katie, I think you are a fantastic and wonderful woman, and again, I really do like you a lot."

I replied to Eric that I really like him also. "You're the most caring, and nicest guy I have ever known." Then I stepped back, smiled and walked away. What I really wanted to do was to run back to him and fall right into his arms, never leaving them. I wanted to tell him how good I feel about myself, and that I think I had fallen in love with him, but I stopped myself. It was time to go back to reality, back to work.

I had to walk past Sue at the service desk. As always, she just smiled at me as I walked passed her. I noticed she had Gene over to the service desk to relieve her. She went into the Coffee Shop and sat down with Eric. I watched curiously, hoping she wasn't telling him about what Danny did to me last night.

I confronted her about this after the workday ended, by asking her what she and Eric were talking about. She came up with a fast story about sending out some paperwork to corporate headquarters. She didn't want any mistakes on it. I told her I'd see her tomorrow. She asked me if I was going with Mr. Sommers to the meeting.

I said, "Yes, he asked me to go. We will be gone for the whole day I guess."

She replied, "It seems to me Katie, you really deserve a relaxing day."

When I got home I found Danny there. He told me he found another apartment on the other side of town. The apartment downstairs from his brother and girlfriend was available for rent. I didn't want to move; I loved it where we were.

I said, "Don't you think living downstairs from your brother, who you fight with half the time, is not such a good idea?"

He said that it is a done deal. I thought silently to myself about how it wouldn't work out. I also knew he wanted to move, just so he can beat on me without interference.

Since we had a month to month lease with Mr. & Mrs. Willis, Danny gave them a months notice. Danny left the next morning for work earlier than usual. I still had an hour left before I had to leave. Mrs. Willis softly knocked on my door and I answered it. She said, "Danny told us this morning you both will be moving in a month. Katie, I hope it isn't because of us."

"Oh, no," I started to say.

Mrs. Willis interrupted me, "You know Katie, me and my husband hear you and Danny fighting a lot of nights. And we think he's hitting you. Is he?"

"It'll be okay. I can handle Danny." I replied.

Mrs. Willis continued, "Katie, no man, if he truly loves you, should ever lay a hand on you."

I said, "I know, but really, I'll be okay."

"They never change Katie. What if he hurts you really bad someday?"

"Thank you for being so concerned Mrs. Willis. He wouldn't do anything really bad to me." I knew I was lying to her, but I didn't want her to worry. I hugged her close to me and said, "I'm really going to miss both of you, you know." I couldn't stop the tears from flowing down my face. It was a very emotional scene. "I'll keep in touch, and besides, who else is going to teach me how to knit?"

She smiled and wiped the tears from her eyes with her apron. "Wait here for a moment Katie." She went over to her apartment and returned with an angel pendant. "Keep this pinned on your shoulder; it will keep you safe, and most of all believe in yourself Katie."

"I will always treasure this Mrs. Willis. Thank you."

It was time to leave for work. I put the angel pin on the collar of my dress. On my drive to work, I felt a little anxious. The song "My Eyes Adored You" came on the radio. I thought about what a romantic song it was. It made me think about Eric. I don't know why I was so nervous. It was just a meeting we were going to. Then again, it was going to be just Eric and me in his car alone.

As I pulled up to work, Eric was just getting out of his brand new red convertible Mustang. I had to check in first with Sue at the desk before we could leave. As I got out of my car, Eric rushed over to greet me. "Hi sunshine, ready for a day on the town."

I looked at him and smiled, saying, "Yes, anywhere with you will be fun, even a meeting."

He replied, "Well, it can be fun when you're with the right person." I blushed as we both walked in the store at the same time. Not surprisingly, Sue and Joan were both at the service desk huddled together, scheming and plotting something. They both had smiles as wide as could be, as if they knew something we didn't.

"Well." I said, "I just came to check in." Mr. Sommers went up to the office. Sue and Joan put their arms around me and told me they wished that they could trade places with me. They gave me all the papers I needed to take to the meeting.

After about five minutes, Eric came downstairs from the office and said, "Well Katie, are you ready?"

I turned to Sue and Joan and told them I'd see them later. They were both acting silly as I turned around and smiled, waving goodbye.

We got out to the parking lot and went over to Eric's car. He came around to my side and opened the car door. I thought to myself, "I'm not used to this type of treatment. Usually, Danny slams the door on me or he's pushing me out of it." When I got in the car, I noticed a beautiful bouquet of springtime flowers next to my seat. As Eric got into the car, he presented me with a small wrapped box with a tiny red bow on it, and a cup of tea!

I was speechless, "What's all this for?"

He replied, "I love to watch you smile Katie, and I remember you telling me you didn't like roses because Danny always gave them to you after a fight. So, I brought you some bright cheerful flowers instead. I hope you like them."

"Like them, I love them! Thank you so much Eric. But you shouldn't have."

Then he stopped me to say, "Open up the box Katie."

"It's beautifully wrapped." I said. I didn't know what to expect, so I took off the bow and started to unwrap this small and mysterious box. I couldn't believe my eyes. It was an exact duplicate of the class ring that Danny threw away on me! I started to ask, "But how?"

Eric began to tell me that Sue told him about what happened to my class ring, and how devastated I was when I couldn't find it. "I wanted to do something really special for you Katie. I love to see you smile." He proceeded to tell me that Sue got in contact with my sister Cindy, to find out the exact description of the ring.

I had a stream of tears running down my face as I thanked him by saying, "That was the sweetest gesture that anyone has ever done for me." As he pulled me towards him to embrace me, I spilled my tea on his dashboard. I said, "Oh, I'm sorry, I'm so sorry."

"Don't worry about it Katie, I'll clean it up." He held onto me gently, as I watched the warm liquid from the tea make its way down the dashboard. I felt so wonderful and comforted in his arms that I never wanted this moment to end. Finally, I moved back to my seat and started to wipe up the spilled tea. Eric laughed and said, "Go ahead, if it will make you feel better." He took the ring out of the box and said, "May I," as he slipped it onto my finger. It fit like a glove! I couldn't stop thanking him!

It was time to leave for the meeting. As we drove off, Eric reached over and put a cassette in his tape player. The song by Joe Cocker entitled "You Are So Beautiful" began to play. We listened to the entire song. As we approached a red light, Eric turned to me and said, "Katie, this song was meant for you. It's few words have a lot of meaning."

My face must have been as red as his car as I replied, "You are the sweetest guy I ever knew. You have such a big heart Eric." At this point, I became overwhelmed with emotions that I didn't know how to handle. I asked Eric if he could please tell me why he was being so nice to me. "What I mean to say is, I will remember this day forever. But I have to tell you, it's making me feel very attracted to you and I think I'm starting to......Oh Eric, I'm so sorry. This whole thing is getting really complicated."

Eric pulled the car over to the side of the road. "Katie, don't be sorry for how you feel. I'm feeling the same way about you, and have been for quite awhile." He leaned over and we hugged each other.

I cried on his shoulder while saying, "What can we do? Danny will never let me go. He's crazy."

"Let me take care of you, Katie. I'm not afraid of Danny, but I still want you to be safe."

"That word doesn't even exist in my world with Danny." I looked at the time and told Eric that we had to get to the meeting or we would be late. Eric kissed me and we drove off, but first he said, "Don't worry Katie, we'll figure something out."

The meeting was at the corporate headquarters. I was a little nervous sitting at the table with all the top executives. Seated next to Eric I kept silent while taking notes. They served beverages and pastries, but all I wanted was something to drink. Whenever Eric and I made eye contact, he'd smile at me. That made me feel very comfortable.

The meeting went on for the remainder of the morning. When lunchtime arrived, an elegant buffet was set up provided by the company. Eric and I along with some associates Eric knew sat together. They were a friendly group of people who cracked a lot of jokes.

When lunch was over we returned to the boardroom. While taking notes, I thought about how I was learning quite a bit about myself today.

The meeting was expected to last the whole day, but it adjourned about two hours earlier than anticipated. Eric and I gathered up our belongings and headed out the door. We got back to his car and Eric suggested we swing back to his house for a minute. He needed to pick up a couple of papers for work to bring back to the store. Upon approaching Eric's house, I could see a long winding driveway, leading up to a beautiful house! "Wow." I said, "What a gorgeous home." "Is this yours?" I asked.

Eric said, "No, it's not mine, I'm just renting it for now. Do you like it Katie?"

"Yes, it's beautiful!" I said. "It looks like a mansion." The landscaping was phenomenal! I said to Eric "I love to garden. Being outdoors with nature brings on such a peaceful feeling."

Eric teased me saying, "Oh yeah, well maybe I'll hire you to be my groundskeeper."

I just laughed and said, "Sure, I'd love it."

He asked me if I wanted to come in.

Being very curious about the décor, I said that I would. The inside of his house was even more beautiful. I asked him if he did all the work himself.

He said, "No, most of it was already furnished and decorated. I just had to bring my belongings in. Would you like a glass of wine or some tea?"

I replied, "No thank you I'm fine." He showed me to the back of the house from the rustic kitchen and I said, "What a beautiful view!" The house was on five acres of land. On the back patio was a huge hot tub. About 20 feet away was a built in swimming pool. For a winter's day, the temperature was unusually high, about 57 degrees. With the sun out it felt even warmer.

Eric told me he'd be right back and went to retrieve the papers he needed. I took a couple of deep breaths, breathing in the aromic scent of the warm spring-like air. When he returned he said, "We have some time before we have to get back. Do you want to sit out here for a few minutes? We can talk."

I told him to lead the way. As we sat down together, we both just stared out into the distance, of what seemed to be acres of endless trees and land. I told him that the scenery is breathtaking.

He said, "Not even half as breathtaking as you are Katie." He took both my hands, put them into his and said, "Talk to me Katie, is Danny still hitting you?"

"Eric," I said, "I don't want to spoil this moment talking about Danny. Can we please change the subject?" He looked over at me with such concern, and then slowly leaned over and kissed me. I felt a strong connection to Eric that I'd never felt with anyone else before. I dreamed about him every night, but now my dreams have turned into reality. I kissed him back. He was such a wonderful kisser. I think we broke all records for kissing that day; I could have let it go on for eternity.

Eric said to me, "I love you Katie. I feel so alive and exhilarated when I'm with you."

"I love you too Eric." We just sat there, embraced in each other's arms, until I realized how late it had become. I told Eric that we had to leave. We freshened up and unwillingly decided to go. As we walked toward the car, Eric put his arm around my shoulder and pulled me in close, as I leaned my head onto his shoulder.

I knew this probably wasn't the right thing for me to do, especially with my Catholic upbringing. On the other hand, I think that even God would have forgiven me for how I was beginning to feel about Eric. I just couldn't help myself. Eric was everything I ever imagined dating and real love should feel like. I missed so much during my teenage years being with Danny. He had robbed me of my youth; I never experienced romantic strolls, or the safe, secure warm feelings you experience with someone you love. When I allowed myself to stop daydreaming and come back to reality, I thought all of this would be just a memory, permanently branded into my mind forever.

Eric held the door for me as I slid into the seat. Before he put the key into the ignition, he looked over at me with those beautiful expressive eyes and proceeded to say, "Please Katie, don't let this be over. I don't want something wonderful that just started to end already."

I told Eric, "I think you know how I feel." I put my face into my hands and cried.

Eric comforted me by repeating, "It'll be okay. I'm not giving up on us. We were meant to be together forever. We're soul mates Katie, I can even tell what you're thinking and feeling."

We ended our long and loving embrace because we had to return to the store. At every red light, we gazed at each other as he put his hand over the top of mine. While approaching the parking lot Eric asked when would be the next time we could get together, and if he could call me.

"You can't call me Eric!" I blurted out. "If Danny answers and you hang up, he'll automatically think it's a guy calling me."

"Well then I guess I'll have to settle for seeing you at work for now. I'm a very patient guy. I can wait forever, as long as I know you love me Katie."

I said to Eric, "I have never in my life been so in love or felt like I do when I'm with you." It was a very emotional moment, seeing a tear run down Eric's face as he hugged me.

He asked me if this meant I would leave Danny.

I told him that I needed some time to figure out what I could do.

Eric pledged to me that he's not a violent man, but if Danny lays one more hand on me, no jury would convict him for what he might do.

That was exactly what I thought. I know now, that I could NEVER let Eric find out about Danny hitting me again. I told Eric that I had to do a lot of soul searching.

He replied, "It's going to be a tough night sleeping, just thinking about us."

I said, "I'm going to be up all night myself." I wanted to be with Eric so bad, my whole body ached at the thought of never being a part of his life!

I told Eric that I knew Danny never really loved me, because he's incapable of it. "I've just become his possession. He has to be in control of me at all times, and it is with that kind of sick passion, that drives him to do irrational things. Danny has no morals or values; he's just a cold-hearted person." I proceeded to tell Eric about witnessing fights between Danny and his father. "In their cellar they would start by swearing at one another, then progress to physical violence. One time, Danny shoved his father so hard that he fell against a pole. The clanking sound was so loud; it seemed to ricochet throughout the whole cellar. While watching him lay there, I thought he was dead! Danny with no concern, started kicking and taunting him, while ordering him to get up. He would say, "Get up, you dirty old man, before I kill you.""

Surprisingly, his father grabbed Danny's leg and forced him down. I was so shook up and scared; all I could do was yell at them to stop. It was as if I wasn't even there. Danny continued by raising his fist above his father's head. I remember turning around running as fast as I could up the steps, and bolting right out of that house."

Eric was speechless at first. He just couldn't believe Danny and his family could be so violent. Then he continued to say if I stayed with Danny, he would probably hurt me permanently.

"I've managed to stay alive so far," I said. I didn't know what my greater fear was, to be without Eric, or to have Danny find out about us, and kill us both!

Eric continued, "I don't want you to live in fear anymore Katie. Move in with me. I'll protect you from Danny, always. We'll move you out in one afternoon. All you need is your personal belongings. I'll get you everything else; including a lawyer, who can get you an order of protection. You'll divorce him on the grounds of cruel and inhuman treatment."

My head was spinning. I assured Eric that I trusted him one hundred percent and that I would go home and pack. The idea of being with Eric all the time would be like a dream come true. I gave him a kiss and then we both got into our cars. Again I thanked him for the ring, telling him that I will always treasure it!

Eric told me he loved me as he helped me into my car.

"I love you too, Eric." I said as I drove away.

CHAPTER 14

On my way home, a song came on the radio that always made me feel so alone. Since I've met Eric, I will never feel alone again.

Knowing Danny wouldn't be home yet, it was the perfect opportunity to quickly go through my belongings and gather them up. From inside our closet, I retrieved a hidden strong box that I had found by accident one day. I was always curious about the contents, but never had the courage to look inside. Today I would search it, to ensure none of my missing silver bars were in there. The key was taped to the bottom of the box, so I opened it. My eyes widened as my heartbeat rapidly increased. The box didn't contain my silver. Inside was a small, loaded handgun with a supply of bullets. Since I was sure this was not a legal gun, and not wanting to know what else was in that box, I removed the bullets putting the gun back into the box, after wiping off my fingerprints. Then I retrieved a small envelope in the box that caught my eye. As I picked it up, I could smell the scent of strong woman's perfume. It was addressed to "Dannycakes." I opened it up and began to read it. "Hey baby, had fun the other night. It was quite memorable. But then again, every week is memorable. Meet you at our usual place lucky number 35! Love and Kisses, Shelly."

I thought to myself, "He's been cheating on me again." Then it occurred to me who Shelly was, she's a waitress at the restaurant/hotel where he works. Whenever Danny and I would stop in and have dinner, he would always make sure we sat at her station. It wasn't my imagination when I thought they were flirting with each other. One time I even confronted him about it at the restaurant. At first he smirked, then he grabbed my hand turning it towards the bottom. He placed his hand over the top of mine, and slammed my hand down really hard on the table. It hurt so badly. I thought he had broken my knuckles. He then gritted his teeth and quietly said, "Shut your fucking mouth up about Shelly. And don't ever ask me that question again. Do you understand me?"

While my hand was still in his grip, I said, "Okay, okay, I'm sorry." I knew it wasn't that he was upset that I suspected him of this, it was because of the restaurant's policy, not to have employees who are dating or married, work the same shift. If his boss found out about this affair, they would both get their schedules switched around. I also knew the rooms number 35 that Danny and Shelly had their affair in, was on the far side of the building away from the restaurant. It was a perfect hideaway for them.

Now that I knew about the gun, I was even more scared than ever before! While putting the box back where I found it, I thought for a moment about what he would do to me or Eric, if I just packed up and left. He's even more psycho than I ever imagined. Why did he have a gun? Would he ever use it on me? Is that why he bought it? All these questions raced through my mind as I fumbled to put everything back the way it was. I knew what I had to do—something drastic – quit my job. I had such strong feelings for Eric; I was totally in love with him, but I couldn't let anything happen to him. Right now, I could not worry about myself. In my heart I knew that it would be the only way Eric and I would both be safe. Knowing the more I see him the harder it would be for me to, "step over that line" and make love to Eric! Now, I can only dream about it being one of the most beautiful and loving moments, something Danny could never take away from me.

The next day at work I went into Joan's office and informed her I was giving in my two weeks notice. She was shocked. "Why Katie, is it Danny?"

While trying to compose myself, I told her that I needed to do this.

"Do you have another job?" Joan asked.

"I'm thinking of applying as a waitress at a restaurant near my new apartment. I'm not sure yet."

Joan approached me putting her arms around me and said, "Katie, we're all like family here. When you hurt, we hurt. You know you can tell me anything."

I broke down and cried, "Joan, I don't know what to do."

"Does it have anything to do with Eric? He really loves you, you know."

"I really love him with all my heart and soul. I want to be with him for the rest of my life, but I can't."

"Why not?" Joan asked. "Just leave Danny. It's not like you have many possessions accumulated."

"It's not that. If we did have any, he could have all of it." I decided to tell Joan about the gun, the sleazy note, and everything else. Afterwards, I made her promise not to tell Eric or anyone else. She was great at keeping secrets, a great quality in a friend; I really trusted her. I knew she understood but she still tried to get me to change my mind.

She promised to come up with a story to tell Eric after I leave.

I asked her if she could also promise not to tell anyone else I was leaving.

She agreed on one condition. "You will always keep in touch with me?" She asked.

"Just try and stop me." I replied. We both had tears filling our eyes.

She hugged me and told me that there will always be a place for me here, if I ever changed my mind.

I knew it was going to be a rough couple of weeks. Although I love Sue, I decided not to tell her. She wasn't good at keeping secrets and I couldn't risk Eric finding out yet.

Joan was really going out on a limb for me, having to conduct interviews for my replacement in secret. She assured me everything would be fine.

Eric arrived at work later that day. He wanted to talk to me in the coffee shop. While feeling like I was about to betray the man of my dreams, we both slid into a booth. Knowing exactly what he was going to ask me, I just couldn't look him in his wonderful, trusting, caring eyes. He asked me if I got all my things together.

Not knowing what to say, I told him that it would take awhile. How I wished I could tell him everything, especially about the gun. All I could see was a tragedy, one that I could prevent.

Eric told me to report for work on an unscheduled Sunday; he had a surprise for me. I couldn't resist; he can be so persuasive. I told Eric I would be there, knowing Danny never knows my work schedule from week to week. Whenever Eric looks at me, I just melt. He then softly and sweetly said, "I love you Katie."

It took all of my emotions not to break down and cry. "I love you too Eric! But I have to get back to work. I'll be counting the days until Sunday." I thought that it would be our last time together. Hoping I would have the strength and the courage, I plan to tell Eric on Sunday that I was quitting the store.

The days seemed to drag, only four more to go. Keeping his promise, Eric never called my house. Every chance we got though, we would flirt with each other. It was so fun being at work. I was really going to miss the store and all the people that I've grown to love. I'll especially miss Eric, and the fairytale life I have always dreamed of. People take love and life for granted. Being in an abusive relationship makes it hard to get up every day, and go about your daily routine much less worry about love. If I was able to be with Eric I know that I would treasure every day we had. I wondered how I was going to go on, knowing how good it feels to have someone love me so much, versus Danny, whom I despise so much. I guess some people would think that I should have my head examined, but what they don't know is how fear can rob you of your life.

CHAPTER 15

After a sleepless Saturday night, Sunday finally arrived. Danny had to work, and also thought I did. He was so exhausted, or so he said. Danny said that he and Tim were out until 4:00 a.m. When I asked him where they were, he told me it was none of my business. I knew him and Shelly spent the night in Room 35, as usual, and I didn't even care to confront him about it.

After Danny left for work I proceeded to get ready. Butterflies fluttered around in my stomach as I headed for the shower. After having a relaxing shower, I put on the radio and listened to my favorite songs. I felt like a teenager again, but I also knew I was only fooling myself. It was a beautiful day outside, and I felt like the angels in heaven were rooting for me! As I drove to meet Eric, my mind was racing with thoughts of what I would tell him. I guess I would know the answer to that question when I saw him, maybe I would change my mind.

As I pulled into the parking lot, Eric stepped out of his car waving and smiling. He looked great! I parked next to his car and he opened my door, taking my hand and said, "Hey sunshine, how's it going?"

I laughed and told him how sweet he is. He led me over to his car and helped me in. Just like before, he had a cup of tea waiting in the cup holder. I thanked him.

He turned to smile at me and said, "You look really beautiful Katie, I hope you'll like what I have planned for us.

I told him how I just like being with him. We drove for awhile and we talked all the way to our destination. He was so considerate, not wanting to spoil any of our precious time together by mentioning Danny's name, unless I brought him up.

Our peaceful journey led us to a beautiful scenic park. Eric parked his car and we got out. As we strolled hand and hand, we went through a path that led us to a trail. Ahead of us was a gazebo with an antique bench in it. Eric ran ahead and sat on the bench, gesturing for me to follow. It was so serene and peaceful sitting there, enjoying the warm and wonderful day. I noticed Eric was getting fidgety, constantly checking his watch. Minutes later, a man dressed in a white tuxedo approached us in a horse drawn carriage; he pulled the reins on the horse and stopped right in front of us. Eric had this huge smile on his face while the man stepped down from the carriage, and came over towards us. I asked Eric if this was for us.

He replied, "Yes my lady," and extended his hand out to mine and helped me into the carriage.

I thought, "Oh my gosh, how romantic!" Eric took his place next to me, as the carriage slowly departed. There was a chilled bottle of red wine with two glass goblets and a bouquet of spring flowers in the coach. I smelled them and said, "Flowers, my very favorite. All for me! Thank you so much Eric." I leaned over to kiss and hug him. We cuddled during our romantic ride through the park. I was so wrapped up in the moment. We watched the kids playing and the ducks with their young waddling behind. Lovers were scattered throughout the park, strolling hand in hand, stopping every so often to sneak a kiss. It was magnificent; I wanted to pinch myself to see if this was all a dream.

The world could have ended at that moment and I would have died happy. Our emotions were flying. Eric said to me "Katie, I love you more than life itself. Someday, I would like you to be my wife."

I replied, "Eric, I love you more than you'll ever know." I knew this wasn't the moment to tell him this was all going to end. It was probably selfish of me to want to enjoy the rest of this day, knowing it would probably never happen again, or how much it would hurt us both.

After an hour passed, our "Cinderella" coach ride ended. The driver dropped us back off at the gazebo. While thinking this was it, Eric asked me if I wanted to sit down for awhile and talk. He began by asking me when I would be moving out of the apartment.

"I wasn't sure." I cowardly told him.

Eric asked me if I wanted to change anything at his house, or get anything new for it.

"Oh Eric, I think your house is beautiful just the way it is."

After we sat in silence for awhile, he spoke of getting a couple of cars ready for an upcoming car show.

"When do you have time to prepare cars and paint them?" I asked.

He said that in his spare time he goes down to a friend's collision shop, and uses his facilities.

"You sure do great work. It seems that everything you do, you put your whole heart and soul into. You're a very passionate guy. They don't come any better than you Eric." I said. He kissed me again; it was great!

Just then we heard the sound of a plane overhead, and Eric made sure we stopped to look up at the beautiful sky, while he kept checking his watch. He told me not to take my eyes off the plane. Within seconds, streams of white smoke came out of the plane spelling out the words: I LOVE YOU KATIE. WILL YOU MARRY ME? LOVE FOREVER, ERIC.

I was speechless. Could this day get any more romantic? I couldn't believe someone would do all this for me. My head was about to burst and I started to feel faint. I felt like I was having a panic attack. In the back of my mind, I knew what I had to do, but my heart and body were saying something else. Hearing Eric's voice calling my name brought me back to reality.

I said to him "Eric, I love you, and if I had to count the ways, it would go on into infinity. You are the greatest gift I have ever received. Everything you did for me today will live within my heart and dreams forever." I looked back up into the sky, as I watched those beautiful words that were written in the heavens for me, start to slowly fade away. As tears streamed down the sides of my face, I tried to quickly wipe them away.

Eric asked me why I was crying. "Didn't you like our day together?" He asked.

I said, "Words cannot express what you have done for me today. I loved this day so much, and that's why I hurt so badly."

"What do you mean Katie?"

"I don't know how to tell you this Eric without hurting you, but I can't leave Danny right now, and as of tomorrow, I won't be working at the store anymore."

His eyes grew wide as he asked if it was something he did, or if he was going too fast. "I can slow this down. Please, tell me it isn't so Katie." He had tears in his eyes and at that moment I could no longer compose myself.

I totally lost it and broke down and cried like a baby. I cried so hard and for so long that my body began to tremble. "How could I do this to such a wonderful guy?" I thought to myself. Not knowing what Danny would do to us both, I knew in my heart it was safer for Eric if I leave now. Thinking about the gun, I could have taken it, but Danny would have easily replaced it. Then, all of my worst fears would become a reality, and Danny would get his revenge!

Eric asked me why I had to quit my job.

"If I don't we'll probably both be dead! I knew it would only be a matter of time before something happens between us. Seeing you every day Eric would be too much for me to take." I knew he wanted to take me away from Danny to keep me safe, but in the end, Eric let it be my decision. He didn't want to control me, or force me into anything the way Danny does!

Again he assured me and said, "You'll be safe with me Katie."

I replied, " I know you feel that way and I believe you Eric, but Danny is a force to be dealt with to the death, and I can't take that chance, I love you too much. "I really do have to go Eric."

"Can I at least call you when Danny's at work, I need to know you're alright Katie?"

"As long as I don't rock the boat, Danny will leave me alone, but I assure you, he will not let me leave him. While turning to walk away, I felt a sudden yearning to come back and hug and kiss Eric one last time! "I will always love you Eric, and someday, I hope you can find it in your heart to forgive me."

I turned around and ran toward the park exit in search of a telephone, to call for a taxi ride back to my car. A river of tears streamed down my face. I slowly looked back and saw Eric sitting down on the same bench where my fairytale day had began. His head was down in his hands. "Oh God, what did I do?" I felt like my whole world ended that day.

I was able to flag down a taxi outside the park. After it dropped me off at the store, I drove back to my apartment where I broke down and cried. Danny is the devil himself; he has no soul. I began to despise him more and more. My stomach began to ache, and I was feeling very nauseous. I vowed some how I will get rid of Danny, and I prayed to God, that he would forgive me.

CHAPTER 16

I needed to conjure up the nerve to tell Danny I quit my job. I knew I could get a job as a waitress, but I didn't know how he would feel about that. It really doesn't matter anymore; I just exist on this Earth now.

To keep my mind off Eric, I began packing. Our move to the new apartment was to take place this weekend. While marking a box, I heard Danny slam the door muttering under his breath. Then the muttering escalated to yelling about what a crappy day he had. Knowing he was grouchy from being overtired, I wanted to ask him if he and Shelly had fun screwing in Room 35, but I just didn't feel like being kicked around like a rag doll today.

Surprisingly, Danny started to help me out. We packed one room at a time. Danny asked me why I was so quiet.

"I don't feel very well." I answered. After what seemed like hours of silence and packing, I decided to tell Danny that I quit my job.

At first there was dead silence, and then came the storm. "What the hell did you do that for? Are you an idiot? We have bills to pay. Why did you do this?" He demanded.

"I'd like to waitress. I think I could make more money doing that."

"That's your problem Katie, you shouldn't think. Not that anyone could really accuse you of that. It does require a brain. You've got two days to get a job, or you will answer to me."

It didn't even take me two days. My brother got me an interview with the owner of a fancy restaurant. He hired me on the spot and asked if I could start the following day.

When Danny came home from work that night I told him about my new job and how I was hired on the spot.

He fired back with his usual demented comments. "What did you do to get this job so fast? Did you screw the owner?" While kneeling over a box I was packing, Danny grabbed my hair and jolted my head up. "Let me tell you something here you little slut. If I ever find out you're screwing anyone else, I'll kill you both." He uttered those words very calmly, and with such conviction. "You do believe me Katie. Don't you?"

While he was tugging my hair one more time I cried out, "Yes, yes, I believe you. Now please let me go. That hurts."

Then he brought his face down to my level, put his cheek against mine and said sarcastically, "Honey, you don't even know the meaning of the word hurt yet. Cheat on me even once, and I promise you, I'll make sure your pain will be very slow and intense." His breath almost made me puke; I thought I would pass out from holding mine so long! "Just keep on packing. I'm going out." He said.

I thought to myself, "It's 11:30 p.m. Did I even have to guess where he was going?" I didn't care, as long as I didn't have to be in the same room with him; it suited me just fine.

The next day I started my new job. I knew I would like it because I really enjoyed waiting on people. The tips were great! When I got home Danny made sure I handed him over all my tips. He actually frisked me and rummaged through my purse to make sure I wasn't holding back. I ended up having to hide my tips in my shoes, as he never checked there.

As the week came to a close, we were moved into our new apartment, downstairs from his brother and girlfriend. The first night there, Danny and his brother got along great. As the weeks passed by, they both started to annoy each other, just as I predicted.

Danny was starting to get bored with his restaurant job, and decided to apply at a bus company. Coincidentally, Shelly also left her job at the restaurant, amidst rumors about her being pregnant. I could take a good guess as to who the father was! Danny probably had enough of Shelly and threatened her. I'm sure of that. He can scare anyone with his monstrous, cold-hearted temperament.

CHAPTER 17

After about a month passed, Danny came running into the house screaming; he practically busted down the door. "I got the job! The confirmation arrived in today's mail." So now he was going to be a bus driver. He said that the restaurant could shove their lousy pay and no benefits right up their ass. He then grabbed me and threw me on the bed. I knew what was coming next. In the past, we had always used protection, not wanting me to get pregnant. Today, it didn't seem to matter. He jumped right on top of me.

"Stop." I yelled. "I don't want you to do this Danny. I don't feel very well." I would have used any excuse possible.

He replied, "Screw you. This is going to happen."

I begged him to at least use protection.

"Nothing is going to happen. So just shut up." He then forced himself on me anyway in his rough and mechanical way, without emotion. Thank God it was fast. I thought about how making love with Eric would be absolutely wonderful, gentle and loving.

As the weeks progressed, I started feeling sick every day. After missing my period, I suspected I was pregnant. I went to the drugstore and bought a home pregnancy kit. After hiding it, I went about my daily routine. I didn't want Danny to know anything about this yet. He was adamant about not wanting kids for a long time. I decided to do the test in the morning, when the reading will be more accurate. As the night dragged on, I watched the hands on the clock tick away the minutes. I tossed and turned, praying and hoping that the test stick would not turn blue.

Danny had left for work before I got up. I sat up slowly and went to the closet to retrieve the hidden pregnancy kit. I followed the instructions carefully, which stated that positive results show within ten minutes. While putting the solution on the bathroom sink, I prayed the test would be negative. During the ten minutes it takes for the results to show, I kept myself busy. It seemed like ten hours. When the timer went off, I was a bit startled; my stomach was in knots. I proceeded toward the bathroom. From a distance, without even having to enter the bathroom, I could already see the solution had turned blue; it was positive.

So many emotions were racing through my head, which for once excluded Danny. While pausing in front of a mirror, I felt my stomach. As I turned sideways, I thought to myself, "I'm actually going to have a baby. A tiny little person was going to be growing inside of me, and I was going to be its mommy. It will be a tiny little life that I could love and take care of and it would love me back."

Immediately, I telephoned the gynecologist's office. They had a cancellation for that afternoon, or I would have to wait a couple of weeks for an appointment. I told the receptionist I would be there this afternoon. Not completely trusting the home pregnancy test, I needed to be one hundred percent sure.

While driving to the doctor, I started to wonder how Danny would take this news. "Would he be pleased and change for the sake of the baby? Is this a blessing in disguise?" No, I will never love, much less like Danny, in this lifetime or any lifetime!

The doctor performed a thorough examination. When he finished he smiled and said, "My guess is that you're pregnant. But to be sure we'll do a blood test. You'll have the results later today." He gave me some prenatal vitamins and some brochures. I thanked him and when he left the room, I got dressed.

Upon exiting the examination room, the nurse led me to a lab to have my blood drawn. After the test, I was instructed to set up another appointment with the receptionist. The receptionist informed me to call back later for my test results. I thanked her and left.

While leaving the building I paused on the top step and took a breath of the spring-like air. Not feeling like going home right away, and knowing that I was so close to the store I used to work at, I got in my car and headed towards it. I thought about how much I missed Eric and all my friends there.

While driving towards the store, I reflected on my last conversation with Sue, who calls me often and keeps me abreast of everything that's happening there. At first, she was upset with me for leaving, she really wanted Eric and I to get together. Apparently, some of the others in the store are upset with me for quitting so abruptly. Sue told me that she wished she were allowed to tell them the whole story, confident they would understand.

I told her that I've already dragged enough people down with me. I cannot get over how much I hurt Eric, even though the time I shared with him was the most beautiful of my whole life, short-lived as it was. "I've never experienced a more wonderful, heart-filled love like Eric's."

"You're not being very logical." Sue said.

"Love isn't supposed to be logical, but then sometimes life doesn't seem fair either."

Sue told me that she knows Erie still loves me. She can see the twinkle in his eyes whenever my name is brought up, which is often. "Do you know how hard it is to find a love like that Katie?" She tells me Eric is always asking for details after she talks to me. He wants to make sure Danny's not abusing me.

I never reveal that side of my life to Sue anymore; therefore, she thinks all is well with me. I've hurt Eric way too much already; he doesn't need to keep worrying about me. Sue said that Eric is so sad all the time; everyone is very concerned about him. He has been asked out by some of the girls in the store, but he always gracefully declines. Instead he works long hours and pursues his hobby of restoring old cars. Sue said he's supposed to be getting a car ready for a car show, but he's not sure he'll have it finished in time.

Upon arriving, the first thing I saw was Eric's car. I parked right next to it, hoping to get a glimpse of him. Pausing for a moment, I wondered what I was doing there. I missed him so much. Not a day goes by that I don't think about him. After I told Eric goodbye, I went into such a depression that I lost five pounds. Focusing on my new job didn't help, my memories of Eric keep me barely going. Eric will always be in my heart and dreams forever. I started to cry as I remembered my conversation with Sue. I felt so guilty for having hurt such a great guy. I felt I deserved whatever life has in store for me now, since I was powerless to change my situation. At least a glimpse of Eric's car made me feel close to him, even if for just a moment!

After strolling down memory lane, I headed back for home. It was late afternoon, time for me to call the doctor's office.

"How may I help you," answered the receptionist.

"I'm calling for the results of my pregnancy test."

She asked me for my name and then put me on hold. When she returned, she informed me the results were positive. "Congratulations Mrs. Jenkins, the Doctor will be seeing you in about a month, at your next appointment."

I thanked her and hung up. I thought about how the hard part is yet to come, telling Danny. He usually arrived home from work about 5:30 p.m. In the month since he started his new job, all he does is complain about how stressful it is. I don't think anything pleases him. He's destined to be an unhappy, miserable person for the rest of his life.

He arrived home accompanied by Tim. They were yelling at each other; they must have got into another fight. He stomped over to our door and slammed it shut after he entered. I thought to myself that this would be a good time to tell him about the baby. Danny's always in a foul mood anyway, so I might as well tell him now that he was going to be a father. Without saying hello, he went straight to the refrigerator, got himself a beer and proceeded to sit down in the chair in front of the television, all while yelling at me to get his dinner.

I stood in front of the television and told him that I had something to tell him.

"Move the hell out of my way." He shouted.

I just blurted it out, "Danny, I'm pregnant."

He spit the beer out of his mouth yelling, "How the hell did that happen? You little whore, you got yourself knocked up by someone else, and you're going to try to push it off on me."

I screamed back, "You're the father. I've never slept around with anyone else, ever, unlike you with Shelly. I heard you got her pregnant too, and that's why she left her job."

He became enraged and lunged at me. I turned around and ran to his brother's apartment knowing he was home. Luckily Danny tripped on an end table, otherwise he would have caught up to me. The door was unlocked and I ran right into Tim's arms, sobbing for protection. Tim stood between Danny and me, demanding to know what the hell is going on.

Danny screamed, "Ask the little slut. She says she's pregnant!"

Tim pushed Danny into a chair and told him to sit down. He turned to me and smiled. "Katie, are you pregnant?" Tim asked.

I replied, "Yes, and Danny insists he's not the father. I didn't sleep with anyone else Tim, honest."

"I believe you," Tim said. He then looked over at Danny in disgust, and asked him why he thought he wasn't the father.

"Because we always use something." He shouted.

I interrupted his ranting, to remind him of the day he came home with the news of his new job; he threw me down and told me not to worry about one time without protection.

"Danny, do you remember that?" Tim asked.

"Yeah, so, but…"

"But nothing, it only takes one time. You should be happy Danny. I'd love to have a baby with Michelle, but she wants to wait."

Danny replied sarcastically, "Well, Michelle's smart then."

While feeling protected for the moment, I told Danny if he wants a divorce he could have it, because I am not going to abort this baby.

"Divorce! I told you Katie you are mine. I'll kill you first."

Tim shouted back to Danny, "You are just like dad! I feel sorry for Katie."

"Stay the hell out of our business Tim or I'll…."

"Or you'll what," Tim shouted back. "Or you'll hit me. At least you'd be hitting a guy instead of a helpless pregnant girl! Does this give you a surge of power Danny to beat up on Katie all the time? Do you feel like a man? Think about it Danny, you're out of control!"

Danny was silent for a moment then lashed back at me. "I never, ever, want to hear you bring up Shelly's name again. Do you understand?"

"No, I don't understand. I want to know if you've been sleeping with her?"

He replied, "If I did or I am, it's really none of you damn business!"

"Yes it is," I dared to shout back. "It's not fair to me. Please, just let me go and you can sleep around with a hundred girls."

He shouted in my face, "I told you Katie, I will kill you first!"

Tim was starting to grow tired of this whole mess, but yet he still felt compelled to protect me. "Danny, why do you feel you can do this to Katie? She's supposed to sit back and count off all your affairs as you have them."

"Shut up Tim," he shouted. "In some countries men can have as many women as they like, and the women still respect and honor them. The men own all those women."

I jumped in with, "This is America Danny, and I'm not like those other women. I don't have to take this. You and I are married and you never show me any respect!" I was getting totally exhausted at this point. I told him that I had to go back to the apartment and lie down.

Tim asked me if I wanted to go to his bed and rest, while things cooled down.

Just as I thought things had finally calmed down, Danny blurted out, "Why Tim, do you want to screw her too? She's coming back downstairs with me."

Tim said, "Danny, you're a demented asshole! Are you calmed down enough to leave Katie alone so she can rest?"

"Yeah, yeah, Danny snarled, Just go downstairs. You're looking pretty sickly anyway. Just make sure you don't puke on my side of the bed."

I walked slowly to our apartment. Feeling so weak, I saw the bed and just collapsed onto it!

CHAPTER 18

When I woke up, it was morning and Danny was already gone. I got up and found I still had another couple of hours before I had to leave for work. The phone rang and I answered it. Whoever it was hung up very gently.

I imagined it was Eric, as I am always thinking about him anyway. Sometimes, whenever I go to a mall or supermarket, I wish I could see Eric, even just for a moment. I know a lot of people say your heart does go on, and ultimately it does, but in a whole bunch of broken pieces. It's like a puzzle, never to be fit back together again, no matter how hard you try. Having a baby coming reminds me I have to go on. He or she can fit some of those pieces of my heart back together again, but there will always be one piece that will never fit, and that piece will always belong to Eric!

I thought that maybe a shower would invigorate me, but as I got out of the tub I felt a little light-headed. I paused for a moment, took a deep breath, and it passed. I finished getting ready and left for work.

After my shift ended about 7:00 p.m., I once again felt compelled to drive over to the store and park by Eric's car, knowing he worked the evening shift on that day. His car was there and I parked right next to it and just sat there. Daydreaming seemed to become my second life now. I stared at his car while rewinding my mind back to when we were together in it. Putting my head down on the wheel I started to cry for what seemed like hours, not the few minutes it really was.

Suddenly my door opened! I look up and discovered Eric hovering over me. He told me to move over and slid in next to me. He hugged me and asked, "Katie, are you okay? Why are you crying, and what are you doing here all alone?"

"I'm so sorry Eric. I never meant to hurt you. It's just that I can't get you out of my mind."

"Katie, I feel the same way. I know that I promised not to call your house but I do, just to hear the sound of your voice."

"I was hoping maybe it was you Eric, but I wasn't sure."

"Please Katie, can't you reconsider us? I really need you."

I hugged him back so tightly, not wanting him to ever let me go. I did break away to tell him my news. I told him about how last month Danny came home and forced himself on me and from that, I am going to have a baby. I continued telling Eric how I hate Danny touching me....

He politely interrupted, "You're going to have a baby Katie. How do you feel? Are you okay?"

"Yes, I have a little morning sickness, but otherwise I'm okay."

"Katie, this doesn't change the way I feel about you. Come with me and I'll take care of both you and the baby."

"Eric, I can't! I decided to tell Eric about the gun.

He pulled me even closer to him and said, "You're not going back to him Katie."

"I have to I replied. As long as I stay with Danny and do what he says no one gets hurt, especially you."

"Katie, you've been staying with Danny all this time because you don't want me hurt. Oh Katie, I'm not worried about myself, only you."

"No," I said to him, "He will kill you or me or both of us. I know this like I know my own name. So the only relationship I can have with you will be in my dreams."

Eric hugged me even tighter and we kissed, It was spectacular! Eric said, "I love you and it will always be forever Katie!

I replied, "When you love someone, that love is the very best part of you. You Eric, are the best part of me. But now, we both need to get on with our lives." I must have cried a river of tears.

Eric said, "I know I can't force you but please Katie won't you change your mind? Trust me when I tell you, I can make sure Danny will never bother you again!"

I didn't even want to know what that meant, I just said, "Right now I can't Eric."

"Well then, I'm going to be your guardian angel! You won't know when, you won't know how, but I will be around. When you need me I will always be there for you. I'm also promising you this, I know we will be together someday soon."

Katie said, "I'm wishing that too with all my heart. I'm just waiting for a reprieve. Right now, the time is not right."

Eric said, "Look Katie, lets stay together but on your terms. You can call me when Danny's not around and we'll get together when he's at work."

"I can't do that to you, Eric. You can't go on with your life if you're waiting for me."

"I can't go on without you either. So I'll take whatever special moments we can have! You never know how much time you have together, so you have to make every minute count."

"I would love to do this Eric, maybe this will work out. Would it be selfish of me to ask you to hold on until I felt the time was right."

"Katie, I'm basically a loner. I'll find other things that can occupy my life like my cars and my job, but I need you too. You've changed the way I feel about life. So I'll step back for now and I'll look forward to our special moments together."

We embraced tightly, fearing it would be the last time for awhile. Eric wiped the tears from my eyes and I stroked his face softly and said that I won't say goodbye. Eric slowly got out of the car, stroking my hand one more time, and left.

CHAPTER 19

As time progressed, my morning sickness subsided. I threw myself into my work. It seemed to be my only excitement, besides my morning wake-up calls from Eric. When I'd answer Eric would say, "forever and ever". I'd reply with, "ditto" and we'd both hang up!

My birthday was fast approaching and I knew I'd be working that day, which is how I wanted it. Danny never did much for my birthday anyway. At the end of the day he would say, "Oh yeah, it's your birthday huh." That would be the end of it. At least my family would call me and my sisters would take me out to lunch. I always looked forward to at least that.

The day before my birthday Danny and I had went to bowl in a league we had joined with his brother and girlfriend. It was somewhat fun, something to do. Since my average wasn't that great, I was a good handicap for the team. Our bowling night started fine, until Danny and Tim decided to down a couple of shots with their beers. I hated it when Danny drank, but I couldn't control him. As the evening progressed, the more intoxicated they became.

Although I wasn't particularly close with Michelle, we shared the same opinion about how the guys were acting. That night was the first time we ever had a chance to talk alone; it was really nice. She told me about how her and Tim fight often and how she hoped the noise didn't bother me. I graciously told her that the noise doesn't bother me, and asked her if she hears Danny and I fight.

She said, "Katie, I know me and Tim fight a lot but it's usually just words. If you don't mind me saying, how can you stay with Danny and take such physical abuse? Tim says you've been abused for seven years already. Is that true?"

"It's okay, you just get used to it. I guess Danny has a bad temper, I just have to learn not to make him so mad."

"But that's no way to live Katie, being in fear for your life all the time. It must be like walking on eggshells. I'd leave Tim in a heartbeat if he threw me around like that."

"Tim isn't quite like Danny. I mean he has a temper and I know he's verbally abusive to you. Danny has this horrible rage inside of him; he's mad at the whole world. When a mood comes over him, I'm always his target! His eyes get so vicious and his face changes so rapidly. He becomes positively evil looking."

"Katie, you don't think he'd hurt you while you're pregnant, do you?"

"I hope not."

Michelle then asked me why my family has never intervened.

I told her that they don't know anything because of Danny's threats to kill them if they did. "I put on a good face for us all, I've become quite the actress."

All of a sudden we were startled by the sound of breaking glass! Danny had got into a fight with some guy at the bar. Tim was trying unsuccessfully to pull Danny back. We ran over to see what the problem was. The guy that Danny was fighting with already had a bloody nose. Danny had smashed the end of a beer bottle and was ready to slash it at the guy. The bartender informed Danny that he had called the police. Danny flung the bottle across the room, and took another punch at the guy. He decked him so hard that the guy fell over a chair and landed on the ground!

Danny told Tim, "Let's get the hell out of here." As he was pulling me by my shirt towards the door, the police arrived. They accosted him and took him back to the bar. The injured man was just getting up, with the help of his girlfriend. The cops started questioning everyone, starting with the man Danny assaulted.

He said, "My girlfriend and I were sitting at the bar. I left for a moment to go to the bathroom. When I returned I found this jerk hitting on my girl. She told me that he said, he thought she smelled good, and had a nice ass. Then he asked her to dump the loser boyfriend, and that he'd meet her later so she can have some great sex with a real man. I came in just as she was slapping him across the face. When he raised his arm in the air to retaliate, I jumped on him. Wouldn't you have done the same thing officer? She was just sitting there minding her own business and this jerk hits on her."

Danny slurred, "She's a slut! All women are!"

The officer asked the bartender if this is how it happened.

He said while pointing to Danny, "Yep, that guy, started it all. I don't blame this guy for wanting to protect his girl. She was just sitting there minding her own business."

The officer asked him if he wanted to charge Danny with assault.

He said, "Yes I do, and I'd probably be doing society a favor."

The police cuffed Danny and told us they were taking him down to the station, and booking him with assault.

"Hey Katie," Danny said, "Do something right for a change and get me a good lawyer."

Everyone just shook their heads in disgust. One of the cops leaned over to me and quietly said, "Maybe you should consider a good lawyer for yourself too, if you're married to him." After that, they took him away.

I didn't feel sorry for Danny one bit. Tim and Michelle took me home with them. Tim offered to call a lawyer, but I told him thanks anyway, but I would take care of it.

CHAPTER 20

The next morning was my birthday, and it was the best birthday I've had in seven years! It was such a peaceful night's sleep without Danny. I woke up and wished myself a happy birthday, which is more than I would have got from him. My whole family called to wish me a happy birthday, as did Sue and Joan from the store; it was great talking to them! They wanted to take me to dinner, but I wasn't sure what time I was working until. Also, I wasn't sure if Danny was going to be back home tonight, and if so, what kind of a mood he would be in. Sue and Joan kept pressing the issue, "Come on, Katie, just come out with us for one drink, or in your case one soda."

I said, "Maybe just one." Joan set it up for us to meet at a pub on the outskirts of town, a place from my younger days. It had a beach right behind it.

I really didn't want to call a lawyer; I wished that Danny would stay in jail forever! I put the task off until 2:00 p.m., one hour before the start of my shift. The lawyer asked if I would be able to pick Danny up. I replied that I had to work. While hearing hesitation in his voice, I thought he would understand why I didn't want to pick him up.

When I arrived at work, I saw it was pretty busy. As the evening died down, all my co-workers started wishing me a happy birthday. They even brought me a cake and sang to me. I was so surprised! At around 7:00 p.m. a deliveryman arrived carrying a floral arrangement. He asked the hostess where Katie Jenkins was. She called me over, and the deliveryman handed the flowers over to me. All my co-workers were commenting on how beautiful they were. I felt so special! I opened up the card and read it, "Katie, a very happy birthday, forever and ever, Love, E.S." They were from Eric! All the girls assumed they were from my husband and I wanted to keep it that way. They didn't know about my personal life at this point.

As the customers dwindled down, my boss asked me if I wanted to leave early. I thanked him and called Sue to tell her I would be early. She said that would be great.

I also called Tim to see if Danny was getting out of jail tonight and if so, would Tim be picking him up. Tim informed me that Danny has to spend one more night in jail. He assaulted a police officer while he was being booked. Tim told me that he doesn't think Danny is ever going to learn to control his temper. "He has a short fuse and has been lucky until now, considering how many times you could have had him thrown in jail."

I cut him short, "Well, I just wanted to know. I guess I'll call his lawyer in the morning to see when I can pick him up."

Feeling relieved about Danny being in jail, I was really looking forward to seeing Sue and Joan. I arrived at the pub a few minutes early and decided to stroll over towards the water. It was a gorgeous, warm night. The tide was moving in very slowly. I stood there for a moment gazing out over the water, and took a deep breath. I went back into the restaurant and found Joan and Sue grinning from ear to ear. They both hugged and kissed me and asked me how I was doing. "I'm doing great and I'm so happy to see you guys. I've really missed you both."

Joan said, "Before we forget Katie, Eric told us to give this to you so you don't get in trouble for the flowers. It's another small card from all of us at the store. When Danny asks you where you got the flowers from, you can tell him they were from us. Now you have the card to prove it! It must be very hard for you not to wear the school ring Eric had duplicated for you."

"Yes it is. I put everything he's given me in a special hiding place."

Sue said, "Let's get a table facing the beach."

Joan pulled me back and told Sue to go on and get a table. "We'll be there in a moment. Katie, we have another surprise for you, but you have to wait a little bit. What time do you have to be home? I don't want to get you in trouble with Danny."

"Oh don't worry, I can stay out all night if I want to!"

"What do you mean, Katie."

"I'll tell you when we get inside."

We proceeded to find Sue at our table. We sat down and our waitress came over to take our orders. I just had a seven-up, since I wasn't hungry. "So Katie, what is it you were going to tell us?" Joan asked.

"Well, last night Danny and I were bowling, and he started a major fight with some guy there. So now he's sitting in jail!"

Sue asked, "What was it all about?"

"Supposedly he was hitting on this guy's girlfriend and the guy didn't like it. Then after they took him in to book him for assault, he hit a police officer. He was really drunk."

"Too bad they can't lock him up for good and throw away the key." Sue said.

I told them that I have to pick him up in the morning. "I'm sure he'll be in a foul mood when I get him."

We talked about work and all the people there. I asked Sue if she and Mark started dating yet.

"That's funny Katie, me and the stock boy."

"He's really nice and he seems to like you a lot."

"He's asked me out, but I don't know what to do. Maybe I'll shock him and say yes." Sue said.

I added, "Besides, I thought he was doing this work part-time and going to college."

Sue said that he is.

"Well, I think he's really cute and you should give him a chance."

Sue said, "I've been going out with this other guy named Kenny. He loves photography and I really like him a lot."

"You're still seeing him?" Katie asked.

"Yeah, that's why I'm not accepting a date with Mark yet."

"Well, if you're happy with Kenny that's all that matters."

Joan said, "Katie, look who's giving happiness advice!"

We continued to talk and laugh and had a great time. Joan looked at her watch and told Sue they have to go to the bar for a moment. "We'll be right back Katie."

As I waited, I stared out the window mesmerized by the twinkling stars in the skies, and watched the water slipping across the sand. Just then, I heard the song "You are so Beautiful," by Joe Cocker come on the jukebox, and I recognized the scent of a familiar, sweet cologne that had filled the air. Chills ran down my spine as I felt a light tap on my shoulder, and a voice I surely knew, this could only be Eric! "Happy birthday Katie, my beautiful girl." Eric was standing there with a huge smile on his face. I got up and hugged him. I looked over towards the bar and saw Joan and Sue wiping tears from their eyes. I don't know who was crying more, them or me. They finally returned and said, "Surprise."

We all sat down, but I couldn't take my eyes off of Eric. He was wearing black fitted pants and a white tee shirt, with a black suit coat over it. He knew it was my favorite outfit of his. He looked so sexy and smelled so good! "What a great birthday! Thanks you guys." We all talked for awhile, and then Joan and Sue announced they had to leave.

"You guys set this all up, didn't you?" I asked.

Joan said, "Just enjoy your birthday sweetie." They both gave me a hug and said that they loved me.

I replied, "I love you too guys, and thank you for the best birthday I have ever had!"

I was a little bit nervous sitting back down with Eric. The way he looked and smelled I didn't know how I was going to contain myself. "Thank you so much for the beautiful flowers. I love them."

At that moment, he pulled a small box out of his pocket. "This is for you Katie, Happy Birthday."

"No Eric, you've already done enough for me."

"Please Katie, open it." I hesitated at first, but then opened it slowly. The sparkle of the contents seemed to light up the room. It was a gorgeous diamond tennis bracelet!

"Oh Eric, this is really beautiful, but you shouldn't have."

"I bought this for you, because it sparkles as big and bright as your eyes and your smile."

"Eric, I can't accept this. It's way too expensive."

"It's a gift that comes from my heart. Please take it Katie, I love you. Here, let me put it on your wrist."

I extended my arm to him and he kissed me and clipped the bracelet around my wrist. "Thank you. This is the most beautiful bracelet I ever saw." After I got up to hug him, he pulled me onto his lap and we kissed. I said, "Thank you so much for a dream come true. You're always there to rescue me, even after I tell you I can't see you anymore, there you are. I love you so much Eric.

Eric asked me if I wanted to go for a stroll along the beach and I agreed. He said, "I hope you don't mind, but Joan told me a little bit about Danny and how he ended up in jail."

"Of course I don't mind." As we walked along the beach through the sand, I put my head on his shoulder and he wrapped his arm tightly around my body. We didn't even have to speak, our being together was enough. As we approached the end of the beach, there was no one else in sight. It was just me and Eric, and the sound of the waves, with the light of the stars guiding our way. Life just couldn't get any better than this. Now I know what paradise must be like! We sat down on a rock near the water, staring up at the sky, and kissed under the light of the moon and the stars.

"Make a wish, Katie, on the biggest star in the sky." Eric said.

I responded, "I don't have to make a wish, because my wish already came true tonight."

Eric took my hands into his and asked me if I wanted to spend the night at his house.

I surprised myself by replying right away, "There's nothing I'd love more than to spend an entire evening with you Eric." We stayed on that rock, still amazed by the sky. Eric took off his jacket and placed it over my shoulders. If I never believed in fate or angels before, I do now. I felt that whatever I had done wrong in my life, I must have done something right too. The angels were leading me to a better place. It was such a peaceful night.Eric and I got up and walked over to my car. He told me to follow him back to his house. I didn't know what was going to happen tonight, but I knew it was quite exhilarating to feel so alive! As I approached Eric's driveway, I had no apprehension about the night ahead of me. Eric quickly got out of his car and came over to open my door. We walked to his front door and he unlocked it, while deactivating the security system.

"Can I get you anything to drink?" Eric asked.

"I'd love some water. Thank you." As he left to get our drinks, I picked up his jacket and smelled it. It was an enchanting fragrance, which had Eric's scent all over it. He returned with our drinks and asked me if I would like to go out on the patio. I agreed. The evening was still quite comfortable, with a warm breeze blowing. We just stood there wrapped in each other's arms, enjoying the moment. I looked over at the hot tub; it looked so inviting. Eric asked me if I would like to go in it.

"I'd love to, but I don't have anything to change into." I said.

"If you feel comfortable enough, you can go in it wearing your underwear." Suddenly I felt terribly shy. Eric being so perceptive said he would get us a couple of towels, and I could get in before he returned. I quickly undressed and stepped into the hot tub. It felt wonderful. Eric returned with the towels, disrobed, and got in. I couldn't help just staring at him. He had an awesome physique! I must have turned every shade of red when he scooted over next to me. Sensing my embarrassment, Eric did everything he could to make me feel more comfortable. At the push of a button, we had soft music. Another button turned up the water jets. He was careful not to turn the jets up too high. Eric then looked at me and said, "Katie, you look so beautiful. I love what you're wearing." My underwear was red, trimmed with white lace. He added, "It almost looks like you're wearing a bathing suit."

I blushed and said, "I think you're the most wonderful man I have ever known. I must be the luckiest girl in the whole world to have you love me." Eric quieted me for a moment by kissing my neck. I got chills up and down my spine. He moved his lips toward my ear, and then he pressed his lips to mine. We kissed in the warmth of the hot tub so passionately that it felt like the water temperature rose to the boiling point! Eric gently began to pull my bra strap down, and kiss me lightly on my shoulder.

I've never felt like this before; that night is etched in my mind forever! We made love under the stars. It was the most beautiful and loving experience I have ever felt. I had never imagined such love and warmth in my wildest dreams, being so close to another person, and feeling as though you are one. It was incredible!

While we were exiting the tub, I noticed my skin was shriveled from being in the water so long. Eric held me close and wrapped a huge towel around us both. He looked into my eyes and said, "I love you so much. I hope this won't change the way you feel about me."

I said, "Eric, I love you more then you can ever know. Now I feel like I'm a part of you too." We strolled back into his house and went upstairs to his bedroom, where we ended up making love all over again, and again, until the wee hours of the morning. I never imagined that being in love could be so grand! I learned a lot that night. Love should never hurt. It should be gentle and loving. That is what everyone was put on this Earth to feel, a strong bond of love, not just physical lust, but an inner feeling of being totally complete.

The next morning as the light shone through the window it awakened me, and I wondered if I was dreaming. I looked over to see if Eric was lying next to me and discovered he was gone. I remember just two hours ago lying in his arms drifting off to a peaceful sleep. I sat up and rubbed my eyes for a moment until my vision came back into focus. Eric was standing beside me with a silver tray containing a cup of tea, a muffin, fresh fruit with whipped cream, and a bouquet of flowers. "Hey there sleeping beauty. How do you feel?" He said cheerfully.

"I feel wonderful! You are so thoughtful Eric. Did you get any sleep?"

"Maybe an hour or so. I just couldn't help watching you, as you slept. You looked like an angel. I wish I could wake up next to you every morning."

I replied, "That is a wish I will always be asking myself for too. What time is it? When do you have to be at work?"

Eric answered, "It's 7:00 a.m. I don't have to be at work until four o'clock this afternoon." He handed me the tray and sat on the bed next to me.

"This looks wonderful Eric! I feel I should be doing something nice for you."

"Just you being here is enough for me. I'll do anything for you Katie. Don't you know that?" I smiled at him as he picked up a strawberry, dipped it in some whipped cream, and bought it to my lips. I opened my mouth to taste it. The berry was sweet and delicious.

"May I?" I said as I reached for another strawberry. I dipped it into the cream and playfully teased him with it. As I raised it up to his lips, I smeared the whipped cream all over his mouth! We both laughed.

Eric said, "So, you want to play." He put his hand in the whipped cream bowl. Knowing I was in trouble, I got off the bed and started to run. Eric quickly caught me and we both tumbled down to the floor. While pining me down gently, his messy hand hovered over my face. Suddenly, he got a serious look on his face and said, "I just can't do this." He leaned over and kissed me instead. We made love again!

I was surprising myself with my newfound sexuality. How complete I felt to have Eric love me so much. I believe now that true love is the glue that bonds all lovers together. As we embraced, I felt I never wanted to leave. I just wanted to stay in Eric's arms forever.

As the morning progressed, I knew my fairytale dream would be soon ending. Eric asked me if I wanted some lunch. I told him that I wasn't really hungry. He held onto to me so tight and said, "I don't want you to go. I don't like it that you're going to be with Danny." Again Eric told me he could put Danny out of his miserable life. Again, I didn't ask him what he meant.

I said, "I don't know how I'm going to walk out this door and leave this all behind as just a beautiful memory."

Eric said, "It doesn't have to be just a memory of the past. I need you to be my future. I need to be certain that we'll be together soon, and that you'll be safe Katie."

I said. "I want that too, but right now my future is anything but certain. I don't want Danny near me. I'm hoping he'll just go away and find somebody else. All I know is nothing will ever be the same. I will find a way Eric, I promise. We will be together. But please know this, I can't expect you to wait for me forever either. I'd understand if you want to…"

He put his finger up to my lips and said, "I know what you're going to say and that will never happen. I will always be here waiting for you, but I need to know you will always be safe. I will never let Danny lay another hand on you now, or ever again!"

We kissed and hugged as Eric pulled me back one more time and said, "I have such dreams for us. I want to complete that circle of life and have a family together. Do you believe in miracles Katie?"

I said, "Yes I do, because a miracle already happened for me when I met you. I will love you forever Eric!"

"I will always love you too Katie."

I kissed him and walked towards my car. I could barely see the driveway because my eyes were flooding with tears. As I got into my car I turned back towards Eric. He was wiping tears from his eyes as he blew me a kiss. All the way home I thought about Eric and our night together. I know for sure, that I could never stomach Danny near me again.

CHAPTER 21

When I arrived home Tim came running over to me blurting out the details of Danny's continuing saga, like I even cared. He asked me where I was and added that Danny's been ordering him to have me call him.

"What did you tell him?" I asked.

Tim said, "Nothing. Where were you last night Katie. You weren't home."

I hated to lie to Tim, so I told him I didn't want to be alone on my birthday, so I stayed overnight at my sister's house.

Tim told me to call Danny's lawyer, saying, "He should be sprung today, unless he had another run-in with the law."

I thanked him and went into the house to compose myself before I made the call. I didn't have much time to relax because the phone rang right away; it was the lawyer. He told me the steps necessary to obtain Danny's release. They expected me to come up with bail money, and I didn't have any idea where I was going to get it. Tim walked in the door when I was on the phone, and offered to make bail for Danny. He explained that he owes Danny one "get out of jail free card" from their younger days when Danny had bailed Tim out. I couldn't imagine Danny helping anyone but himself.

We left our house and went down to the jail to pick Danny up. While I was filling out the papers I was thinking, "Just keep him and throw away the key." My heart felt like it was in my throat as I watched an officer escort Danny out to us. He had this smug smile on his face as he pulled up his pants. He looked horrible; his face sported a scruffy, two-day old beard. It was apparent to us as he got closer that he didn't look very happy.

As we all walked back to the car, Danny asked Tim if he got that guy from the bowling alley and his whore girlfriend's names and addresses for him.

Tim told Danny to leave it be; they weren't even regulars.

Danny said, "Screw you, Tim. I'll get it from the police report myself."

I interrupted him to ask why he wanted to know about these people.

He said, "Because I want to kill them both!"

"You're kidding. He's kidding, right Tim."

Danny started to laugh and said to me, "Katie, you're such a naïve and stupid girl. You know I'm not kidding. I'm gonna get them."

Tim calmed Danny down for the moment by changing the subject to their mother, the only thing that Danny cared about.

Danny asked, "What about mom?"

Tim replied, "She's not feeling well lately and she's been asking about you."

Danny said, "You didn't tell her about me being in jail, did you?"

Tim said, "Of course not. It would really hurt her."

Danny replied, "Quick, take me home and I'll get cleaned up and then I'll go see her. Katie, did you call my work and tell them I was sick."

I wanted to say mentally sick, but I assured him that I did.

I was supposed to be at work at 5:30 p.m. but Danny informed me I was to call in sick, to accompany him to his mother's house.

I asked "Why can't you go alone?"

"I'm not asking you, I'm telling you. So just do it!" He shouted.

I really hated going over to his mother's house. She totally ignores me and makes me feel invisible, like I have the plague. Her behavior makes me feel as inadequate as he does.

When we arrived home per Danny's orders, I called in sick. After Danny freshened up, we left for his mother's. We walked in the door and discovered her on the couch. Then the dramatics started. "Danny, oh hi baby. Where have you been? I've missed you. When you didn't call mommy I was so worried."

I thought I would be sick. She's so nauseating. Just the sound of her voice gives me the chills. A few quarts of cheap beer were lying on the floor next to her. Again, she didn't acknowledge me, even after I asked her how she was feeling. She just turned her head away from me and asked Danny to come over and give her a big hug. Then she told him she needed him to take her to the bathroom, since she couldn't make it there on her own, being as drunk as she was. I figured he would walk her there and wait outside the door, but instead she had him go in with her. They are both demented.

After they emerged, he helped her back to the couch. She blurted out to Danny, "Why did you have to bring her with you?" She was slurring her words. "I mean, me and you don't get a lot of time alone together anymore. It's just that I miss you honey."

Feeling very uncomfortable and wanting to leave, I told Danny, "I'm going to take a walk over to my parent's house."

Knowing I hated being there, Danny told me, "Just go sit down in the kitchen and shut up!" I looked over at his mother and noticed she had the most vindictive smile on her face. It let me know that she was still more important to Danny than me, and always will be.

I went in the kitchen and sat down at the table. While trying to block out their voices by plugging my ears, I closed my eyes and thought about Eric. My thoughts of him took me away from this nightmare into a calm and wonderful place. One thing Danny can never destroy or take away from me is my thoughts and dreams; they are buried deep within my heart.

After what seemed to be hours of glorious daydreaming, Danny came back into the kitchen and startled me. He slapped my head and announced that we were going. He covered his mother up with a blanket, and asked her if she needed anything else.

She replied, "Yes, a great big hug and kiss from my best boy." I watched in dismay as he leaned over and gave her a hug. She clenched him as he kissed her, trying to make it last. I had to turn away; it made me sick.

As we were leaving he nudged me and said, "Go give my mother a hug."

I thought about how she makes my skin crawl and just said, "I hope you feel better Mrs. Jenkins. Goodbye." I could tell Danny was pissed off.

After we approached the car, Danny pushed me against the door. He yelled, while pointing his finger in my face, "Don't you ever treat my mother like that again."

"How? She treats me horrible, Danny. I think she hates me."

"Well, do you blame her?" He yelled. As we were standing by the car door arguing, I looked up at the window and saw his mother had miraculously made it off the couch to spy on us. She made sure I saw her smiling. When I told Danny to turn around and look, she had pulled back the drapes.

Danny verbally abused me all the way home. He said, "You better start treating my mother better. She's a sick woman. Do you hear me?"

I yelled, "Yes she may be sick, but everyone knows it's because she's an alcoholic!"

Danny slammed on the brakes and punched me in the face. "I told you to shut up about my mother" He screamed. I held onto my face with both hands. He had hit my eye, and at this point I just about had it, I couldn't take anymore of his abuse! I didn't know what came over me as I jumped from my seat, and clobbered Danny as hard as I could with my fist to his face. His nose started to bleed immediately! He couldn't even scream at me because the blood was refusing to stop. He grabbed every napkin he could find, before he needed to use his shirtsleeve!

Danny didn't say a single word to me the rest of the way home. We got out of the car and I could feel that my eye had already began to swell. I got into the house and went to the freezer to get some ice for my eye. Danny, still silent, cleaned himself up before retreating to the bedroom. I knew there would be consequences for what I did, but it was worth it! A few minutes later, Danny emerged from the bedroom, with a smirk on his face. He said, "So Katie, do you think you're so tough now?" He grabbed me from behind, and with his other hand he quickly held a gun to my head saying, "Katie, I'd like you to meet my friend here," as he rubbed the gun against my face. I didn't know what to expect when he stated, "I'm going to kill you! Cocking back the trigger of the gun, he played his own little game of Russian roulette with me! Clicking the gun twice he laughed saying, do you still think three is your lucky number Katie?" I didn't cry, and I didn't beg for my life, I just wouldn't give him the satisfaction. He said, "I'm not sure what I'm gonna do with you yet Katie. If you ever piss me off this bad again, I can guarantee, you'll smell the scent of gunpowder on your way out of this life!" Again, I felt so belittled. The fact that I was four months pregnant really scared me. How could Danny be so cruel to me while I'm pregnant. I now know he isn't going to change his treatment of me ever!

Danny ordered me to start dinner. After we were done eating, he told me to get ready because we were going back to that damn bowling alley. "I hope I see that slut and her boyfriend there again. I'll kick their asses good this time."

I told him that I didn't feel very well and that I would be staying home, not wanting to see any altercations tonight.

He screamed back at me, "Oh yeah you're going Katie. Are you trying to get sympathy from me? Well, too bad. That's reserved for my mother."

I argued back with him again, "Look at me Danny, my eye is swollen. Don't you care that you did this!"

"You deserve everything you get." He said.

"No I don't, you could have hurt the baby!"

He said, "Oh, you mean the one you trapped me into. Get ready!"

I said, "I'm going to lie down. You would leave your mother alone if she asked."

"That's it!" He screamed. He grabbed me by my shirt and started to pull me towards the bedroom.

"Stop Danny you're hurting me." He threw me on the bed and pulled me up again. I struggled with him and told him to leave me alone. He pulled me by my hair and shoved me into the bedpost. My stomach hit the corner of the post so hard I fell down to the floor. He screamed at me to get up, but I couldn't. My side and stomach began to feel sharp pains. I curled up in a ball, hoping the pains would subside. While crying uncontrollably, all I could think of was my baby.

Within moments, Tim came crashing through the door. He must have heard us fighting. "Danny, what is wrong with you. What did you do to Katie?"

"None of your business. Do I come crashing into your apartment when I hear you and Michelle fight?"

"At least I don't beat on her. You're friggin' nuts, Danny." Tim turned to me and said, "Honey, can you get up?" He pushed Danny aside and helped me up. My cramping was getting worse. Tim helped me to the bathroom and stood guard at the door. As I pulled down my underwear and noticed blood, I let out a loud scream! Tim came running in. "What is it?" He stopped himself as he noticed blood dripping onto the floor.

I cried, "I'm going lose the baby. Tim, I love this baby. Please help me."

"Damn you Danny. We have to get her to the hospital." Danny went to get the keys and Tim carried me out to the car. He also grabbed some towels. Tim reassured me, "You'll be okay Katie," as he ordered Danny to drive faster!

During the drive to the hospital Danny said, "Shit Tim, you'd think she was your wife the way you're acting."

Tim said, "Just shut up and drive Danny." He then instructed me to take some deep breaths."

I told Tim, "It's starting to hurt worse. I'm so scared."

"You'll be alright. He pushed the hair out of my eyes and noticed my shiner for the first time. "Jesus Danny, did you see what you did?"

"Look, you don't know her. She pisses me off all the time."

"Danny, everyone pisses you off. Why don't you just admit it, you have a big problem. You're addicted to violence. Don't they have a name for that? They have a name for everything else." Tim looked over at me and saw the extreme pain on my face. "Hold on Katie, we're almost there."

As Tim was helping me to the emergency room entrance, Danny told us both to be silent about what had happened. He said, "I'll do all the talking."

As we entered the hospital, a nurse spotted me and brought a wheelchair right over. She asked me what had happened.

Tim said, "She's in her fourth month of pregnancy and bleeding badly. She ordered another nurse to get me inside right away. They helped me into a hospital gown.

A doctor was at my side within seconds. He examined me thoroughly and then delivered the grim news. "I'm very sorry. Your baby has already started a spontaneous abortion. We have to let you go through the contractions and deliver it. We will also be doing a procedure called a D & C afterwards. It will cleanse out the uterus."

I was numb. It was like my whole world came crashing down. I felt as though I let this sweet, little unborn baby down. As I struggled with my thoughts, I heard the doctor tell me to push, and out came this tiny, lifeless fetus. He told me it would have been a boy. A nurse covered my tiny baby up with a towel and carried him away. I broke down and cried for him. "I'm so sorry."

The doctor asked me, "Mrs. Jenkins, if you don't mind, can you tell me what happened? And how did you get that bruise on your right eye?"

Danny was listening outside the door. He forced his way in the room, starting to tell his rendition of what happened.

The doctor interrupted him, "By the looks of your eye and the bruising on your side…We're you beat up Mrs. Jenkins?"

I was shocked that he asked that question so directly. My eyes widened and my face flushed. I wanted to tell the doctor that my husband did this and to charge him with the murder of my baby.

Danny grabbed my hand and squeezed it so hard. "No, my wife is so clumsy. She tripped on something and fell against the bedpost."

The doctor asked, "How did her eye get so bruised?"

"Oh, when she fell it shook the nightstand and a heavy lamp fell over and hit her in the eye. She's lucky it didn't knock her out cold."

You could tell Danny was sweating this one out. His face and hands were perspiring. The doctor looked at me in disbelief. "I'll get you prepped for the D & C, Mrs. Jenkins." You could tell he didn't believe a word of what Danny said. The doctor left the room.

Danny let my hand go. "Man, they're awful nosy around here. They don't get paid to butt in." I was still sobbing. "What's that doctor talking about, a D & C. What is that?"

"It will clean out my system." I started to shout, "After what you did. I lost my baby boy because of you. You're a murderer!"

He told me to keep it down. "Wait, did you say it was a boy?"

"Yeah Danny, you just killed your son."

He sat down and looked almost human for the first time. "Katie, I'm really sorry. I didn't mean for you or the baby to get hurt."

"I hear this story over and over again Danny. You're always sorry, until you're ready to beat on me again, and forget it when you drink, then everyone is in danger."

"What if I stop drinking?"

"Danny, you've said that, done that, and went back to it. It's the same thing over and over again."

At that moment, the nurse came in the room. It was time to go into surgery. She told Danny he could wait down the hall. It would be a short wait.

The last thing I remember was being backed into a room. As I awoke from the anaesthetic, I tried to focus my eyes on my surroundings. Danny and Tim were next to my bed. The nurse came in and said that as soon as I could drink something and urinate, I could go home. She also brought me a cold compress for my eye. "That's a pretty bad bruise you got there. Keep this on your eye; It will keep the swelling down a bit. She looked at Danny very suspiciously. As long as his story held up, nobody could question it.

After about an hour, I was able to leave the hospital. They had to wheel me down to the front door in a wheelchair. The nurse, who was with me the whole time, stood with me until Danny and Tim brought around the car. She quietly said to me, "My daughter was in a very abusive relationship until he broke her jaw for the second time." She retrieved from her pocket a card. Listed on it was the number of a place I could call if I ever needed help. "These places protect girls when men abuse them." I opened my hand to take it. Tears poured down my face as I lowered my head and thanked her. She gently squeezed my hand and said, "When somebody loves you, and you have to be very careful not to make them angry, honey, that's just not love." Our car pulled up and Danny and Tim got out. I stood up from the wheelchair and wiped my eyes. I looked back at the nurse, and quietly she said, "Call the number." I managed to smile, but deep down inside I was feeling so empty.

When we got into the car, I felt totally numb. I didn't want to talk. Danny and Tim made small talk all the way home. I just sat in the back seat and closed my eyes. I thought of how my little boy would have looked, and what he would have turned out like. In my mind I named him Jason Eric. I liked that name. I knew from this day on, that little angel of mine would be in heaven, and I would pray for him every single night.

When we got home Tim started to help me out of the car. Danny pushed him aside and said, "She's my wife. I'll get her."

I told him, "I don't need help. I can get out myself." I didn't want him to touch me. Tim went his way and we went ours. I just wanted to lie down. Danny asked me if I needed anything and I told him that I didn't.

I showered and threw away my bloodstained underpants. Afterwards, I fell into bed and started to doze off, I was so exhausted. My thoughts drifted into memories of Eric and my little baby, who didn't have a chance.

In the morning I awoke to a warm bright room, but Danny was still there; he must have taken the day off. "Why are you still home?" I asked.

He said, "To take care of you Katie."

I thought to myself, I would rather be alone. He had went out earlier and picked me up a dozen red roses. I have really grown to hate red roses! I just said, "Thank you. You really didn't have to."

Danny took my hands and told me, "As of this day, I vow never to hit you again. I'm even going to give up drinking too. I'm sorry about the baby, Katie. Will you ever forgive me?"

I paused for a moment as I contemplated my answer. I was afraid that if I said no he would beat on me again. "Sure Danny." I said.

He came over to me and gave me a hug; it made my skin crawl. "Maybe when you're better we can start on another son. What do you think?"

The thought of him fathering another child with me made me shudder. Again, I told him what he wanted to hear just so he would leave me alone.

Danny told me he had to run out for awhile, but would be right back. All I could think of was how I wished he'd never come back. I waited until he left and opened up my jewelry box. I took out the crisp $5 bill my parents gave me, upon hearing the news of my pregnancy, and put it in my purse.

I had an urge to go to church. I've always found solitude sitting in the church alone. When I arrived, I found the doors open and the church empty. I entered and proceeded to the front row. I just sat there and cried, praying for my baby boy. Afterwards, I got up and took the money out of my purse. There was no better place to leave this as a remembrance of my baby. I lit a candle and quietly whispered, "I love you baby Jason Eric. I'm so sorry. I wish I could have been stronger." Mysteriously, at that moment I almost felt "enlightened." I believe the saying that "tears can wash your soul clean." If that's true, then mine must be spotless from all the tears I've cried since I've met Danny.

I left the church and returned home. Danny still wasn't back yet. I made myself a cup of tea and laid back down. Since it was my day off anyway, I decided to stay in bed. I pretended to be asleep so I wouldn't have to talk to Danny. I called my parents and told them about the baby. They wanted to come over right away, but I couldn't let them see my swollen, bruised eye. They certainly would have questioned me. I told them I would call if I needed anything. My parents both told me they loved me; I told them that I loved them too.

After hanging up, I went back to bed. Danny returned, but he thought I was asleep. He left me alone the rest of the day. Tim came down to check on me a few times. I overheard them talking. Danny told Tim that he really wants to try to watch his temper.

Tim replied, "You better. Katie is a great girl and you are so lucky to have her."

All I could think about was how much I loathe Danny. I didn't want him then, or ever! While tossing and turning, the only thing that would relax me was to think about Eric. Finally I drifted into a peaceful sleep.

CHAPTER 22

The next morning Sue called. I told her I lost the baby. She asked me how. "Was it Danny?" She asked. I was silent for a moment. Sue continued, "It was, wasn't it? Wait until I tell Eric. What did Danny do to you Katie?"

"Sue please, don't, you can't tell Eric! You can tell him I lost the baby, but please Sue, please…I'm begging you not to tell Eric anything because if you do, my chances to be with Eric will be lost. I'm so close to getting rid of Danny. Promise me, Please."

"Okay. I promise. Do you want me and Joan to come over?"

"Thanks, but I have to go to work today. I've already missed a couple of days."

"Are you sure you're okay?" Sue asked.

"Yes, I'm fine. How is Eric doing?" I asked.

Sue said, "He really misses you. Boy, your birthday must have been great. Eric was on Cloud Nine at work the next day. We could have all asked him for a raise that day and got it! You've made him so happy Katie."

"He's made me feel like the luckiest girl in the whole world too. I really love him so much."

Sue said, "We can't wait till you get together for good!"

"I feel like it's so close, but all of a sudden Danny is trying to act like Mr. Nice Guy."

"Yeah," Sue said, "For maybe one day. No – wait – change that to one hour. If he can keep his fists against his sides."

I told Sue that I had to go, but to tell everyone there I miss them."

Sue laughed, "You mean Eric, don't you."

"Especially Eric, but I really do miss all of you too."

"I'll call you soon Katie. Love you kid."

I finished getting ready and left for work. Upon my arrival, my boss asked me if I was all right to work. "We're really sorry about your miscarriage," he stated.

"I'm fine Mr. Roberts. I would rather be working; it takes my mind off of things."

He smiled and kissed the top of my head. "If you feel you can't make it through the day, just let me know." He's really so nice; he reminds me of my dad.

Just before my shift ended, I got a phone call. It was Eric, sounding very concerned. He asked me how I was feeling.

"I'm great. Just hearing your voice makes me feel so much better. Really, I'm fine."

"What happened Katie?" He asked.

"I had a miscarriage. It's not uncommon for the body to reject the fetus during the first pregnancy." I was choking up a bit, but I knew I had to remain strong. I couldn't let him know. He asked, "Katie, are you sure Danny isn't responsible for this?" I assured him he wasn't.

"When can I see you?"

"Not right now, but really soon. Danny's being especially suspicious right now, but you just never know when Danny's luck will run out."

"I'll still be calling you Katie, every morning. If Danny isn't there, can we talk?"

"I was just going to say that. Sometimes I think we're on the same wavelength. If I pretend you're a salesman, then you'll know Danny's there."

"I love you, Katie."

"I love you too." Then, we hung up.

CHAPTER 23

For the next few months my morning call was the only thing I looked forward to.

So far, Danny had kept his promise not to hit me. But he also knew I hated to have him get close to me. I would lie still whenever we had sex. He might as well have gotten himself a blow up doll. When Danny would want sex, he would just do it fast, jump off, zip up, and he was done. Now, all of a sudden, he wanted to slow it down. Sex with Danny was still for himself; it was just a little more dragged out. It was horrible! He doesn't know the first thing about love and passion.

Up until the time I met Eric, I didn't have a clue either. Since I've been with Eric, I truly know the meaning of unconditional love. It was so hard not seeing him. It's really sad that so many people in the world are so unhappy. You get just one chance to live your life. Nobody has the right to challenge how you want to live, or whom you like to live with. As adults, some of us still let people manipulate our hearts and minds. In my case, Danny used his own strategy with me. Because I was young when we first started going steady, his threats, beatings, and mind games worked on me. As we entered our twenties, the pattern still hadn't changed. So many times I felt like being dead would be better than living with Danny, but I got stronger, and wouldn't give him the satisfaction. I knew deep within my heart that someday Eric and I would be together, but I also decided I would always go on, but for myself first.

Danny started working out more often at the gym, in order to prepare for a body building contest. It wasn't smooth sailing all the time; we still got into some fights. When he would raise his hand to me, a voice from within must have told him to stop. I was not convinced this was going to continue. Earlier in our relationship, he could contain his anger temporarily.

One day I discovered a strange letter in our mailbox addressed to me. Its return address was from Texas, where I didn't know anyone. I brought it in the house and opened it, first checking to see who wrote it. It was from Shelly, the waitress Danny had the affair with. I was mystified as to why she was writing to me and proceeded to read it.

"Katie, I'm writing this letter to you so you can show it to Danny. If I had addressed it to him, you probably would never have known about this letter or us. You see Katie, when we both worked at the restaurant, Danny and I were sleeping together. I'm sorry I have to tell you about this now, but you would have found out sooner or later. I know you're a nice girl, despite the fact that Danny portrayed you as a slut who didn't understand him. I know now that was not true.

But now, I must ask Danny to get a blood test done to prove he has a baby daughter. He got me pregnant, then abused and threatened me when I told him about it, by dislocating my jaw; luckily, the baby survived. Now I am seeking child support, I can't do this alone, since I had to move away because of my fear of him. Please show him this letter and I will get back in touch with him. My apologies to you Katie, Sincerely, Shelly."

I wasn't even in shock from the letter, since I already knew they were sleeping together. I remembered the rumors that she was pregnant with Danny's baby. This confirms it. Not wanting to lose the letter or have Danny tear it up, I ran down to the drugstore and made a copy of the letter, which I put in a safe place.

As the evening approached, I just sat and waited for Danny to come home. He arrived complaining about some guys at the gym annoying him. Just to make conversation with him, I asked what happened.

"Are you really concerned or are you…."

I stopped him right there. "Danny, I have something that came in the mail today that was addressed to me, but it was really meant for you."

"What do you mean Katie? I don't like riddles."

I told him to wait here for a moment, as I went to retrieve the letter from Shelly. "Here," I said and handed it to him.

He began to read it and started to squirm. After he finished the letter he said, "Well, I suppose you're going to give me some kind of lecture about this." He slammed his fist on the table and said, " This is bullshit! I'm not her kid's father."

"Are you telling me you've never slept with Shelly? I know awhile back I put the question to you, and you told me it was none of my business. So now I'm asking you again. "Did you ever sleep with Shelly during our marriage?"

"Look Katie, don't talk to me or ask me questions like that."

I could tell he was starting to get angry. You can't miss that demeanor, which I've seen a hundred times. "Danny, I would believe you if you told me you didn't sleep with Shelly." I had to lie or suffer the consequences!

Danny said, "You'd believe me."

"Yeah, you're my husband." I thought I'd choke on those words.

"Come here, Katie." He said. I didn't know what to expect. I walked over to him and he grabbed me and said, "Let's go into the bedroom."

"Oh no," I thought, "How did I get myself into this and how do I get out of it?" He put me on the bed and started to take off his clothes. As he approached me, I told him to wait.

"For what?" He said.

I said, "I don't feel very well."

"So, what does that have to do with it?" He said.

I think he knew I didn't want to sleep with him. He started to get rough and pushed me down. I thought about how I'd rather get beat up than to sleep with him.

"You're going to do as I tell you." That night ended up being another nightmare!

CHAPTER 24

The next day Danny left for work. I didn't have to go in until later. Eric called me in the morning and we talked for a long time. He told me that he needed to see me and asked me when I could get away.

I said, "I wish I could see you tonight. I miss you so much." I told him about the letter.

"Katie, can you get out now, before you go to work?"

"Sure, I still have almost six hours before I have to start."

"Where would you like to meet?" He asked.

"How about our favorite spot?" I suggested.

He said, "You mean in the store parking lot?"

We both laughed. "Yeah" I said, "I love starting out there."

Eric said, "I'll meet you there in a half an hour. Is that okay?"

"Just try and stop me." I had already showered so I just did my hair and makeup fast. I went into my hidden jewelry box and retrieved the ring and bracelet Eric had given me, and put them both on. While feeling like the luckiest girl in the whole world, I got into my car and hurried to my destination. I became so excited to see him, I thought my heart was going to pop out of my chest!

When I pulled into the parking lot, Eric was already there waiting for me. I pulled alongside his car. Smiling, he got out and opened my door. "How's my beautiful girl doing today?" The sound of his voice was so soothing to me.

"I'm hanging in there," I replied. We hugged for a long time after he helped me out of my car. I could have hugged him forever.

"Come on Katie." He took my hand and led me to his car.

"Where are we going?" I asked.

"What's your favorite spot to be at Katie?"

"The beach. Why?"

"You'll see," he said. We drove to the same beach where our first magical night started, the night we first made love. As we got out of the car, he took my hand and led me along the beach. There was a ramp with a beautiful yacht parked at the end of it. As he led me to the ramp, I was thinking we were going to admire the yacht. "Do you like it, Katie?"

I said, "Yes, it's great!"

"Well then Sunshine, let's get on board."

I was so surprised! I asked him if we were going on it to look.

"No, we're going to take it for a ride. My friend is allowing me to use it today."

I was astounded! The yacht was huge. It had a big deck with steps that lead up to an even higher deck. There was a cabin down below. Eric gave me a tour of it. There was a kitchen and a game room with a television, VCR, and a stereo system. I was in awe of it all. Then we toured the living room, bathroom, and bedroom. It was so beautiful, like being in paradise! There were dozens of springtime bouquets everywhere. I smiled and said, "Oh Eric, this is so wonderful. When did you have the time to do all this?"

"Well Katie, I'm magical."

I replied, "You know, I do believe you are. Do you know how to drive this?"

He laughed and said, "Yes I do, but it would take up too much of my time with you. So another friend of mine will be coming aboard to set sail for us."

"You have a lot of nice friends Eric, but that doesn't surprise me. You are so wonderful and generous with your heart."

Eric said that he felt so fortunate and fulfilled, and that he loved me with all his heart and soul. He added, " I wish everyone in the whole world could find someone special to love, as much as I love you. What a great world it would be."

"Come here next to me," Eric said before he kissed me. Gosh how I loved the way he kisses, the way he smells and the way he holds me. It's enough to fuel the fires of passion that burn within one's soul.

As we kissed, I heard someone board the yacht. He yelled, "Ahoy mates."

"That's my friend Roy. He's a real character. Come on, I'll introduce you to him." He took me by the hand and we proceeded upstairs. They greeted each other and shook hands. I said hello.

Roy said, "This pretty filly must be Katie, the girl who has stolen our Eric's heart. You know, Eric has really fallen hard for you. I can honestly say we have never seen him like this before. Our Eric is a great guy and an equally great friend. We're glad you came into his life Katie. Well, We'll only be sailing for a couple of hours. Eric tells me you both have to go to work later. So enjoy your cruise and leave everything to Captain Roy. You're in good hands with me."

He left us and went to start the engine. We stayed on the top deck for awhile, enjoying the sunshine and the warmth of the gentle breezes.

After a few minutes, we decided to go downstairs. Eric closed the door behind us. It was just like a dream. We sat down for a moment on the beautiful handcrafted couch. It had windows all around it so we could see right into the water. I was totally enthralled with the moment. Eric put on some soft, romantic music and asked me if I wanted a glass of wine. I nodded my head yes. He poured it and we raised our glasses to make a toast.

He noticed I had the ring and bracelet on that he gave me. "The bracelet looks great on you Katie. I'm so glad you can wear it."

"I only wear it for special moments."

"What do you want to toast to Katie?"

I said, "To our love and the day I can totally be with you."

Then Eric toasted, "I can't imagine my life being anymore fulfilled than it is right now. When I see your smile and I hear your laugh, I fall in love all over again. You have made me so happy." We took a sip of wine, and then we put our glasses down and started to kiss. "Would you like to dance, Katie?"

"Yes, I'd love to." As we danced very slowly, our bodies seemed to melt into one. We began kissing softly and gently as we continued to dance. Eric started to slowly massage my back as he moved his lips up and down my neck. We danced over to the bedroom, where we could still hear the music play. We made our way to the bed and made the most beautiful love on the high seas. I said, "I wish I could lie here forever with you."

Eric replied, "Then I wish I was a genie, because I would grant you that wish, for a very selfish reason, being to always have you with me." We kissed again.

Eric said to me, "Wait here for a moment," as he jumped out of the bed, put on his shorts, and left the room momentarily. He returned carrying a small black gift box, with a tiny red bow on it. I sat up and he put his shirt over my shoulders. He opened the box, and inside was the most beautiful, sparkling diamond ring I have ever seen! Then he said the most beautiful words to me, which I'll never forget, he said, "I never wanted a woman as much as I want you. You make my days brighter and my nights warmer. I can see right into your soul. I'm nothing without you. I love you to the depths that my heart and soul can reach. Katie will you do me the honors and marry me?"

My eyes filled with tears of joy as I hugged him and said, "Yes Eric, I will." He placed the ring on my finger and we embraced. We stayed in that position, as we peacefully watched the water flowing passed us through the window.

After awhile, we decided to go to the top deck and enjoy what was left of our day together. Everything was perfectly timed. As we approached the deck, Roy was starting to steer us back to shore. Roy smiled and winked at me, "Hey Katie, maybe you and Eric can go out with me and my wife sometime."

"That would be really nice," I replied.

Eric took my hand and we walked up the steps to the higher level of the yacht. We got to the edge of the rail and he stood behind me, wrapping both of his arms around my body. He said to me, "I love the way your hair smells," while he kissed the back of my neck. I got chills up and down my spine. He's so romantic. We stood there for the rest of the journey, enjoying the warm breezes and watching the birds soaring through the sky. Thoughts of just running away with Eric began racing through my head.

Eric then asked me the question I knew was coming, "I don't want to force you to leave Danny, because then I would be no better that he is, not allowing you to make your own decisions. Do what you feel is right and when you feel it's right. But I hope it's soon, because I can't take much more of you being with Danny. I know you tell me he's not abusing you anymore, and I believe you. Just the same, I know it's still a horrible life with him."

I told Eric that I need just a little more time, hoping if Danny was still not abusing me, that I could reason with him, and talk him into counseling to control his temper. After that, I will leave him and take my chances. All I know is that the more I saw Eric, the stronger and braver I became. I was starting to get my self-worth back, and realized that I am a human being, and that I should be treated with dignity and respect.

As the boat pulled up to the dock, Roy stopped the yacht, came over to us and said, "Well kids, our tour is now over." He seemed like such a fun guy.

I said to him, "You were a great captain. Thank you so much for a wonderful cruise."

"The pleasure was all mine Katie."

Then Eric shook Roy's hand and said, "Thanks Buddy, I owe you one."

Roy laughed and said, "I think I still owe you a few more first."

As we departed from the boat, we realized we still had some time left before we had to go to work. We walked up to the Beach Restaurant and Eric asked me if I would have an early dinner with him. I said that I would. We got a great table by the window facing the water. When our dinner arrived, we decided to have a glass of wine to accompany it. Eric raised his glass to make a toast, "I promise this to you Katie, I will never hurt you. When you're free for us to be married, our marriage will last a lifetime."

I said, "I believe it will go on past a lifetime." We both professed our love again as we kissed. It was approaching the time for us to leave. I always felt my heart was breaking every time I had to say goodbye to Eric. We saw each other so seldom, but when we were together, it was spectacular!

We got into his car and headed back to reality. Eric drove me to my car, and asked me if I was going directly to work.

"Yes," I told him while admiring the beautiful diamond ring he gave me. He took the box out of his pocket and opened my hand to put the ring away. Then he brought my hand up to his lips and kissed it. "I will always cherish this Eric, and every moment we're together. Even when I can't wear it, it will always be a part of me. I love you." We hugged each other. He opened my car door and helped me in. Then he leaned over and kissed me.

"I love you, Katie." I pulled away, while wiping tears from my eyes, and thinking about how much I love him.

CHAPTER 25

Work was fairly busy, yet I was able to leave on time. I returned home to find Danny slugging down a can of beer. "Here we go again," I said to him, "I thought you gave up drinking."

He hideously laughed, "Yeah, the same way I gave up sex. Be serious Katie. Come here. Sit right down next to me," He said while patting the sofa with his hand.

I thought about how I dreaded this. He was watching a XXX sex flick on a movie screen.

He said, "Watch this, maybe you can learn something." I've never seen such filthy sex acts before. There were threesomes, and even animals doing unspeakable things. I noticed his hand moving under a blanket. He whipped the blanket off and it was obvious he was very turned on by this stuff. He then started to masturbate. I was so disgusted that I started to run out of the room. Danny grabbed me by my shirt and told me that I wasn't going anywhere. "Sit here and watch it." I closed my eyes and listened to him grunting, making animal-like sounds. It scared me to think what I was in for. Noticing I had my eyes closed, he slapped my back and told me to open them.

I cried, "No, I hate this Danny."

He pulled my hair backwards and clutched onto my face really hard. He spewed spit at my face as he yelled, "I'm sick of you not obeying me.

Now you watch this, and then I'm going to quiz you on it so you can show me what you've learned. Do you understand?"

He pulled my hair harder until I answered him, "Yes, okay Danny." I couldn't shake the thought of just slipping poison into his beer, and contemplated how, and if, I could really do it.

The next morning I felt so depressed and used. How can a human being treat another person with such disrespect and degradation? I always felt like a prostitute around Danny, and now more than ever, I was determined to never let Eric find out about Danny still abusing me.

Eric called as usual the next morning, but Danny was still home nursing a hangover. He didn't go to work. I whispered into the phone that I couldn't talk, and Eric let me go immediately!

Looking at Danny so pathetically lying on the couch, I felt like I was living in hell with Danny, and in heaven with Eric, so I knew I had to get rid of Danny for good. I did a lot of soul searching in those days while sitting in church praying for some guidance, and possibly a miracle! What I realized is that God gives us the strength and love when we need it, but he also gives us our own free will, to do what we feel is the right path to take. I think that has to be our own decision, and it has to come from deep within our own hearts and souls. I also knew the path I will take will come with a price!

CHAPTER 26

As a couple more months passed by, I was starting to feel a bit under the weather. Eric called me one morning sounding a bit odd. He said that he needed to see me and asked if I could come over to his house that night. I could tell by his voice that something was wrong. I told him that I would take the night off and arrive there by 3:00 p.m. "That would be great Katie. I love you." Those words were so reassuring to me. Still, so many thoughts were racing through my head. I was thinking that maybe he didn't want to go on like this anymore, which I couldn't blame him for. Maybe he found someone else. I had to stop imagining the worst; maybe I was worrying for nothing.

After Danny left to go out, I headed over to Eric's. Danny thought I was going to work. Eric was waiting on the front porch when I arrived. My heart felt like it was in my throat and I suddenly got very scared, until I saw Eric with a huge smile on his face, when he came over to help me out of my car. "I'm so glad you could come," he said while giving me a strong hug. I asked him if anything was wrong.

His eyes started to tear as he broke the news to me. He said he was being transferred to the West Coast for about a year and that it was a big promotion for him. I was in shock for a moment, and then asked him when he would have to leave. He said in three weeks.

"Three weeks," I gasped, "They're not giving you much time to get ready." Then I switched gears because I didn't want to make him feel bad. "Oh Eric, if this will be a big opportunity for you how could you turn it down?"

He replied, "I want to go because it is a great opportunity, but I want to ask something of you."

"What is it?" I asked.

He said that he wanted me to come with him to California.

"I would love to, but I just did something too. I enrolled in cosmetology school and I will be starting next week. I had to put over half of the non-refundable tuition down already. I'm sorry Eric, it's just that I wanted you to be proud of me! Doing hair is something I've always wanted to do."

"Katie, I'm always proud of you, but I cannot take away your dreams of becoming something you have always wanted. I'm not going to take the job in California, I don't want to leave you here alone."

"You are so sweet Eric. But I can't let you do that, you have to go, or I will feel really bad. I promise I will be all right! My parent's took out an insurance policy for me when I was born, and I never told Danny about it, so I cashed it in to pay for my tuition to beauty school.

Eric said, "I think it's great that you want to be a hairstylist."

I said, "It's because of you that I can accomplish this. You've given me a newfound confidence. Ever since I was a little girl, I've wanted to do hair. I even use to cut my sisters and my 'Barbie Dolls' hair all off! Even back then, I had it in me!" I asked Eric, "What about your house? Can someone rent it on such short notice?"

"Well Katie, I have another surprise for you. I know how much you love this house, so I purchased it for us.

"You bought it for us!"

He said, "Yes, and my brother and his girlfriend will stay here for the year and take care of it for us."

I was so excited; I practically pushed him over when I jumped up to give him a huge hug. We kissed and I told him that he couldn't be for real. "I still think I'm going to wake up someday, and all of this will be just a dream!"

Eric assured me that it wasn't a dream and that he will always be there for me. Then he stated, "I'm going to be having a barbecue on Sunday and I would like to introduce you to my family, can you come to it Katie?"

"I thought your parents live in Florida?" I asked.

"Yes, they do, but they are coming in to visit along with my younger sister. I don't get a chance to see them very often. I know they would love you."

I asked him if they knew that I was still married.

"Nobody knows that yet, not until you say the word. I don't want you to feel uncomfortable Katie."

I asked, "How big is your family?"

Eric replied, "I have three sisters and two brothers."

"It sounds as big as my family. I'd love to come! Your parents must be really special people to have turned out a son like you."

Eric held me close and we stood there and hugged. "I really wish you could come with me Katie. I will call you every morning, and almost every weekend, I will fly into town to see you."

I replied, "A year can go by really fast, especially when you're busy. I will miss you so much, but you might not have a lot of time to fly back very often."

He looked at me and said, When something is important to me, I make the time. You are the most important person in my life now and always."

I just smiled, gave him a kiss, and told him that I will always see him when he comes into town, no matter what."

He changed the mood and asked, "Do you want to go swimming?"

"I'd love to, but I don't have a bathing suit."

Eric said, "Wait out on the deck. I'll be right back."

I gazed out at the endless amount of trees in his yard. It was a beautiful sight which put me into a trance. Eric appeared behind me and told me he had a surprise for me. I turned around as he handed me a beautiful wrapped box with a big red bow on it!

"What's this?" I asked.

"Open it and see." I opened it slowly, trying not to ruin the wrapping. Under the red tissue paper was an elegant, silky white bikini with a matching beach robe.

"Oh Eric, I love it!

He said, "Go ahead and try it on."

I ran into the bathroom and put it on. It fit like a glove. When I came back outside, Eric snapped a picture of me. He whistled and said, "Katie, you look beautiful. Even Venus, the Goddess of Love couldn't do that outfit justice the way you do."

I could tell I was blushing while I said, "You are so good for my ego."

He said, "Let me take a couple more pictures of you out by the pool." We went out there and I playfully posed for him.

I told him that it was my turn and proceeded to snap some pictures of him. I said, "I wish I could get us together in a picture."

He said, "Your wish is my command." He went into the house and retrieved a tripod. We posed together while his camera did all the work of snapping our picture together. We had so much fun!

Eric jumped into the pool and swam the entire length. "Come on Katie, jump in. Follow me." I was very apprehensive. I just walked around in the shallow part and then froze in my tracks. Eric was so receptive. He immediately swam over to me and asked what was wrong.

Feeling ashamed, I told him that I couldn't swim.

"You never learned in school?" He asked.

I said, "When they built my school, it was supposed to have a pool, but that part of the budget never got passed. So there was no pool and I never learned how to swim elsewhere."

He asked me if I wanted to learn how to swim. "I'll teach you," he said.

"Yes, I've always wanted to learn, but I've been afraid I wouldn't be able to do it." Eric taught me how to swim that afternoon. He was so patient. I was diving off the edge into the deep end by the end of the afternoon. Feeling so excited, I must have thanked him a hundred times. It was a big stepping stone for me to accomplish something that I should have learned in my childhood years.

Eric said to me, "I'm really proud of you. You're such a fast learner. Come on. Let's go soak in the hot tub for awhile and just relax." We got out of the pool and stepped into the hot tub. It was so soothing. I leaned my head into his chest and he bought my face to his and kissed me. "How can I manage being away from you for so long?" He said.

I said, "This job may be a way to a better future. I want you to know I can hang in there as long as I know you love me."

Eric responded, "My heart knows nothing else but to love you forever." We got caught up in the moment, as he picked me up and carried me to the bedroom, where we made the most passionate love ever. Afterwards, we dozed off for about an hour wrapped up in each other's arms. We woke up to the same beautiful music we fell asleep to. "Hey Sunshine, did you have a nice catnap?"

I said, "Yes, it was so peaceful."

We both sat up. Eric asked me again if I could definitely come over Sunday for the barbecue.

"Yes, I wouldn't miss it. I'll get my sister to cover for me. Cindy and Danny don't get along, so he won't call there to check up on me. Besides, it's his Sunday to work anyway."

"Great, then it's all set."

I said, "I think I'm going to be a bit nervous meeting everyone."

He reassured me, "Don't feel that way. They'll love you."

I asked Eric if I could help plan the party.

He asked, "Do you really want to?"

I said, "Sure, are you cooking too?"

Eric answered, "Yes, I cook often. You learn a lot about cooking when you're a bachelor. So what do you think we should serve?" He caught me staring at him. "What's wrong, Katie?"

I said, "I have to say whenever you talk about you or us, you always include me. You really make me feel so special. I'm so overwhelmed by you. Sometimes I feel I don't deserve you Eric."

He put his finger to my lips and said, "Please don't ever say that. I know Danny made you feel worthless and unloved. That's going to be his loss. He's clueless to both your inner and unblemished beauty."

I teared up and hugged him. "I love you so much."

He replied, "I love you too, with all my heart. Someday you'll believe in yourself as much as I believe in you."

I said, "Eric, you always make me feel better. I want to say thank you for everything." After we finished making plans for the party, it was time for me to go home. Home, that seemed so inappropriate sounding for a place you hate going to. We said our good-byes and Eric walked me to my car.

"So you'll be here Sunday right by my side."

"Just try and stop me." I said.

Then Eric leaned over, kissed me, and whispered "I love you, I'll see you soon, Sunshine."

CHAPTER 27

I was quite surprised to find the week went by quickly. Danny experienced his usual foul mood swings. Not wanting to get hit anymore, I played along with him and coddled him as he ranted and raved to me about work, the gym and me. I told him that on Sunday I was going to a hair show with my sister and it would be an all day event.

He replied, "I don't know why you want to do hair anyway Katie, you'll probably goof up everyone's hair. Besides, how are you paying for this so-called beauty school."

I lied to Danny and just said, "I got a new charge card and I can get another job to pay it off."

He came back with, "Just make sure you don't have my name on it or skimp on the money you make at the restaurant for me. You know while I'm bodybuilding I need all my protein drinks and vitamins."

"I'll work it out," I said.

"Good, just as long as you have it straight. I'm not giving up anything I'm doing now for something you want. Do you understand?"

"Don't worry Danny," I said as I was thinking about how I needed to call Cindy, and fill her in on what's been going on in my life. I feel I can trust her now, and I know she'll be happy for me having someone special like Eric to love me so much.

The next morning the phone rang at the usual time. Eric said, "So Sunshine, are we still on for Sunday."

"Yes, and I'm getting my sister to cover for me." After he told me what time the barbecue started, I asked him if he wanted me to come early to help.

"Katie, I always want you here with me."

I laughed and told him that I would be there about 11:00 a.m., one hour after Danny leaves for work.

He said, "The barbecue starts at 3:00, and I would like you all to myself for awhile, before the guests arrive."

Sue also called me that morning, wanting to know how I was doing and if I was all right. I told her I was great!

"How are you taking the news about Eric leaving?" She then asked, "Why won't you go with him. It would be the perfect solution to finally breaking free from Danny?"

I said. "When he told me I thought my heart was going to drop down to the floor. It is a great career move for him. I would go with him in a heartbeat, and it's not just the fact that I signed up for beauty school, you know Danny would try to kill my sister Cindy, to make good on his threats."

Sue said, "Katie then how will you and Eric ever end up together?" I said Danny will be taken care of very soon, just trust me." Sue replied, "I do believe Danny has pushed you too far, and payback time is here; and he deserves everything he gets! Katie, I have to tell you what has been going on around here at work. There's these two girls who got hired here a couple of months ago. They both have major crushes on Eric."

I stopped her, "Do you think he'd like to go out with either of them? Does he have coffee with them?"

Sue interrupted me, "Before you get upset, I'll tell you Eric doesn't even give them the time of day. One of them even goes out of her way to look like a tramp. Eric has shot down any advances they've tried to make, nicely, of course. I think they think he's available, but because he never talks about his life or is seen with any girls, their speculating that maybe he's gay. Joan and me laugh about that. Katie, you will never have anything to worry about with Eric. He's totally devoted to you. When Joan, Eric and I take our breaks together, he lets loose with us. Joan and I wish we were in your place sometimes. You guys are like Romeo and Juliet! It gives us a chill just thinking about how strongly two people can be so in love, against all odds. He always says he knows that you and him will be together really soon."

I replied. "Yeah, if we kill Danny."

Sue said. "If I had it in me, I would do it for you! Eric has a plan for when he gets back from California. He knows it has to be your decision to leave Danny and he especially knows how scared you are of him. But he says you won't have to ever worry or be scared of Danny again."

"What do you think he means?" I asked.

Sue said, "I don't know. When we ask him he just smiles and says that Katie and I will definitely be together."

"Wow, maybe he really has plans to kill Danny." Sue and I both laughed. I said "Hey, I'm going to be meeting Eric's family on Sunday!"

Sue said, "Wow, that's a big step. Are you nervous?"

"A little bit, but when I'm with Eric I feel I have nothing to fear. I prayed so hard everyday that I can be with Eric soon. I imagine there's a reason why I'm not totally with him yet. But, as the saying goes, all good things come to those who wait, and I'd wait an entire lifetime for Eric." I told Sue that I had to go and she made me promise to call and give the whole scoop of the party to her and Joan, which I promised I would.

Then Sue added, "You know Katie, your whirlwind romance with Eric is what keeps me and Joan going. You guys are like a book with a new chapter for us to look forward to. We feel like we're living our lives through you."

"I love you Sue." Tell Joan I'll talk to her soon."

"Love you too Katie. I'll be waiting for your call."

The weekend was finally here and I worked that Saturday at the restaurant. It was pretty busy. I decided to stop at the mall on the way home from work to get a new outfit to wear to Eric's the next day. I browsed through every store possible, while thinking about how lucky I was to be a part of Eric's life. Although our time together is short, every moment we have is very precious. I got teary-eyed thinking how I will handle Eric leaving, since I had always been so comforted by the fact that Eric was nearby if I needed him. Now he's going to be hundreds of miles away, but I also knew he would try to be here almost every weekend!

In the middle of the mall was a booth where a man was airbrushing tee shirts. He had a long, curly ponytail that came halfway down his back; it would surely make some women envious. I politely interrupted him and asked him if he could airbrush a shirt with a cherry red, 1934 Ford three-window coupe? I knew Eric was such a car buff and that was one of his favorites. The guy said that he could do it without a problem. I told him that it was going to be a special gift and that I had one more request, putting "Eric's Toy" on the license plate of the car. He said that was all right and it would be ready in an hour. I thanked him.

I couldn't wait to see it and give it to Eric. He's given me so much already. I really wanted to give him something special. As I walked around, I found a store that was having a huge sale. Upon realizing an hour had passed, I headed back to the airbrush place. It looked dynamite hanging up waiting for me. While I paid the guy, I thought about how much Eric would like the shirt. I thanked the guy a hundred times and told him what a beautiful job he did. Then, I headed back home.

I had to hide the tee shirt in my car until Sunday, so Danny wouldn't see it. He arrived home about an hour after I did. My stomach was feeling a bit queasy again, which it has been for quite awhile now. I hoped I wasn't coming down with something; I wanted to feel great for tomorrow.

Danny told me he was going to the gym. Noticing lately that he was looking puffy in the neck and face, I asked him point blank if he was taking steroids to bulk up.

He got furious and lashed out at me, "Do you really think I couldn't do this on my own?"

"I don't want to fight with you. I'm just asking. Those drugs can be dangerous."

"Like you really care. I'm going." He proceeded to slam the door behind him. I was relieved not having to sit with him all evening.

What I did want to do was wrap up Eric's tee shirt. After I retrieved it from my car, I wrote a poem inside a blank card, sprayed it with perfume, and put it inside the box. It read, "Dear Eric, your love has made a difference in my life. You mean everything in the world to me. You have touched my life in so very many ways I cannot even begin to count them. I've lived as a prisoner in a torture chamber paralyzed by fear, seeming always to be in imminent danger. But, because of your undying love and affection, I have been set free. You're my window into heaven, my pot of gold at the end of the rainbow. I can honestly say that I have been freed, and now I am a better person because of you. This is why this poem comes from deep within my heart and soul, where you will always hold a very special place. With all my love to you always and forever, Love, Katie." Sentimentally I cried, putting the whole package together and then I put it back in the trunk of my car.

CHAPTER 28

The next morning I got up extra early, after a restless night's sleep. I felt like a little kid who was anticipating the excitement of Disney World for the first time. I showered and dressed in a conservative outfit, to change out of after Danny left for work. When he finally left, I put on what I was really planning on wearing. I got my jewelry out from its hiding place and put it on. The ring was so beautiful!

I started the drive to Eric's house while listening to my favorite cassette tapes. Suddenly, I got butterflies in my stomach as I pulled into his driveway. Eric came out of the front door as I pulled up. He had the biggest most beautiful smile on his face. He came over to my car, opened my door, and practically jumped in with me. "Hey beautiful, how are you?" He said.

I said, "Great, now that I'm with you." He threw his arms around me while gently pulling me up from my car and gave me a long, romantic kiss. We started to walk towards his door, but I stopped him and ran back to my car.

"You're going already," he kidded.

"I have to get something out of my trunk." I opened it up and pulled out his gift. "Here, this is for you."

"Katie, you don't have to get me gifts."

"Please," I said, "Just open it."

He smiled and said, "How can I ever turn you down." He sat on the front porch and opened the box. He kidded with me and said, "Something sure does smell great in here, are you sure you weren't in this box Katie."

I laughed and said, "I put my perfume scent on it so you'll always remember me."

"I could never forget you." He pushed aside the tissue paper and took the shirt out of the box. He was speechless for a few seconds.

I said, "I hope you like it."

"Like it, I love it. It's the nicest gift I have ever received." He hugged me and thanked me. "You had this detailed so great. I love these cars. They're my favorite! How clever, you had my name put on the license plate. That's really cool. Would you mind if I put this on now?"

"I'd be honored; and besides, I love watching you take your shirt off."

He smiled and winked at me as he changed the shirt he was wearing, replacing it with mine. "So, how does it look?"

Gazing at him I said, "You look absolutely great in anything."

Eric picked up the box to smell the scent again and noticed the card. "What's this?"

I said, "Open it up and see."

He opened the card and began reading it. Being as sensitive as Eric is, he began to have tears in his eyes, which he tried to hide by turning away. He then embraced me ever so tightly. I didn't think he was ever going to let me go. Eric took my hands into his while facing me and said, "Katie, you are an angel. I never thought I would find someone like you in my whole life. But here you are so sweet, and loving and inno-cent. Your heart is as pure as gold. I can't imagine my life ever without you. This poem you wrote me I know is from the deepest depths of your soul, and I will always treasure it. I believe we were meant for each other. I have found everything I'll ever want or need in you. I love you so very much. This transfer to California is really causing me pain." Tears starting running down his face.

I moved closer to him and kissed him as I wiped the tears away. "Eric, I'll be alright. You said you'll be calling me, and I promise, anytime you come into town, I will always get away to see you. So, it will almost be the same."

He took my hand and asked me to follow him. We went up to the bedroom, where he said there was a surprise waiting. The picture he took of me in my swimsuit had been made into a huge, life-sized, poster placed on his bedroom wall!

I said, wow that's a big picture. Do you use it as a dart board."

Eric laughed and said, "You're so refreshing Katie." He proceeded to get out his wallet and show me all the pictures he had of me in it. "I keep these in here so you'll always be with me."

The moment was perfect, for a morning-long love making session. Afterwards, Eric asked me if Danny was leaving me alone.

I told him that he's been occupied with his bodybuilding, so he does-n't have time for me.

"He better keep it that way." Eric said.

It was getting late, so I suggested we go downstairs and start prepar-ing for the festivities. To my surprise, he had everything finished. When I asked him why he didn't wait for me to help him, he just smiled and said he wanted every moment we had together.

Eric asked me to come into the other room. We sat down on the couch and he pressed his body close to mine. He had turned on the tel-evision and VCR to my favorite movie, "Grease" after serving popcorn and Iced tea. We relaxed and watched the movie. I always felt so com-forted being in his arms. Eric told me I could take the movie home and watch it whenever I wanted to. The time seemed to fly by and before we knew it, the doorbell rang. "Well Katie, that must be our company."

While getting up, I told Eric I suddenly felt a little nervous.

"Don't worry about it. My family is a bunch of characters, and they're really a lot of fun to be with. Besides, they'll love you." He held my hand as we approached the door. Behind it was standing almost his entire family. They rushed in to greet Eric by hugging and kissing him.

His dad looked over at me and said, "So this is Katie. Wow, quite a looker you got there Eric," as he elbowed him.

I smiled and said, "Hello."

Eric's mom came over to me and paused for a moment. I flashed back to the disastrous first time I met Danny's mother. I greeted Eric's mom and to my surprise, she gave me a big hug and said, "Hi Katie. Eric has told us a lot about you. Now we know why he's taken such a fancy to you."

Eric's brother Rick, who was the police officer, introduced himself and his wife Carol. I thought about how Eric's family is so loving and affectionate. Now I know where he gets it. They all seemed very sweet.

Eric led them inside, while taking their luggage and jackets, asking them where Randy and Meg were.

His mom replied, "Your sister wanted to spend last night at Randy's place, but they'll be here soon, along with Lynn, Randy's girlfriend."

Eric informed everyone that Sherry and Heather will be over soon with their families.

I helped Eric get things situated as he told his family to make themselves comfortable. His parents and Meg would be staying for a couple of extra days before returning to Florida.

His Mom walked into the back of the house and said to Eric, "This is really such a peaceful setting back here. I always love to sit out here and relax when we stay with you." I knew exactly how she feels, it really is beautiful.

The doorbell rang again. It was the rest of the family, including two nephews and one niece. Eric brought out some snacks for everyone. By the fireplace was a circular bar where Eric served the first drink. Afterwards, everyone could help themselves.

The kids and the younger sister wanted to go swimming. They suited up and jumped in the pool. The rest of the party quickly followed outside, where it was easier to keep an eye on them. The kids were having a great time. All the adults were commenting on how inviting the hot tub looked, and that they'd probably be going in later. It was big enough to seat 12 people.

Eric sat down for a moment right next to me, as he put his arm around my shoulder and whispered in my ear. "Are you okay?"

"Better than okay. This is like being with my family. When we all get together, there are over 40 people present, and the number is still growing. I can't wait to introduce you to my family, I know they'll love you."

His parents sat next to us and struck up a conversation. His dad asked, "So Katie, Eric tells us you come from a big family."

I replied, "Yes, my parents have seven kids. I was just telling Eric how our family parties number around 40."

"My goodness, how do you all fit in the same room?" his mom asked.

"We manage. When we were little we always went to my grandparents' farm. It was amazing. My mom came from a family of ten brothers and sisters; and everyone met there for the holidays. In those days, there were over sixty people there.

"Wow," his dad said. "That's a party in itself."

"Yes," I replied, "everyone would bring something so my grandmother wouldn't be cooking for hours. But, she would anyway. It was the greatest feeling being there."

"Your grandparents had a farm, Katie?" Eric asked.

"Yes, they had cows, chickens, and horses. We would always get to ride the horses, and help my grandfather milk the cows! It was so much fun. My grandparents were Polish, so they used to go to an open-air market and sell their produce, eggs, and chickens. My mom took us there all the time when we were little. We became hysterical though upon witnessing the chickens getting decapitated, having just played with them hours before."

"I know what you mean." Eric said, "My grandparents were also Polish. I was practically raised on a farm myself, always going there to help them out. It was really a hard life for people back then. But given the chance to choose, they would do it all over again."

Eric was so pleased that everyone was hitting it off. He got up and announced that he was going to start dinner. I offered to help and followed him. We were alone in the kitchen when he grabbed me and pulled me close to him. Kissing me repeatedly he said, "I can't tell you how happy I am with you. I know my parents like you a lot, especially my mom. She's very proud of her heritage. When we were little my parents had to struggle to make ends meet."

I said, "I know what you mean."

Eric continued, "Then my dad got a lucky break by getting employed by a big company and worked his way to the top. He's a very hard worker and it paid off. Now, although they're very well off, my mom's good values have kept them very down to earth. I'm proud to be their son."

I said, "They've done great with all of their kids. I feel the same way about my parents and couldn't imagine growing up in any other family. We've both been blessed."

It was time to return to our guests. Everything, including dinner went great. We swam in the pool and relaxed in the hot tub later that afternoon.

Eric's brother Rick, the police officer, and his wife Carol had their own house in a new development. They didn't have any kids yet, but Carol was due to have a baby in three months. They were both really nice to me. Carol told me that she's a hairdresser and I told her that I just enrolled in beauty school. Afterwards, we talked about hair for a long time, and she gave me a lot of advice about the world of the beauty industry.

In the early evening, we all played volleyball and then took a walk to a creek that ran through the back woods. I was really starting to get tired and wanted to stay and help Eric clean up, but I also knew it was getting close to the time that I would have to leave. If Danny arrived home before me, he just might call my sister and I didn't want him bothering her. Eric's parents seemed a little disappointed when I told them that I had to go, since it was still early. Eric covered for me and told them I had a family engagement party I had to be at. I could tell he really didn't want me to leave either.

Everyone said their good-byes and told me it was really nice meeting me. His parents got up and gave me a big hug, telling me to stop in again before they leave for Florida. I smiled and said my good-byes and said I would try to get back. Eric walked me to my car and jumped in the driver's seat; I sat on the other side. He then proceeded to drive down the driveway. "What are you doing?" I asked him.

"I want to make sure I could kiss and hold you without an audience." We kissed for about five minutes!

"I had a great time. Your family is so nice."

"They like you a lot too." Eric said.

I asked him if he wanted a ride back up the driveway.

He laughed, "Katie, you're so cute. I'll walk back and call you in the morning. I love you."

"I love you too, Eric." I said as I drove away.

CHAPTER 29

Luckily, I got home before Danny. I changed, showered, and sat down to watch Grease. When Danny arrived I was about halfway through the movie. He immediately stopped it and asked me why I was watching such a pussy movie.

"I love this movie." I said.

"I got one that's even better." He left the room to retrieve it and put it in the VCR. It was another dirty, XXX rated film. I got up and started to walk out of the room, but Danny stopped me cold in my tracks. "Where the hell do you think you're going?"

"I'm tired and I want to go lie down." He got up and pulled me back by my hair. I ended up on his lap. "Danny, I hate these kind of movies. I don't want to watch it!"

"Just shut up and watch." I closed my eyes and could tell he was getting excited.

"At least let me go get some protection." I begged. I always carried them in my purse from the supply in my drawer, for Eric and I to use. He started to laugh hysterically. "What's so funny?" I asked.

Sarcastically he said, "Well those things won't do you any good."

"What do you mean?" I asked.

"I knew you didn't want to get pregnant again so soon, so I poked a hole in every one of those things while you were at work one day."

I shouted, "How could you do that to me?"

He yelled, "I want a son again! You couldn't keep the last one in the oven, so I thought I'd bake us a new one." I started to cry and ran out of the room. The last thing I wanted now was to have Danny's baby. "Just forget it," he shouted from the other room, "you spoiled my mood anyway." He continued to watch the video anyway, and I could hear the animal sounds and grunts coming from him, while he masturbated himself.

I laid in bed thinking about how could a person be so despicable! A loveless marriage is like living a death sentence. It kills you every second, every minute, and every hour. After dozing off I suddenly was jolted awake. Suddenly it dawned on me that if Danny poked a hole in every rubber, it could mean there's a huge possibility I could have become pregnant with Eric's baby! Then I thought about how sick I have been for the last couple of weeks. My period did arrive, but it was very light and lasted for only one day.

After Danny left for work the next morning, I purchased a pregnancy test kit from the drugstore and took it right away. I walked away from the bathroom where I had laid the vile on the sink. Pacing back and forth, I couldn't stand the suspense any longer. Slowly I walked back to the bathroom. My heart beat faster as I looked at the vile. It was pure blue!

I ran from the bathroom into the bedroom, fell onto the bed and cried. What do I do now? Whose baby is this? Oh God please let it be Eric's, or I'll be tied to Danny forever! I decided not to tell Eric yet. If he knew there was a possibility that I was carrying his baby, he may not go to California. That job was an opportunity of a lifetime for him and I wasn't going to spoil it. On the down side, it could be Danny's. Could my life get any more complicated?

The ringing of the phone brought me back to reality. It was Eric. He immediately detected something in my voice. "Katie, is everything alright?" He asked.

"Yes Eric, everything is fine." I assured him.

Eric asked, "Can you come over within the next couple of days? My family has been asking me when they can see you again."

I choked back my tears. Maybe I'll try tomorrow. I'll see what I can do. We talked for awhile longer and I told him that I had to go.

"Katie, are you sure you're alright?"

"I'm great. I have an appointment in a little while with the Beauty School. Can you call me later?"

"I sure will. I love you sunshine."

"I love you too, Eric."

When I hung up, I had to wipe the tears away. I called my gynecologist and told the receptionist that I needed an appointment as soon as possible, since I had a positive reading on my home pregnancy test. She scheduled me in for the following week.

I couldn't face Eric yet, so I called him back to tell him I wouldn't be able to get away. "Tell your parents I had a really nice time and I can't wait to see them again."

"I understand." He said. "Can we get together a few more times before I go?"

I told him that would be a definite date!

The day of my doctor appointment arrived. The doctor told me that he cannot be sure I'm pregnant until the results of my blood test come back, but it appears I'm about six weeks along and to call the office for the results.

Later in the day my suspicions were confirmed; I was pregnant. I retrieved the journal I hide under the mattress and counted back six weeks. That was one of the weeks that Eric and I were together a lot. I thought about how he could really be this baby's father. Suddenly I felt great warmth within my body. I still couldn't tell him though, in case it wasn't his. Also, I was not planning on telling Danny yet. So I kept the news to myself for now.

Eric and I were able to get together a couple more times before he had to leave, and on his last day, I managed to spend the whole day with him. We made love all day long. At night we laid by the pool just watching the stars light up the sky. If I could wish upon any of those stars, it would be that I was carrying Eric's baby.

He told me that he wanted to show me something, so we both got up and walked into the house, where he asked me to wait on the couch. He returned holding a photo album. It was engraved with our names on the cover, "Katie and Eric." Underneath was the date of our first time together. "I have one for myself Katie, It's an exact match." I opened the album and discovered it was filled with the pictures he took of us.

"This is wonderful, it's just what I needed Eric. I will always hold these close to my heart."

Eric said, "These pictures will always be with me wherever I go. I'm really going to miss you." His eyes started to water.

I broke down and cried. I didn't want to upset Eric, but my hormones must have been out of control. "Oh Eric, I'm going to miss you so much."

"Katie, if you want me to stay just say the word. I'll do anything you want."

I know that when guys tell you these things, in the back of their minds they really don't mean what they say. With Eric it was different; I knew he really meant it. I said, "A year will go by really fast and besides, I'll still be seeing you every time you're in town." Changing the subject, I asked, " When is Randy and his girlfriend moving in?"

"They're coming in tomorrow. My brother will be taking me to the airport."

Suddenly, my stomach felt very queasy, like I was going to be sick. While covering my mouth I ran to the bathroom and made it just in time to vomit into the toilet. Eric heard me and opened the door asking me if I was all right.

I said, "Yes, I'm probably just coming down with the flu or something."

"The flu in the summer?" He asked.

"I'll be alright. Maybe it was something I ate that didn't agree with me."

Eric said, "Promise me Katie, if this keeps up you'll go to the doctor."

"I promise." I said.

Eric left the room and returned with a glass of ginger ale. He hugged me and said, "I just can't seem to let you go. When I get back things are going to change for us. Danny won't be bothering you anymore Katie, I promise."

I answered, "When that day comes I can tie up my past with Danny and start on my future with you. That's when I know the hand of the Lord will be on my shoulder. All my prayers will finally be answered."

Suddenly, I had to throw up again. Besides being pregnant, my being upset about Eric leaving was probably the cause of this. Eric was so worried even though I told him not to be because I was just getting worked up over his leaving.

"Maybe I should stay." he said.

"No really Eric, you have to go. I'll be fine." I started to feel a little better as I rinsed my mouth out with ginger ale, and sucked on a mint.

Eric said, "I'm still going to call you every day. If you need me for anything at all, you can page me at this number."

"I will. Thank you so much for everything. I love you very much." The tears were flowing down my face.

"Katie, I love you too. I also love your poem so much, I even laminated and framed the card and beautiful poetry you wrote to me, I will always treasure it, and you know I always wear the tee shirt."

We kissed our last kiss for the night. As I left Eric said, "I'll call you Katie." I smiled at him and waved goodbye as I blew him a kiss. I could see he was wiping tears from his eyes.

CHAPTER 30

I cried all the way home, but had to compose myself before arriving back to Danny. I told him that I was visiting my sick godmother with my parent's, and that she lived an hour away. He had to work anyway and I knew he wouldn't call my parents house. When I got home he wasn't there. I took the opportunity to go lie down.

The next morning I got up around 7:00 a.m. and Danny still was not home. His side of the bed had not been slept in. I imagined him having been in an accident, and laying unconscious somewhere. What a great fantasy that was! I know I wasn't raised to think that way but sometimes you just can't help yourself. I probably would have thought about suicide, but then Eric came along, and it was like he threw a life raft to me. He saved my life by making me feel worthy and valuable. His love inspires me to know that everyone born here on this earth has the right to be respected and feel accepted. He also taught me that I can stand on my own two feet, and against all odds with my newfound strengths that he has helped me to achieve; I will prevail against Danny.

The phone rang and it was Eric. "Hi Sunshine, how's my favorite girl doing this morning?"

"Hi Eric, I'm always better when I hear your voice."

He said, "I thought I'd call you before I have to leave for the airport. I'm going to really miss you Katie. I'm already trying to schedule a few weekends to get back and see you."

I replied, "I can't wait. I will be thinking about you every minute of every day." Just then, I heard the door unlocking. It was Danny. "Danny's here, I have to go."

"I love you," Eric said, "I'll call you soon."

"Me too," was all I could say back. Danny walked into the room looking awful. I didn't want to question his whereabouts, since I really didn't care to know.

As usual, he had to start on me. "So Katie, what time did you get home last night?"

"I didn't look at the clock probably around 7:00 p.m.," I lied. It was more like 9:00 p.m.

"I called your parents' house at 6:00 p.m. How come you weren't there?"

I said, "Because we returned right after that. Afterwards, I stopped at the store." All I could think of was that this is a trap, he had quizzed my parents and they had told him they haven't seen me. Luckily, he didn't pursue it any further, except to find out why I didn't want to know where he was.

"What's up with you, Katie? Aren't you going to ask me 24 questions about where I was?"

"No," I boldly dared to say loudly.

He came over to me and clobbered me with his arm into the side of my head.

I screamed, "Stop it Danny!" He yanked me by my hair as I pleaded some more for him to stop. I knew right now that this is where I would have to tell him that I'm pregnant, or he'll surely kill this baby too. As he dragged me across the room, I blurted it out as his fist was raised in the air ready to hit me. I screamed, "Danny don't, I'm pregnant!"

He brought his arm back down. "What did you say?"

"I'm pregnant."

"Why didn't you tell me? When did you find out?"

"Just today," I lied.

"How far along are you?"

"Six weeks. I'll tell you right now, if you abuse me while I'm pregnant, I'm liable to lose this one too. It might be that boy you've always wanted."

He collapsed onto the bed and started to cry. "Katie, I don't know why I do this to you. I just can't help myself sometimes. I mean, you make me so mad. It's hard to stop myself."

I've heard this all before; his tears mean nothing to me. He's sorry because I make him so mad, so he beats me up. That's logical only to his sick mind.

"Come here," he said to me as he sat on the bed, still sobbing. I dreaded every step I took towards him. He clutched his hands around my waist and pulled my breasts close to his head. "I'm so sorry. I love you and I don't know why I do all these bad things to you Katie."

I said, "When people do bad things they have to own up to them Danny. Otherwise a distinctive sense between right and wrong is shattered." I don't even know if he understood a word that I said.

"Katie, I promise I'm really going to try not to hit you while you're pregnant. I need to have a son. My mother would be so proud of me."

I said "Oh, so after I have this baby you'll resume the abuse." He looked puzzled saying, "I have to get ready for work; I start early today."

I waited until Danny left to wash up. While standing in the soothing pulsating shower for what seemed like hours, I thought about how long I could put off telling Eric about this baby. Since Danny has a rare blood type, it will be easy to tell who the father is. I prayed for the miracle of having this little angel I'm carrying inside of me, to be Eric's baby.

The days and weeks passed. When I approached my sixteenth week, I decided it was time to tell Eric. He continued to call me every morning, but this weekend he was coming in for a visit. I was hardly showing yet; however, I knew how quickly a pregnancy could become apparent. This was such a dilemma for me, because I knew he'd want to return home instead of finishing his work in California.

I prepared my story for Danny so I could escape to see Eric this weekend. I thought about telling him I had to work both days, and then ask my boss if it was alright if I had the weekend off, promising to work a double shift the following weekend. I proceeded to call him; he said that it would be all right and he would arrange sufficient coverage. It worked out perfect, because one of the waiters wanted to go away the following weekend. Everything was all set!

Danny kept his promise about not hitting me since I was pregnant, but his temper still flared up. Sometimes he would punch the wall, or throw a chair. This was all right, as long as it wasn't me that was the target. But now, his new game of torture was to totally ignore me, little did he know, I enjoyed his silence. He had started to wash all his own clothes and dishes, leaving mine intact. One day I had to ask him a question about a bill while he was watching television. I stood right in front of him, trying to get him to at least answer my question, but he totally ignored me, like I was invisible. I stopped asking him anything anymore.

Eric called me the day before his arrival. "Hey sunshine, I'm really missing you something fierce. Will you be able to come over to the house?"

I told him that I was all set for both days. "How's your job going?"

He said, "Great, I got a surprise to tell you when I see you."

"Eric, can you tell me now?"

Eric replied, "I want to see you in person when I tell you."

"Okay." I said. " What time will you be at your house tomorrow?"

"Bright and early, I wanted to spend as much time as I can with you."

"Alright, I'll be there about 10:00 a.m."

I was so excited about Eric's upcoming visit, wondering what he wanted to tell me.

While searching for a screwdriver to fix a bathroom cabinet, I discovered it was not in its usual place. I proceeded to search Danny's dresser for it, and came across some hidden bottles and a syringe. I looked at the writing on the bottle and it was just what I suspected, steroids. I knew he was taking something to bulk up, and probably has been for some time. His face and neck always looked so swollen. I got a frightful feeling inside. If this were Danny's baby, how would the steroids affect it? Danny told me that he's never taken that stuff. I ran to the phone and called the doctor's office to see if he could give me some information on this drug. I got a recorded message stating the office was closed until Monday morning. I would have to wait for the weekend to pass before I got the information.

When Danny arrived home from the gym that evening, he seemed especially moody. He made himself a protein drink that had a few more ingredients than usual: raw liver, raw eggs, and a few other unrecognizable items. It looked and smelled disgusting. He then true to form, went into the bedroom and locked the door. Now, I knew for sure the poison he was injecting into his body.

His mood worsened as he progressed from hitting me to ignoring me. I'd rather have this kind of abuse, him pretending I just didn't exist. What he didn't realize was that his mental games were suiting me just fine. It was like history repeating itself; his parents did the same thing.

Right now, all I could think about was seeing Eric tomorrow. It was going to be great seeing him both days, especially with Danny being in his own little world of weights and drugs. He rarely checked up on me these days. He probably thought that nobody would want me anyway, being pregnant. Although he's told me that since I've known him. But now, since I've been with Eric I know that I am a valuable human being just looking for a way to love and survive. I'm so tired of walking on eggshells, worried about my fears always turning into terror.

I think that everyone should look deep within himself or herself, and find out what they truly want in their lives to change, and what it would take to accomplish it. With the strength and love that God gives you, you could probably move mountains, but you also have to learn to count on yourself for answers!

CHAPTER 31

The next day Danny left for work without saying goodbye, as usual. I showered and happily got ready to go and see Eric. I still got butterflies in my stomach every time I knew I'd be seeing him; it was a great feeling!

Upon entering the long driveway, I discovered Eric standing there with his thumb out. I stopped the car and kidded with him, "Going my way handsome."

"Always," he answered and hopped into the car and gave me a huge kiss. "I've missed you so much."

I was like putty in his arms. "I've missed you too, Eric."

"Let's drive up to the house. I've got a surprise for you." After we approached his front yard, we stepped out of the car and walked up the front steps. Eric told me to stay where I was and to cover my eyes. I couldn't imagine what the surprise was. He went into the house briefly. I heard him come right back out, as he asked me to keep my eyes closed, and to put both of my arms out. He placed something warm and fuzzy in my hands and said that it was all right to open my eyes. It was an Alaskan malamute puppy!

"Oh Eric, it's so adorable."

"Surprise! Do you like her?" He asked.

"Yes, I love her." I said.

"Good, she's yours when you move in here for good. You'll both be here forever. What would you like to name her?" Eric asked.

I thought for a moment and said, "How about the name Roxy? I think she's really beautiful."

Eric said, "So is her new owner. I like that name too."

I smiled at Eric as we watched the little puppy run all over the place. She was so full of energy. Eric told me that his brother would take care of Roxy for now. "They don't mind, they love dogs." That was really nice of his brother and his girlfriend to take care of her for so long. Eric still had quite a few months left in California. We hugged, and I thanked him for the special surprise.

Eric announced that he had another surprise. All I could think of was that being with Eric was like waking up to Christmas morning every day. He said that instead of being away eight more months, it would only be four months and that he would be coming home more often. "The stores are coming along ahead of schedule. They're really pleased with our efforts."

I was so excited I almost knocked him over. He'd be here in time for the baby's arrival I thought! I knew I could no longer keep this news a secret from him. I told Eric that his news was the best ever, but now I had some news for him. "I want you to know that I am happier than I have ever been in my whole life." I just blurted out the news, "Eric, I'm pregnant!"

He didn't know how to react. "Katie, I know how Danny is and I know you willingly wouldn't let him touch you anymore, but Danny needs to be put in his place. He's a menace to you and to society.. Maybe I'll just put him out of his misery for good. Then he'll never hurt you or anyone else again." He then took me in his arms and hugged me. "I love you so much Katie. I promise you this nightmare will be over very soon. I also want you to know I will help you take care of you and your baby. When are you due?"

I told him that I have something else to tell him. "I'm due in four months."

He paused for a moment and smiled saying, "Do you mean I could be the father of this baby Katie! But I thought we always used protection?"

I interrupted him, "Danny told me he wanted a son, so he poked holes in all my condoms."

Eric stopped me, exclaiming, "Katie, this baby could be mine! " He sounded so excited. "Even if I'm not the father, I will still love it because it is a part of you."

We hugged as I asked him if he knew what his blood type was.

He responded, "A-positive. Why?"

"Because the day this baby is born I will know who the father is. Danny has a rare blood type. I've been praying so hard every day that this baby will be yours. I don't know what will happen to me when Danny finds out I'm leaving him, but at this point, I don't care anymore."

Eric held me close to him and assured me that there was nothing to worry about. He was going to take care of everything. He said, "Katie, I know I never tried to force you out of your marriage, even though it killed me inside to know you felt you had to be with Danny out of fear. I would have felt guilty about not letting you make your own decision. Now that I know you freely want to be with me, the wheels are in motion to get you away from Danny. Our love is strong, and I want you to know that I have never met anyone so sincere and loving as you. This little angel you carry within yourself will be a very lucky baby."

I put my hands to my stomach and said, "I already love this baby."

"I know you do." Eric said.

We stayed at his house and had a wonderful time. His brother and his girlfriend stayed at a hotel for the weekend so we could be alone. I told him that his family was so sweet and considerate. He agreed. We watched the puppy run all over, biting anything that got in her way. We decided to take a walk in the back trails of Eric's land. The puppy loved it. We strolled through the gardens as we walked hand in hand discussing our plans. Eric suddenly picked me up gently and slowly spun me around. "Katie, I'm the luckiest and happiest guy in the whole world! Pinch me to make sure I'm not dreaming." I pinched his butt lightly and he laughed and said that he loved me.

Eric made us a fantastic lunch. Knowing I'm a picky eater, he prepared all the foods I like. There was fresh fruit, chef salad, rolls, steaks, baked potatoes, and grilled vegetables. He topped it off with a Baked Alaska that was heavenly. I jokingly asked him if he wanted me to gain 20 pounds in one day!

He laughed and said, "You're going to look so cute pregnant. I'll have to take a lot of pictures of you."

We cuddled by the fireplace after dinner, while sipping sparkling spring water. There was candles lit everywhere. "You are so good to me Eric, I love you."

He said, "Oh yeah, and just what do you love about me?"

I paused for a moment and replied, "First of all, I love the way you take me gently in your arms and smile at me. I love the way you reach for my hand; I love the sound of your laughter. I love the tender ways you show me you care. It's all so special and sweet. I trust you with my most intimate thoughts. The strength of your character inspires me. I have the utmost respect for you because you allow me to be who I am. You are my very best friend in the whole world and I hope as we grow old together, we will never forget the way we feel today. One thing that will never change for me is how strong my love is for you. I will always be in love with you Eric."

He was silent for a moment while his eyes filled with tears. He took my hands and cupped them into his and raised them up to kiss my hands. "That was really beautiful Katie. You're very poetic. That's why I framed that card you made for me. I love it and I really love you."

I replied, "I know why I love you, but can you tell me why you love me?"

"That's easy. First of all, you light up my whole life. That's why I always call you Sunshine. You are a gift of love to me. I'll do anything for you, or go anywhere with you. Love is a feeling of such beautiful warmth, that only you can bring to my soul from deep within my heart. You stir up feelings of such comfort, fun and magic, yet there are feelings of loneliness when we're apart. You're soft and gentle, yet you're the strongest person I know, given what you've been through with Danny. You still came out of it completely and perfectly unblemished, with as pure of a heart as I will ever know. I want to share all of my hopes and dreams with you. I love you for always knowing what is inside my heart that nobody else will ever see. You will always be a special part of everything I will ever do. I just love loving you. That is why I want to ask you this today, right here, where we professed our love for each other. Katie, will you marry me as soon as possible?"

I was overcome with such emotion. Tears of joy came running down my face as I fell into Eric's arms and said, "Yes, I will marry you!"

The weekend was spectacular. It seemed to go by much too fast. Eric promised to return home very soon and will definitely be there when the baby is born.

Being hopeful of what the future would bring, I stopped being in fear of Danny. I know now that no matter what happens, I will not let Danny take away my happiness. This new life inside of me, my little baby, will never be subjected to being abused by Danny or watching me be abused by him. It's funny how a person can withstand so much longtime abuse from another person, but when your motherly instincts kick in, all your protective shields rise up. You get such strength and courage, enough so that you will protect you're young to the death! I already love this baby that's growing inside of me and I will raise it the way I was raised, in a loving and caring home. The abuse stops now! I became a different person over the past few months and nobody, especially Danny, will ever abuse me again!

CHAPTER 32

As the weeks passed by, I was really starting to show. Eric continued calling me every day while Danny continued to ignore me. I knew that it was only a matter of time before I'd be "going home." Eric had visited a few more weekends. I got to see him and our puppy, who was getting into such mischief at this point. Eric always made me promise on the phone and in person, to tell him if Danny was hurting me. I told him that Danny wasn't abusing me at all, he was just ignoring me, which was great for me!

Danny was told that there would be no sex, doctor's orders. He believed me! It amazed me to watch Danny's eyes when he got into his violent rages; they seemed so evil, so cold and distant. I knew he registered everything I told him, but he never reacted, he just looked right through me with that cold, glazed look. I knew he was a time bomb waiting to explode, so I just stayed away from him, usually in the bedroom reading. He didn't come home until very late most nights, sometimes not at all. I'm no longer naïve and know he's sleeping around, like he's been doing since the beginning of our relationship.

Sue and Joan kept up with the events in my life by meeting me for lunch every so often. I told them about Eric and the baby, and that it was possibly his. They really missed him at the store, and said that the new manager isn't any fun at all. He won't socialize with any of them, and half the time he's out of the store. They say it must be great to be paid a large salary and never have to work. Sue wants to apply for the job! We laughed.

It was the holiday season and I was keeping busy making ornaments for the baby, some ceramic and some cross-stitch. Although I was three months away, I still wanted to have a Christmas tree dedicated to the baby. Danny and I always had a real Christmas tree, so I figured I'd go out and buy a small one that I could carry into the house and decorate myself. About a week before Christmas, Danny decided to break his silence and talk to me. He told me not to dare try to bring a tree into his house this Christmas or he'll throw it away. That was the only words he managed to say; that was devastating to me. I stood there feeling very brave. Thinking that Christmas is my favorite time of year, I decided I was going to buy a tree, put it up and decorate it, with all my special ornaments on it.

I enjoyed the day out looking for that perfect small tree. In the middle of a bunch of large trees was a half toppled over, small, "Charlie Brown" tree. It seemed to be screaming out to me. A worker came over to ask me if I needed any help making a selection. I pointed to the small tree and he laughed while he loaded it in my trunk. I thought it was beautiful! I then headed for home.

It wasn't too heavy to carry inside. The fresh scent of pine seemed to fill the house with the Christmas spirit. I set it up, put white lights on it, and decorated it with my homemade ornaments. Some tinsel was the final touch. The small tree looked like a giant after it was decorated; it was dazzling and beautiful! I couldn't imagine Danny not getting into the Christmas spirit just a little.

I stood there for a moment admiring the tree when I had an urge to page Eric. I needed to hear his voice. He called me right back and was worried that I was hurt. I explained that I had just finished the tree and I wished he could see it all decorated! Eric asked me to take a picture of it to show him. We talked for awhile. "Just a few more days and we'll be spending our first Christmas together," He said. Eric sure has a way of picking up my spirits.

I told him about all the ornaments I made for the baby. "Someday, when he or she gets older, we'll let him or her decorate a tree of their very own. I think ornaments symbolize your life. My parents gave all of us one in our stockings every year. There was a story attached to each one. They were my favorite gifts of all. I even have a cheerleader ornament.

Eric laughed. "My parents did the same thing for us too."

"Really," I asked.

"It's amazing how we have such similarities between our families.

I said, "So, I'll be seeing you late on Christmas Eve, after I've seen my family. We'll be together all of Christmas Day. Will that be alright?"

Eric said, "It's better than alright. That's great. Christmas will be at our house and my whole family will all be there."

"I can't wait to see them again. But wait, I can't hide my stomach. I'm showing a lot more than the last time you've seen me."

Eric replied, "Katie, I have to tell you something. Please don't be upset with me. I flew down to Florida to tell my parents about everything face to face."

I asked Eric, "What do you mean, everything?"

"I told them about Danny's horrible abuse, the rapes, how you've been afraid to get out; I also told them about the baby."

"What did they say?" I asked. "Do they hate me now?"

"Katie, no! They love you even more. A long time ago my mom's best friend Millie was in a similar situation as yours. Her husband beat up on Millie and later attacked her children. One day when Millie and her husband were fighting, he beat her to a pulp. That wasn't enough for him. He then went after their younger son, who was crying for his father to stop. He whacked him so hard and with such force, that it ended his young life that night."

"He killed him!" I cried.

"Yes, he did."

"How horrible for her. Is Millie still alive?"

"Yes, she is. Her abusive husband only got 20 to 30 years for that heinous crime. Millie got the lifelong sentence of never being able to hug her child and watch him grow up to become a man. Even today, she still isn't right. She can't stop blaming herself for what happened, and feels like she should have left when he started beating up on the kids, but she was scared. That's why my parents are more understanding about your situation than you'll ever know."

"Did you tell anyone else about my situation?"

"Katie, I didn't want you to feel uncomfortable around my family so I let them know too. They like you so much and wish you could leave Danny now. My brother Rick the cop, is ready to arrest Danny now. You see Katie, Millie is Rick's godmother and she's always been very special to him. He really wants to put Danny in jail where he belongs."

I said, "You have a very special family."

Eric asked, "Have you told your family yet?"

"Not yet. After all the festivities of Christmas wind down I will sit down with my whole family and tell them the entire story. Especially the part about you."

"Will Danny be with you for Christmas at all?"

"I doubt it. I'm sure he'll either be with some girl or his mother. Since we're not on speaking terms, he wouldn't come with me. That's how I know I'll be able to see you for the holidays."

Eric asked with a little hesitation, "Are you sure that you're okay with me?"

"Yes, I'm more than sure. I love you Eric."

"I love you too sunshine. I'll call you in the morning."

I decided to lie on the couch and watch my favorite Christmas tapes after plugging in the tree lights. The lights seemed to be dancing to the tune of the Christmas songs. I don't think I'll ever grow too old to watch Frosty the Snowman. I guess all the little things in life really do count.

There's a kid in all of us when it comes to the Christmas season, the season of love and giving, expect maybe for Danny.

All of a sudden he came storming in the house slamming the door. He must have seen the tree lights from the outside. He started screaming, "I told you not to put up a tree," and began ripping the ornaments off of it. Grumbling to himself he shook the tree. As the ornaments fell to the floor, he stepped on them.

I screamed, "Stop it Danny. Please don't!" My pleas fell on deaf ears; he continued anyway. Fearing he'd turn his anger toward me and hurt the baby, I sat silently and cried, watching every ornament my parents gave me, and the ones I made for the baby, get totally destroyed. It was like watching a sinking ship go down as the last ornament was mangled. The lights flickered just one last time before completely going out. He picked up the tree base and all, dragging it out of the door. Spilling water everywhere he stomped on the broken ornaments. I sat on the couch and froze, fearing he would return and kill the baby and me. My heart raced as I heard him stamp back into the house. He retreated into the bedroom and slammed the door. After a few minutes, he went into the shower. Afterwards, he got dressed and stormed back out the door.

I still hadn't moved from my spot on the couch. When I knew it was safe, I went over to where the broken ornaments lay and knelt down over them. I put my hands to my face and began to cry. How could Danny be so mean to me? I never did anything to him to deserve this. I searched through the pile of broken ornaments to see if any of them could be salvaged. Even the hand-knitted ones were ruined; slivers of broken glass filled the crevices. The pretty silver tinsel lay tangled up with all the broken parts. I felt like my memories of Christmas past were stripped from me. I got up slowly and dried my eyes. From the bedroom, I retrieved my camera and began taking pictures of the mess, and afterwards I started to clean it up. Pieces of glass were getting embedded in my skin; I continued anyway. The glass-covered knitted ornaments I just placed in a plastic bag. I didn't have the heart to throw them away.

Feeling tired and sick inside, I went to lie down and fell asleep. Thankfully, Danny never came home that night. I could not even stomach looking at him anymore.

Eric called me the next morning. "Hi Sunshine. How's my favorite girl doing?"

I told him that I was fine.

He asked me if I got the pictures of the tree for him to see. I was silent for a moment. "Katie, what is it?" He knew something was wrong. "Did Danny hit you?"

"No," I said, and then I told him what a disastrous night it was. After I finished my story, Eric remained silent. I said, "I'm sorry Eric. I know how hard it is for you to be so far away, but I couldn't lie to you."

"Please honey, don't apologize. You didn't do anything wrong. Danny is a very sick man. Katie, is there any way you can get out of there today? I'll take care of everything, please, just trust me."

I told Eric that Danny never came home last night, so I didn't know where he was, not that I cared.

Eric asked me if I could gather up everything I needed and get over to his house today.

"What about your brother Randy and Lynn?"

"Don't worry. They'll just move out sooner than planned. Besides, they only have their clothes at the house. They are planning on moving back to their old place, which is a cute cottage on Lynn's mom's estate."

I said, "Yes Eric, then I'm as ready as I'll ever be! I will just need to stay here until Christmas Eve, that's just two more days. I promise, I'll be all right; Danny won't even look at me, much less talk to me."

Eric said "Katie, gather up only the things you absolutely need and want to take with you, but I really wish you would leave today! I'll be calling you later to make sure you are all right. I love you Katie."

I said, "I'll be waiting, I love you too Eric."

While Danny was still out, I started searching for all the things I wanted to take with me. I packed the items into some bags, and put them into the trunk of my car. Only my most precious and personal items were packed, along with some photographs, clothes, shoes and undergarments. My most treasured item was my secret box containing all the gifts Eric has given to me, and my personal journal. I felt I didn't need to take anything else, and was afraid of arousing suspicion.

My first thought the next morning was how it was only two more days until Eric's arrival. I wanted to go to the mall and get him something for Christmas. Although I had already picked up a few things for him and his family, I wanted to get something more memorable. Tears came to my eyes as I strolled through the mall, seeing all the decorations, especially the trees. At least Danny couldn't crush my vision of how beautiful Christmas really is.

I had made a lot of tips during this holiday season that I didn't hand over to Danny. The only way he communicates with me lately is through the weekly envelopes he leaves for me on the table. They have dates and the words "tips and wages" written on them in big, bold letters. I was supposed to know what that meant. Very soon, he'll be in for a rude awakening.

The mall was filled with a lot of arts and crafts stands, where artisans displayed their wares. I love hand-made things; they touch the heart with so much love. I stopped at a stand with ornaments displayed. A flashback of what Danny had done hit me, but I didn't let it get me down. I purchased an ornament for Eric with a 1934 Ford painted on it, which I had engraved, "Love, Katie" and the date. Afterwards, I bought a set of turtledoves, which I heard symbolizes purity, hope, and love. You keep one, and give the other to someone special.

Then I found a stand of replica trains and hoped to find one that I knew Eric didn't have in his collection, one he was planning to buy someday. I asked the man behind the counter about it. "Oh yes, that's a good one," he said and led me down the table to a glass-enclosed case. There was the train I was looking for, one of only two left. It cost $200.

The price shocked me, but I had enough money left so I told him I would take it.

A stand selling baby items caught my eye. There was a small tree decorated with knitted booty ornaments. I felt I had to have something for the baby, after Danny destroyed all my ornaments. I picked out an all-white booty with room in the middle to display a small picture. In addition, I picked up a few inexpensive trinkets. Afterwards, I took all my gifts to the gift-wrapping booth. They wrapped up my gifts and topped each one with a big bright bow. After hiding the gifts in the trunk of my car, I left the mall.

The big day finally arrived, Christmas Eve. Danny got up that morning slamming doors and grumbling to himself. In spite of the fact I felt he was going to lose it someday, I still felt hopeful. This would be the last day I would ever have to look at his evil face, except the day of the divorce, when Eric will be right by my side. Suddenly, a terrible thought crossed my mind. What if the baby is Danny's? If so, I knew I'd be stepping into a new dimension of terror, to be dealt with if that day arrives. I prayed every day that the baby was Eric's. Today I wasn't going to let any more thoughts of Danny spoil the best day of my life. I will truly be free from the bondage that Danny had me in for so many years!

I stayed in bed pretending to be asleep. Hearing him slamming things around the house made me think he was trying to awaken me. Instead, I laid still. Finally, I heard him leave the house. At that moment, I felt a huge weight lifted off my chest; it was truly a magical feeling. I took a deep breath and smiled. Slowly I made my way to the front window to make sure he was really gone. I peeked through a tiny opening in the curtains and saw his car was gone. I wanted to shout to the world about how today was a new beginning for me! Eric was leaving this morning to come back here, so I wouldn't be getting my usual morning call. I couldn't wait to see him. All the tears I shed with Danny won't even come close to the laughter my future will hold with Eric.

While taking a shower, I sang my heart out! This would be the last shower in this house, as will every task I do this morning. I was feeling so free. I gathered up a few more things, but I left a lot behind. Eric figured Danny would just think something happened to me, until my attorney served him with the divorce papers. Just my family, Sue and Joan will know where I am. Danny will never find out. He will never abuse me again!

As I was finishing up, the phone rang. I was afraid to answer it, but I thought it might be someone from my family. I picked it up and heard "Hey Sunshine. How's it going?"

I couldn't believe it; it was Eric! I said "I thought you weren't coming in until this afternoon?"

"I still am." He answered.

"Where are you calling from?" I asked.

He said, "From about 1500 feet in the air."

"You're calling me from the plane?" I couldn't believe it I was so excited!

Eric said, "Yes I am. I just had to call you to make sure you were alright."

"Eric, I'm better than alright; I'm great."

"Has Danny left yet?" He asked.

"Yes he did, and I have everything packed and I'm ready to go."

Eric said, "Good, I'll be counting down the hours until I see you. I love you."

"I love you too, Eric." We hung up, and I felt like the luckiest girl in the whole world! As I started toward the door, I kept thanking God for answering my prayers. Fearing something would go wrong I left quickly, without looking back!

CHAPTER 33

When I arrived at my parents' house, they asked where Danny was. Not wanting to spoil the day, I said he wasn't feeling well. My family gathered around and we sang Christmas songs, accompanied by my dad playing the organ. The food was just about ready, so we all sat down at the table. Everyone helped serve the food and clean up the mess. Since I was feeling a little queasy from being nervous, I didn't eat much.

All the kids were jumping around begging to tear open the gifts. Before the gifts are opened, my mom proclaims one thing she's grateful for that year, as my dad does the same. Everybody follows suit from the oldest to the youngest as fast as we can, since the children get fidgety. When it was my turn I said, I'm grateful for "second chances." Some puzzled looks came in my direction. It is so exciting to hear what the children are grateful for. When we were all finished with our gratitude, my mom lights a candle for baby Jesus, as one of the grandchildren would put the baby Jesus in his place, next to Mary and Joseph in the manger. We all sing "Away in a Manger." Even the kids really enjoyed this tradition. It helps them to realize the real meaning of Christmas. Also, each family purchases or makes something special for the needy, so those less fortunate can enjoy Christmas too.

At this point, the kids can't contain themselves any longer, so we opened the gifts. My brothers took turns playing Santa every year; this year it was Sam's turn. Santa would give each child a "special gift."

Wrapping paper was all over the place. Most of the kids were ready to collapse, yet some were still going strong, as if they had little batteries recharging them. It was great! Kids really do make Christmas so very special. I think that there is a child that lives within almost every adult, which comes peaking out every so often to try and capture a little bit of our youth. It can stir up the most beautiful feelings inside oneself.

At this point, I had other feelings stirring up inside of me. I knew it was time to gather up my family and tell them my plans for the future, and about the life I've hid from them for so long. I asked my mom to gather up the immediate family and retreat to another room because I had something important to tell them. She obliged. They all sat around me looking a bit intrigued. It seemed like everything was happening in slow motion. Deep down inside I knew my family would understand; this was my life.

I took a deep breath and began my speech. "I'm sure you're all wondering why I wanted to talk to you tonight. First I want to say that I love all of you…."

One of my sisters interrupted me to say, "Oh my gosh Katie, are you going to die or something?"

I chuckled for a moment. A tear ran down my cheek and I proceeded, "No, nothing like that. As of tonight, I've been given a second chance to live again. This is really hard for me to tell all of you. I want to tell you everything, so if you please, I will just say it first with no questions or comments until the end." The tone in my voice got everyone's undivided attention.

My mom assured me it would be all right. "Go on honey." Her voice sounded so reassuring.

I began the story with how Danny was so sweet, wonderful and caring in the beginning of our teenage relationship. After a few months of dating he changed, and from that moment on, my life took a turn for the worst. It was like I was living a nightmare that I couldn't wake up from, and Danny for whatever his reasons were, felt a need to control and abuse me.

Everyone started yelling at the same time. I was starting to get flustered. My mom stood up and silenced everyone.

My story continued. I told them how he would pull my hair and beat on me daily or weekly, depending on his mood. "There were broken ribs, kicks, punches, bruises, and rapes. I know your all thinking why didn't I leave him? The biggest threat he held over my head was he would kill someone in my family and make me watch. Then he would finish me off if I told anyone or left him."

My brother yelled, "That jerk would not have done anything to any of us."

"Yes he would have. I told them about the incident, when he had his drugged up friend pull a knife on Cindy if I didn't go back to him."

Cindy started to cry, "Mom, she's right. He would have killed one of us or Katie, especially when he was drunk." She looked back at me so angrily. "Katie, you promised me that you would tell me if Danny was still doing this to you."

"I know and I'm sorry, but you might not be standing here alive and well today if I did. He dragged me by my hair to a cliff's edge, where he almost threw me off. I was beat with belt buckles, slapped and punched in the head or stomach, wherever his fist would land. The time I lost the first baby was a result of Danny's abuse."

Both of my brothers stood up looking so angry. "Where is he. We'll kill him."

My dad ordered them to sit down. "I know how scared you probably were Katie, but I wish you would have told us. You never gave us any indication this was happening to you. When I think back to your swelled eye and bruises on your arms, you would always smile and make excuses. I'm so clumsy. Maybe my equilibrium is off. I slipped on ice. I lost my footing and fell down the stairs. I walked into a wall at night."

His eyes filled with tears as my parents came over to hug me. It was a very emotional scene filled with a lot of tears.

I continued. "I'm so sorry. There's more."

My brother Jim yelled out, "I hope you're going to tell us you killed him. If he's not already dead, he will be soon!"

"Please don't talk like that," my mother said. Jim complied, knowing he was upsetting her.

"Danny has been cheating on me throughout the whole courtship and marriage. In spite of everything, I had stayed faithful to him the whole time, until about a year ago. I met the most amazing and wonderful guy. His name is Eric. He was the regional manager at the store I used to work at. We talked for hours in the coffee shop on breaks and socialized at store parties. Eric was always so understanding and sympathetic, and was always there for me when I needed someone. When he found out about Danny's abuse, he wanted me to get out. When I thought I would finally leave, I found a gun. I knew if I left, Danny would use it. So I stayed with him. At the time, I couldn't tell Eric about it. For the past year, Eric and I have been managing to see each other, despite Danny. We fell in love. Eric comes from a family just like ours, unlike Danny's." I then proceeded to fill them in on the gruesome tales, of Danny's family background in abuse and alcoholism. "At a point in time, I thought I'd be better off dead than to withstand Danny's abuse any longer. Eric saved me from that, he made me see how my life was worth keeping!

My mom asked me about the baby. "Is it Danny's baby?"

I knew this moment would be difficult for me. I said, "Danny would just throw me down and rape me. There was no love or passion. It was different with Eric. He's loving and compassionate. I didn't know what love was until I met him. Danny has no idea that this is happening. I won't know who the father of this baby is until it's born; I'm praying its Eric's. He asked me to marry him no matter what. I'll be staying at Eric's as of tonight. I'll be safe from Danny. Eric has taught me a lot, especially about self-worth. And, although I cannot change the past, I can certainly change the future. I hope you all understand. I really love Eric and plan to marry him."

There was a huge silence throughout the room. They say confession is good for the soul. I felt like the weight of the world was lifted off my shoulders. My mom came over to me. Her eyes were filled with tears. "It's okay Katie, I love you and I understand. I'm so sorry we couldn't help you sooner. Your dad and I will always be there for you when you need us. Everyone else gathered around to hug me. It was overwhelming. My sister Cindy, still crying asked me "Why? Katie, you could have told me."

Suddenly, my dad spoke up loudly, "Danny will never hurt you again Katie. That's a promise I will keep." My brothers backed my dad up.

I told them that I would give them Eric's phone number. "Danny cannot know about this. The divorce papers will be served to him the day after Christmas.

My sister Cindy asked me, "What if he fights you on this? Can he drag this on?"

I replied, "I have lots of documentation of Danny's abuse. There are pictures and recordings of his vulgar rages. I have a copy of a letter sent to me, but meant for Danny, from a co-worker he had an ongoing affair with. He got her pregnant and then sent her off scared with a broken jaw. I doubt if they'll let him fight it. I'll be getting a restraining order, but you all know that's just a piece of paper."

Cindy asked, "What about your job? He's sure to follow you home from there."

"Eric told me that I should take a leave of absence. That's what I'll do. At this point, Danny has no clue about Eric and me. Danny still thinks I'm this scared, subservient slave that he has spent years training me to become. Eric's brother is a police officer and he said he'll take care of Danny."

I informed them that I should be leaving and told everyone how much I loved them. Family has got to be one of the single most important thing in anyone's life. They can be your salvation. I asked to use the phone so I could call Eric and let him know that I'm on my way. I hugged everyone and said I'd keep in touch, after giving them my new phone number.

As I drove away, I couldn't help the way I felt. It was a feeling of total freedom, no more dictatorship and abuse. While turning into Eric's driveway, instead of seeing him, I saw a jolly Santa Claus waving at me from the porch. I knew it was Eric!. He came over to my car and opened the door. When he put his white-gloved hand out, I placed mine in his and laughed.

"Ho, Ho, Ho, Merry Christmas, Sunshine."

"My Santa, you are very handsome." He pulled me in close to him and we hugged, although his big stomach and mine got in the way. "Merry Christmas," I said. He pulled down his beard and yanked the pillow out from under his suit. I giggled and said, "So, you're really not Santa Claus."

He said, "No, but I am one of his helpers and I can still bring you anything you'd like for Christmas."

"Santa, you already have." He leaned over and kissed me. As we walked up the driveway, I complimented him on how beautifully decorated his house is!

"You mean our house Katie." He added.

I was amazed as I walked through the door. There was Christmas trees all over the place, big ones and small ones. It was truly a winter wonderland. All I could say was, "Wow, it's absolutely beautiful!" Every tree was lit up with white lights, my favorite.

There was one undecorated tree. Eric said, "This one I saved for you to decorate. I know how devastated you were when Danny destroyed the tree you decorated. Although I can't replace the ornaments you made, I still want to make this Christmas, and every Christmas from now on, very special for you. All the days to follow will be equally ful-filling for you."

I started to cry happy tears. "Thank you so much for giving me my life back. I love everything you've done for me. What makes you so spe-cial, is that you are so sincere and giving. You're everything I've ever dreamed of and more. I love you so much, Eric."

"I told you we'd be together. We're good for each other." He said.

"Yeah, like Abbott and Costello," I said kiddingly.

Eric replied, "How about Romeo and Juliet."

"Yes, I definitely love that."

I wanted to go to my car to bring in my gifts and place them under the beautiful trees. "I still can't believe you did all this for me."

Eric said, "I just wanted our first Christmas together to be memorable."

"When did you have the time to get this ready." I asked.

"All my elves helped me." He said.

We walked to the car and he helped me bring everything in. "Katie, you really didn't have to buy all these gifts."

I said, "I really wanted to buy gifts for your family, and of course for you too. I love watching people open gifts."

"Katie, you're so sweet. For me, you could have just wrapped up yourself. That would have been the best gift of all."

I kissed him softly as we both walked back to the house. My only problem was choosing which tree to put which gift under. Eric said, "You can choose any tree you like; they're all for you. By the way, how did it go with your family?"

"Better than I'd expected. Everyone understood and they are all behind me one hundred percent. They can't wait to meet you Eric! I feel so lucky and want to shout it to the whole world how happy I am!"

Eric hugged me, brought my hand up to his lips, and kissed them. He noticed I had on the engagement ring and the other jewelry he gave me. "I'm so glad you're wearing these."

"I love them. I left Danny's wedding band in the garbage at the other house. The way I feel is exhilarating, like I could conquer anything."

Eric told me that his family would be over tomorrow afternoon for Christmas dinner.

"I can't wait to see them." I said.

Eric said, "Stay right here. I have something to show you." I just stood there taking in all of the beauty. He returned with Roxy, dressed as a reindeer!

"Oh she looks so cute, and she got so big." I got out my camera and took a picture of her. We sat by the fireplace sipping eggnog. Midnight approached; it was Christmas day!

"Merry Christmas, Katie."

"Merry Christmas, Eric." We continued to sit there by the fireplace curled up in each other's arms, staring at the flickering sparks dancing around the burning embers.

"Do you want to go to bed, Katie?" Eric asked. "You can decorate your tree first thing in the morning, if you'd like."

"That sounds great to me." We walked up to the bedroom and Eric had a decorated tree there!

I told him how sentimental he is.

"You make me that way." Eric said. "I love watching you enjoy everything. It's like you take it all in and record it in your mind."

"You really do know me so well." I said.

As we curled up together, Eric whispered in my ear, "I got my wish. I can always wake up next to you every morning forever!"

We awoke in almost the same position we fell asleep in. When we got up, we put on some Christmas music and turned on the tree lights. It was time for me to decorate mine. Eric handed me a box of ornaments. Some of them were gift-wrapped. I said, "These are wrapped so nice."

Eric said, "They're for you. Go ahead and open them."

The first one was a baby's ornament. It was so cute. One of the others looked like one of the ornaments Danny destroyed. I had so much fun decorating the tree. When the tinsel was being put on, Eric reached into his pocket and handed one more gift to me. It was wrapped in bright red paper. "What's this?" I asked, as I gently unwrapped it. It was a beautiful ceramic ornament with our picture in the middle. "Our First Christmas" was engraved on it, along with our names and the date. "Thank you Eric, I love it," as I hung it up right in the front.

We went upstairs to take a shower together. Afterwards, we went downstairs to have breakfast. After eating, I helped Eric prepare for the afternoon's festivities.

Roxy ran over to us barking; she wanted to play. She then retrieved her chew toy and kept tossing it up in the air. I remarked how good she's been staying away from the trees. Eric said, "Come here Katie, I want to show you something." We walked over to the sunroom and I saw a huge toy box filled with every chew toy possible. Eric said that hopefully she'd stay away from the trees if there were enough toys for her to play with. Just like a little kid, Roxy already has her favorites.

Eric led me by the hand to the family room, where we sat by the fireplace. "What an elegantly done room," I said. It was decorated magnificently, truly a thing of beauty. Although it was still early, I wished the day would never end. Eric got up and retrieved some gifts from under the tree. He put on some soft music and served some hot chocolate. "Merry Christmas Honey," he said. I also retrieved my gifts to him. Eric loved all the gifts I bought him, especially the train. He said, "Katie, this is great, but you shouldn't have. This was way too expensive."

"I really loved getting you these thing's Eric."

He came over and kissed me. "Thank you. I love you." His eyes widened as he opened another box and pulled out a Nascar jacket and sweatshirt. Pictures of his favorite racecar drivers were on both of them. He couldn't thank me enough.

Eric said, "Now it's your turn to open my gifts." There were so many of them. "Eric, you really shouldn't have. This will take me all day." He got me beautiful sweaters, a leather coat, a diamond watch, and a matching set of diamond earrings and necklace. I felt like the Queen of England! "Thank you so much for everything."

He said, "Wait here," and went upstairs for a few minutes. He returned wearing his Santa suit holding an elf costume in one hand and a sack of gifts in the other. "Ho, ho, ho little girl, would you do me the honor, and accompany me to the Children's Hospital as Santa's helper."

I laughed. "Well yes Santa, I'd be honored."

Eric said that he's been doing this for about three years now. The kids really look forward to Santa's arrival on Christmas morning. "I get the names and ages of all the sick children, and make sure I get an appropriate gift for each child. Wait until you see the joy in their eyes when they see Santa!"

"You are really something special, Eric Sommers."

"So are you, my soon to be bride, Katie Sommers."

"Wow, that sounds like music to my ears." I proceeded to put on my elf suit. Eric made sure it was loose enough for me to fit into."

When I returned to the family room, Eric giggled. He said, "You are the cutest elf I have ever seen."

I said, "With my big belly, I could have probably played Santa." Eric laughed.

Upon arrival at the hospital, I discovered Eric knew everyone there. Even the doctors greeted us with such warmth. The kids were so excited to see Santa. It really did brighten up their day. Even the seriously ill children smiled. I wondered how I ever got so lucky. Not questioning my luck, I looked up into the heavens and said quietly, "Thank you so much Lord."

After we finished at the hospital, Eric told me that we had one more stop to make. His grandmother was ill in a nursing home. He stops there regularly to see her. She was so very sweet. He leaned over to kiss her and said, "Merry Christmas grandma." He sat next to her and held her hand as he said, "Grandma, I'd like you to meet Katie."

She looked up at me and said, "Hi Dear. Eric has told me a lot about you. Our Eric here loves you very much. You really have stolen his heart. You must be a really special girl."

Eric politely interrupted. "Yes, she is."

His grandmother continued, "Some of the nurses here are always trying to talk me into getting a date with him, or even just a cup of coffee, but Eric always gracefully declines." I thought silently to myself about how sweet Eric's Grandma is, which doesn't surprise me, given the rest of his family. We stayed for awhile and visited with her. When it was time to leave, Eric reached into his pocket and pulled out a present. "Oh Eric," she said, "You shouldn't be bringing me gifts."

"I love to, Grandma." She opened the gift. It was a beautiful pen inscribed with her name. It also had a compartment, like a locket, with a picture of her and her late husband. He also bought her a stack of crossword puzzles, which she loved. She had tears in her eyes, as she seemed to be lost in a trance.

While staring at the picture in her pen, she told Eric that she would always treasure it. "Come here, Eric, and give your old grandma a hug." She kissed him and said, "Thank you, I love the gifts, and I love you." Then she asked me to come closer to her. As I complied, she put her hand on my belly, and told me that I'm going to be having a baby girl. I smiled and she hugged me. She said, "It was very nice meeting you Katie. I hope I can see you again."

I replied, "Yes, you will and it was very nice meeting you too." Then we left.

Eric told me, "I know my grandmother took a real fancy to you, but how could she resist. I know I couldn't resist you."

I blushed the color of the Santa suit and said, "Eric, you're so unbelievably loving."

We returned home in time for the arrival of his family. It was such a busy morning, but a rewarding one. I felt so good on the inside. It's so amazing how you can feel exceptionally rewarded when you do something for someone else. It turned out to be an all around wonderful Christmas Day. After we ate, everyone got to open their gifts. Eric's family loved everything I got for them. They are such special people.

Although I was starting to feel exhausted towards the late afternoon, Eric's mom and I took a stroll outdoors. There was only a slight chill in the air; the sun took the edge off the cold. She told me the story about her friend Millie. Although Eric had already told me the story, I wanted to hear it in his mom's own words. There was such pain in her trembling voice as she began to describe the events that led up to that tragic night, when Millie's husband murdered their son. When she finished she said, "So you see Katie, we are so glad that you got out of your situation when you did. Unavoidable tragedies happen every day, but when you can see a situation and avoid a devastating ending, it will make you stronger."

I said to her, "I can thank Eric for that. He has given me the strength. From the beginning, I knew I didn't belong in that relationship, but I was young and scared. Eric made me realize with a lot of encouragement that I shouldn't have to live that way. He's always held on and was so strong for me, even when I gave up. I really love him very much."

"We know you do and we know how much our son is in love with you. I've never seen him this way before. He mostly used to keep to himself. His job seemed to consume him. He's so happy now. Eric has a good heart! It's no wonder you found each other." She hugged me and said, "You're really good for each other. We're all hoping for your sake that this baby you're carrying is Eric's, so you can have a clean break from your abuser. If it's not his, we're going to love this baby just the same Katie."

I replied, "I do a lot of praying these days, but it's in God's hands now." We decided to return, as it was starting to get a little chilly.

As the evening started to wind down, everyone was getting tired and decided to leave. We all hugged and kissed one another. They told us that they'd be seeing us soon before they went back to Florida. Eric's brother and sister-in-law, Rick and Carol hung around for awhile after everyone else left. Eric and Rick took a walk out back while Carol and I sat in the family room sipping on hot tea, while relaxing and enjoying the warmth of the fire. She asked me how I was doing with my schooling and if I liked doing hair.

I said, "Yes, I love doing hair, but with my due date soon, and with Danny's upcoming rampage, it's safer for me right now, to not let Danny see me at my job or at school.

Eric and Rick returned and joined us. We all sat around and talked until it starting getting late. Rick said to me, "I don't want you to worry about anything from now on Katie." I didn't question him; I trusted both Eric and Rick. I hoped Rick and his fellow officers would be able to put Danny in his place.

After our company left, we decided to leave the cleaning until the morning, both of us were exhausted. Eric threw his arms around me and told me how special I was and how he couldn't believe a person could be so happy and fulfilled.

I told him that I felt the same way and that I hoped I could live up to his image of me.

He stopped me right away, "I never want you to feel inferior to me or anyone Katie. You are such a wonderful human being. Don't let your past abuse darken your pure heart." We hugged, turned out the Christmas lights, and retired to bed.

CHAPTER 34

Two days after Christmas I knew Danny had the divorce papers in hand. The court date was scheduled three weeks after my baby was due. I just went on with my business. Cindy called to inform me Danny had been calling my parents' house numerous times. He was harassing them, demanding they tell him my whereabouts. His language got more vulgar with each call. My brothers informed Danny firmly, that they have a score to settle with him, and that he'd better watch his step from here on in!

After receiving the divorce papers, Danny went to my brothers' bar and started tearing the place apart while demanding to know where I was! That was a big mistake on Danny's part. My brothers, who both tower over six foot tall; to Danny's height of five foot seven, let him have it good! They warned him to stay away from our family or his body would never be found! Then they called the police, who they were friends with. Upon their arrival, they carted Danny off to jail, overlooking Danny's bloody appearance. They told him his injuries would be the least of his worries, after being charged with damaging the bar, harassment, trying to incite a riot, and any other charges they could think of. He complained all the way to the police station, claiming his rights were being violated, and demanded to have my brothers arrested. The police informed him that they had a right to protect themselves and their property. Coincidentally through that incident, my brothers got to know Rick Sommers, Eric's brother quite well. They figured out the connection by his name.

Danny stayed in jail for a few days. Thinking his warning by my brothers wasn't enough, Rick and a few other cops paid Danny a visit in his cell. They told him that they'd make the rest of his sorry days on earth a living hell, if he ever hurts me or bothers my family ever again! Then they added that they'd be doing mankind a favor, getting rid of trash like him. "You'll never know who's trailing you until it's too late," one of the cops told him.

The days and weeks passed. For the first time in years, I was living a dream come true. I was happy to be alive! As far as I knew, Danny was in seclusion. There was only a couple weeks left until my baby was due. I was starting to feel a bit nervous, but Eric assured me everything would be fine. He was in the process of preparing the baby's room, across from ours. We picked Mickey and Minnie Mouse for the theme; their pictures were all over the colorful room. Eric filled the dressers and toy boxes to the brim. Given the situation with Danny, it was decided my baby shower would be postponed until after the birth, and besides, by then we would know if it were a boy or a girl. Eric even took some Lamaze Classes with me, since he was going to be my coach.

My lawyer was going to demand supervised visitation if the baby turned out to be Danny's, and given Danny's violent track record, it should be granted. I thought about if Danny was the father, he would definitely try to cause us a lot of heartache. Given his psychopathic mind, he'd see himself as still being in control.

Eric said, "I promise you he will never control you again, no matter what."

My family and I kept in touch all the time. Even Eric's parents would call to see how I was doing. I finally felt I was back to the kind of life my parents started me off with. Every day I awoke feeling totally incredible!

Unexpectedly daydreaming one day, I thought about Karen and Kevin, friends from my teenage years who were in the same abusive relationship I used to be in. I don't know why women stay in these destructive relationships. Each story is different; I was just plain scared. Karen claims she stayed because she really loved Kevin. I know neither of us knew what love really was back then, but given the choice now, I would rather be alone and happy, than to stay with someone who abuses me, and be totally unhappy. What it comes down to is, Love should never hurt, especially in the physical sense. It does an injustice to the female race to endure any abuse, whatever the reason. I knew that someday I'd get away from Danny. Once a baby entered the picture, things changed. I would never have subjected my child to an imprisoned life like the one I had with Danny. Children are such a precious gift from God, but too often, children are also used as a pawn between parents. He entrusts them in our care and expects us to use our maternal instincts to protect them, even if it means a fight to the death. Female animals protect their young from any predator, even her chosen mate. Maybe we should take a lesson from animals in the wild. It makes me wonder why we need brains to figure out what these animals have been doing for all these centuries.

After another week went by, I started to experience some cramping. Eric timed my contractions, they were 13 minutes apart. I called the doctor and he said to call back when they were closer to being seven minutes apart. Eric was nervously pacing back and forth. It was so cute to watch him press the stopwatch every time I had a contraction. "Can I do anything for you, Katie?" He would ask.

I said "Yes, you can come here and sit down next to me. How about if we watch Grease."

He said "Sure, if it will make you feel better."

"Don't worry Eric, I'm fine, really."

He put the movie in the VCR and we snuggled up together on the couch while he massaged my back. The stopwatch was clenched in his hand. Halfway through the movie, my contractions progressed to seven minutes apart. "Let's go Katie please," He begged. "I don't know how to deliver a baby." He was so nervous, but we both managed to laugh as I got up to call the doctor. We were to meet him at the hospital. Eric said "Well, this is it sunshine!"

Upon arrival at the hospital, the nurses led me to a birthing room. The doctor came in and examined me, and told me that I was close to delivery. I was already dilated eight centimeters. The nurses prepared me for delivery. Suddenly, I felt a little scared, until I saw Eric come into the room. My fears vanished as he held my hand and comforted me through the painful contractions. They were intense at times, but he got me focused. He was a great coach! He brought a tear to my eye when he told me that he loved the baby and me very much.

The baby's head started to show. "One more push, Katie." The doctor said. The doctor let Eric come over and guide out this precious little life. His flowing tears wet his surgical mask as he looked adoringly at the baby in his arms. "Look Katie, we have a baby girl, she is so beautiful!"

After the doctor suctioned her out and cut the umbilical cord, Eric brought her over to me and gently laid her on my stomach. She was beautiful. Her hair was full and jet black. When she opened her big blue eyes, it seemed as if she was looking right at me. I knew in my heart that she had to be Eric's; she resembled him so. While relaxing on my belly, she only let out one cry.

Eric said, "She is as beautiful as her mommy."

"Thank you so much for being here and for being so wonderful Eric."

"Katie, you don't have to thank me for anything. I love being here with you. It will always be like that."

"What do you think we should name her?" I asked.

Eric said, "You pick out the name. I'm sure no matter what name you choose, she will love it."

I said, "How about Ericka Nichole Sommers?"

He said, "That almost sounds like my name."

"Yes, it does. I love your name." I said.

Eric looked down at her and said, "Hi their Ericka Nichole," as he put his finger in her little hand, what a beautiful name for a beautiful girl."

A nurse came over and gently picked her up from my stomach. They had to weigh her and clean her up. The doctor finished with me and said, "Well congratulations, she's a real beauty Katie!"

I said, "Thank you so much. She's a little miracle for us."

The doctor informed me that after she's checked out, they'll start on her blood work to determine her parentage. "I know how anxious you are to find out her blood type."

"Thank you for being so discrete about the whole situation." I said.

"I hope it goes the way you want it. Good luck to both of you," the doctor said upon exiting the room.

A nurse came in and cleaned up the bed and me. After she left the room, Eric joined me on the bed. I was exhausted, yet exhilarated! Eric brought the phone over to me so I could call my parents. They were excited, yet concerned saying, "Danny doesn't know you're there Katie does he?" My mom asked.

I said, "No, and he won't find out either Mom."

She told me to rest and said that they would be by later in the day. I couldn't wait for my parents to see the baby and to finally meet Eric!

Eric reached his parents and they were very excited, especially about her name. They told Eric to take very good care of their granddaughter and me. I thought that was so sweet. No matter what the test results turn out to be, my daughter and I are part of Eric's family.

It wasn't long before they returned the baby to us. This would be my first time breastfeeding. She did really great and took in a lot of milk the first time. After she was finished, we just stared at her, our new wonderful little life.

Eric took many pictures. I thought about how this baby would be constantly photographed. Every first event would be documented.

The doctor came back to my room and my heart skipped a beat. I knew this was the moment of truth. The look on his face was dismal and I was about to cry. He said, "Katie, it's not what you think. I'm very happy to inform you, that both you and Eric, are Ericka's biological parents! Her blood type is A Positive. There is no way Danny could be the father of this baby."

I burst into tears. "Thank you so much, Dr. Scott." He still seemed a little down and I asked him if there was something wrong with the baby.

"No, Katie." He said as he came over and shook our hands. "God bless you both. You have a beautiful, healthy baby."

"Are you alright, Dr. Scott?" I asked.

"Not really," he replied. "I just delivered twins and one of them was stillborn."

I could tell he was depressed about this. "I'm so sorry. It has to be really hard to continue your day after something like that happens. I'll say a prayer for the mother and the baby."

"Thank you, Katie. I'm really glad for both of you that things went your way. Maybe now you can end your nightmare with Danny."

"I hope so."

The doctor told Eric to take care of us as he left the room. It suddenly hit us; Eric was really Ericka's daddy! We hugged and cried together. It was one of the most emotional moments of my life. Eric said, "I can't tell you how happy I am. I would have loved the baby even if Danny turned out to be the father. But to know she's just ours means I'll never have to share her with Danny. I love you both very much Katie." Eric asked the nurses if he could spend the night on the chair next to my bed. The nurses told him that it was all right, if he could stand the late night interruptions.

Eric's family and mine arrived to see us. It was so sweet of Eric's parents to fly all the way from Florida to see the baby. We needed a hall to accommodate everyone! They were introduced to each other; it took forever. My family liked Eric right away. They sensed his love and warmth. When the moment was right we announced that Eric is Ericka's biological father! There was a lot of commotion, a display of happiness. Everyone went nuts when they saw her for the first time. They fussed with her hair, and put it on top of her head like Pebbles from the Flintstones. Everyone wanted to take pictures of her.

The nurse came in to calm us all down. "Wow, so this is the party room everyone is buzzing about."

"I'm sorry. We just had some great news. We'll be quieter from now on." I said.

The nurse said, "This room is probably one of the happiest on the whole floor. Right now, I need to take this sweet little angel to the nursery for some tests. After we bring her back, you can keep her for the whole night if you want."

"Yes, we would love to. I'd feel better if she was with us." I said.

After the nurse took the baby, everyone started to leave. My parents told us this would be a good time for us to get some rest. We thanked everyone for coming, and thanked them for all the gifts they brought. I'll need a truck to bring the entire bunch of balloons and flowers home!

Everyone except Rick was gone. Eric and Rick decided to go for a stroll and said they'd be back shortly. I dozed off for a few minutes, although it seemed like hours. When they returned they asked where Ericka was. I jumped up from the bed and suddenly felt this horrible, sick feeling from deep down inside. Nervously I answered, "She's in the nursery."

Rick said, "We just came from there and they said she would be in your room already."

I was frantic! "What!" I said loudly while starting to shake.

We all ran to the desk to ask where the baby was.

The nurse, who was unfamiliar to them, asked them to calm down. She said, "Which baby are you referring to?"

Eric said, "At first it was listed as Baby Jenkins but it was supposed to be changed to Baby Sommers."

She said, "Our shift just changed so I have to check the charts. Oh yes, her father, Danny Jenkins, wanted to accompany the nurse bringing the baby back to the mother's room."

"What? He's not the father!" Rick screeched. "Did you ask for identification?"

"Yes, we did. But the nurse was there too. He didn't take the baby alone."

Eric cried out, "Where is this nurse? I want to talk to her." Unfortunately, she was nowhere to be found.

Rick ordered the nurse to alert Security and have all the exits sealed because we have a possible kidnapping here. He made this request while pulling out his badge. A description of Danny was given to all the guards. The local police were also called and an APB was immediately put out on Danny.

"He stole our baby!" I cried out.

Eric wrapped his arms around me. "We're going to get her back. I promise."

Rick said, "Katie, we're going to get him good this time. He's not going to get away with stealing my niece."

I ran back to the room to get dressed in order to help find our baby. Eric and the nurses said I wasn't strong enough, but a bulldozer couldn't have stopped me!

After I returned, Eric said, "I promise you Katie, I'll find her and bring her back to us."

I cried out, "She needs to be fed. She needs to stay warm. That monster won't know what to do with her. It's all my fault; she should have never been registered as Baby Jenkins in the first place."

Eric said, "Katie, you had no idea. It's not your fault, they had to put her under your name. The hospital had no right to let him near her. The staff was told about our situation, but the change in the shifts, should have been immediately alerted. I will get to the bottom of this after we get Ericka back!"

We all hugged and Rick said that we are going to do everything in our power and beyond, to get the baby back.

I said, "Time is of the essence. Danny has probably already left the hospital with her. It's been way too long already. I don't know how Danny even knew I was here having the baby."

We left the hospital in Rick's car. He asked, "Where do you think he would go? Do you think he left town?"

I said, "No, he would never leave his mother. Wait! That's it. Let's try Danny's mother's house." Rick called for backup and put on his siren and flashing lights. The dispatcher informed us that Danny was not at his house.

I gave Rick a description of his car upon arrival. We didn't see it parked on the street at his mothers. Rick parked the car and told us to wait in the car. He proceeded to check the garage. When he returned, Rick told us Danny is probably here, his car was parked in the garage. My heart pounded, as the backup arrived!

Rick wanted us to wait in the car. He said to let the police handle this. I pleaded with him to let me see if my baby is all right! Eric agreed with me, and against Rick's better judgement, he did let us come. The police surrounded the house. It was like watching a police drama in slow motion.

Rick was the one who pounded on the door. "Open up, police." After no response, Rick and Eric kicked the door down and quickly searched the house. I stood in the doorway waiting.

Suddenly, I heard Danny's voice, which made my hair stand on end. "You can't take her; she's mine." Danny, his mother, and the baby were huddled in a corner of her basement. The baby started to cry and I ran down to get her. Rick gently placed her in my arms.

The police handcuffed Danny. He was squirming and kicking. Danny shouted out, "I'll see you in hell, Katie. I'll get her back one way or another. This isn't over."

Rick said, "It's over for you pal."

Danny's mother interrupted, in her usual whiny voice, "He didn't do anything wrong."

"Try kidnapping." Rick said.

Danny blurted out, "How can I be charged with kidnapping my own kid?"

I stepped right up to him and said, "That's just the point, Danny. She's not your baby."

"What do you mean she's not mine, and where have you been, you tramp!" He continued squirming around.

I said, "All those years you cheated on me I just closed my eyes to it. And I allowed you to abuse me. But guess what Danny, when you were out gallivanting around with who knows what kind of trash, I fell in love, and conceived a beautiful baby girl with a real man!"

"You slut. You cheated on me." He shouted.

At that point, Eric couldn't contain himself anymore. He grabbed Danny by the throat and punched him in the stomach. "Shut your filthy mouth!" Eric demanded.

Danny's mother grabbed Eric while screaming, "Stop it. Leave my son alone, he's a good boy, give him back our baby."

Rick told one of the officers to take her upstairs. I kept hearing her annoying voice, until it faded into the distance.

Rick said, "We're going to settle this now, boy, before we haul your sorry ass back to the slammer. I hear that's your second home lately, Mr. Jenkins."

"That's my baby and I'm going to get her back from you, Katie."

Eric jumped in front of his face again and said, "That is my baby girl, not yours!"

"What? So you're the slut's boyfriend." Danny spit at Eric.

As calm and gentle as Eric is, he couldn't contain himself anymore. He grabbed Danny again and said, "If you so much as touch or look cross-eyed at Katie or my baby, it will be the last thing you ever do. That's a promise I will keep."

At this point, I was escorted off to the side by one of the officers. I had to feed Ericka, so I covered her ears and gently rocked her as she took eagerly to my breast.

Danny yelled, "Oh yeah, big boy. Tell me this stuff without the handcuffs."

Eric asked Rick for assistance in removing them. The cops said that it would be their pleasure. Danny's cocky attitude would finally be put to rest. Danny's handcuffs were removed and he lunged at Eric. Eric took him down immediately. The cops watched with smiles on their faces.

Eric said, "How does it feel big boy, to have a man stop you." I couldn't believe how strong Eric was. Danny didn't stand a chance! Eric got Danny good as he tried to get up, giving him one last punch! Eric said, "You're no man. You're just a smart-mouthed little punk who gets his rocks off by abusing women. You're a sick, pathetic loser Danny and you need help. You will regret the day you were born if you don't leave Katie and my baby alone. You can't control her anymore so get that through your thick skull, or I'll personally make sure your life is more worthless than it already is!" Eric turned and walked towards me. For the first time, Danny was at a loss for words as he lay on the floor. Rick told the cops to cuff him again, and to get him out of here.

As we walked up the stairs Rick said, "Don't worry Katie. We're going to lock him up. I can't say for how long, but kidnapping is a serious offense." I hugged Rick and thanked him a million times. Then I hugged Eric and said, "Thank you for everything."

We got back in the police car and waited for Rick to finish. He put Danny in another squad car and returned to us.

"Finally, a happy ending," Rick said. "Now its back to the hospital with all of you. He had the dispatcher inform the hospital that the baby was found, and that the mother and daughter were doing fine. He'd be bringing both mother and daughter back safe and sound.

I was so relieved to look down at our baby, who was unhurt by this whole event. I said to her as I grabbed her tiny hand, "What a mixed up traumatic day for your first day in this world. I love you my little angel." I vowed to myself that she would never know about this day.

Upon arrival at the hospital, we found most of the hospital staff waiting for us. A wheelchair was at the door. The Chief of Staff approached us to make his apologies. He assured us this would never happen again. He said, "We still hadn't found the nurse yet, but we will get to the bottom of this."

Rick posted a guard at the door to my room for the duration of my stay. The doctor said that Ericka can stay with me all night, and if she has to leave the room, he will personally escort her.

Eric said, "I will escort her as well."

The Chief said, "that would be acceptable under the circumstances."

The hospital staff decided to give me a different room. The doctor came in and gave the baby and I a thorough examination. After he finished he said, "Quite a day for both of you today. I am happy to say you are both doing fine. Eric, make sure they both get a lot of rest tonight."

Eric replied, "I will. Thanks again." The three of us settled in for the night. I fed her again and changed her. Ericka drifted into a sound sleep. Eric massaged my back and asked me to get some rest. "I'll stay awake all night so you don't have to worry about the baby." He said.

I said, "You need your sleep too. I'm so wound up I don't know if I'll be able to sleep."

Suddenly, Rick walked into the room. He said, "Guess what. They found the nurse. She was locked in a broom closet with her mouth taped up. Her hands and feet were also bound. Danny had knocked her out. When she finally came to, she started moaning and was heard by a doctor passing by. That's another charge we can pin on Danny, and that same nurse said that she's seen him here before. Also, she said someone had been calling periodically to ask if a Katie Jenkins was here having her baby. That's how he found out, purely by coincidence. She's pretty shaken up. Danny threatened to kill her and blow up the hospital if she didn't cooperate. She'll be testifying in court against him. I have to go and file my report now, but remember, a guard is posted at the door."

I said "Rick, before you go, I have a question for you. Would you like to be Ericka's godfather?"

He actually started to tear up. He said, "I'd love to Katie! Thank you for asking me, you're a very special girl, and I'm so glad you and Eric got together. Well, I'll let you both get some rest for now."

We told him how much we appreciated everything he's done for us.

He said, "That's what family is for."

Eric resumed massaging my back and I fell into a peaceful sleep. Before I knew it, a nurse was in my room taking my blood pressure and temperature. It still seemed dark outside, and for a very good reason, it was only 3:00 a.m. I looked in awe at Eric, who was sitting in the rocker cuddled up with the baby. He said that she started to get a little fussy, so he got her out to let me sleep a little longer.

I told Eric that I would switch places with him. "I'm sure she needs to be fed."

As the morning light peeked through the curtains, another nurse came in to check us both out again. Afterwards, the doctor came in and said we could both go home that afternoon. I got on the phone and told my parents that I would be home later today. "Boy, do I have a story to tell you." They asked if I needed anything and I told them that I didn't. "I would like all of you to come to our house tomorrow." My parents agreed.

Later that day we wrapped everything up at the hospital, and together as a family, took our first steps into a new and brighter future. Eric pulled the car around as the nurses and Security stayed with Ericka and I. We buckled the baby in her car seat and loaded up the car with all the gifts. I know now that everything will be all right. My destiny is finally fulfilled; I have that American Dream we all envision!

CHAPTER 35

As the weeks passed by, there was an endless stream of visiting family and friends. Ericka was adjusting fine to a regular routine. She was even starting to sleep through the night. We took endless pictures and videos of her!

Danny got his lawyer to reduce the charges due to temporary insanity. He claimed he was under the assumption that the baby was his. He said that he had no idea it could have been another man's child. Even though his sentence was reduced to a lesser charge, considering the circumstances, Danny was ordered not to come near the baby or me. The judge made it very clear to him not to disobey the restraining order, or Danny would have a high price to pay with plenty of jail time to think about it. He was put on probation for three years with orders to seek psychiatric counseling. There would be a stiff penalty for not showing up.

The day finally arrived to go to court to end my disastrous marriage. They had to postpone it a few times due to technicalities. My parents watched the baby and Eric and my brothers escorted me to court. Eric's uncle was my lawyer. I spotted Danny and his lawyer immediately upon entering the courtroom. He deliberately stared at us as we walked in. Only Danny, our lawyers, and me were allowed up front, where the proceeding would take place. I didn't have to say much, the two lawyers hashed out all the details. I would glance at Danny's table and see his eyes shooting daggers at me. It didn't matter. I wasn't in fear of him anymore, and I think he sensed that when I looked him straight in the eye. His control over me was finally over!

There wasn't much to split up. I had forfeited everything I left behind. He had no rights to Erika when my lawyer produced the paternity test results. I was granted the divorce on the grounds of cruel and inhuman treatment.

When we left the courtroom, I felt so alive and relieved! Everyone hugged me. While walking out of the building, I noticed Danny and his lawyer were not far behind. I turned around and said to him, "So Danny, how does it feel to not have control?" I smiled confidently, as I turned around and left. I knew he wouldn't dare have a single word to say back to me.

As a few more weeks passed, Eric and I announced our wedding date. Life was so grand! Eric turned out to be my soul mate and my knight in shining armor. Second chances really do happen, when you really trust in yourself enough to take that chance!

As more time passed things got hectic. When Ericka was four months old, we had her Christening. Afterwards, it was time to plan the wedding. Our guest list was growing bigger and bigger. Eric wanted a huge wedding to show off as he puts it, his two "beautiful girls" who are the love of his life.

We had our wedding at the same restaurant that we shared our very first kiss. My sisters and his brothers and some friends stood up for us. Eric had a special stroller made to resemble a white coach. Sue and Joan pushed Ericka down the aisle in it, dressed as a little bride. She looked adorable! Limousines chauffeured around the wedding party, while we rode in a horse-driven, chauffeured carriage.

While in the carriage travelling from the church to the reception, Eric opened a small box, and put a beautiful, sparkling heart necklace around my neck. "Eric, it's so beautiful. Thank you."

Eric said, "You stole my heart away. I love you with all my heart."

The rest of the Wedding Day went great. The restaurant was beautiful and the food was superb. We took a lot of pictures. Both of our parents took turns watching the baby. We decided not to go on a honeymoon yet. Instead, we went to a lavish hotel, while my in-laws watched Ericka at our house.

Our wedding night was unforgettable! We truly gave a new meaning to the words "wedding night." The room was spectacular; it had a pool in the suite. We skinny-dipped at 3:00 a.m. Sleep was the last thing on our minds.

After a few more months passed by, I became pregnant again! We had a second daughter as precious as our first. She also had a head full of jet-black hair and big brown eyes, just like Eric's. We named her Victoria Melissa Sommers, we will call her Torri for short. I couldn't imagine my life being any more fulfilled and complete! Eric is a wonderful husband and father; I truly am blessed!

Danny stopped bothering us for now, however, Tim goes into my brother's bar and keeps us informed of Danny's shenanigans. Tim told them that Shelly, the waitress that Danny got pregnant resulting from his affair, is now living with him. He convinced Shelly and their little girl to come and live with him, telling Shelly he will support them totally. Tim said, "Danny still has a problem, even though he has been through counseling. It obviously hasn't helped, since he's beating up Shelly in front of their child, and she's afraid to leave him because of his threats to kill her and their daughter both!" Tim said, "You would think that Shelly would have learned never to trust Danny, after he broke her jaw the first time!" Tim doesn't want to get involved anymore, since him and Michelle split up over family problems. Tim also said Shelly confided in him that when her and Danny fight, Danny calls her "Katie" instead of Shelly. I felt really bad for her and her daughter. I know only too well, of the sick and twisted evil mind that belongs to no other than Danny Jenkins!

CHAPTER 36

One day Eric and I were watching the news, when they announced the arrest of a man named Danny Jenkins, who was accused of shooting and killing his live-in girlfriend. I was horrified! "That could have been me." I shouted! "He really did have it in him to murder someone!" At that moment, I felt such sorrow for Shelly's family, and especially for her daughter.

In the days that followed, Rick gave us the gruesome details of the events that took place on that fateful night. Allegedly, Shelly stormed out of the house after having a huge fight with Danny. Danny stayed home with the child, and waited for her to come home with the lights out, while getting totally drunk. He jumped Shelly from behind as she walked through the kitchen door. They screamed obscenities at each other and had a fistfight. A neighbor called the police after hearing gunshots! When the police arrived, they had to knock the door down. There, they found Danny hovering over Shelly's bleeding body. The gun was still in his hands. She was beaten badly, and had been shot point-blank three times in the chest. Shelly never had a chance. The police said, Danny just kept on repeating over and over, Katie, I told you not to ever leave me. He just kept on repeating my name, over Shelly's body. The worst part was the sight of his three-year old girl, standing in the doorway clutching a blanket in one hand and a stuffed bear in the other. She was crying hysterically, "Mommy, Mommy!" They think she might have witnessed the murder. According to the autopsy reports, Shelly had numerous fractures and scars. She must have endured a lot of abuse." I put my head down and cried for the little girl, hoping she would be all right. Rick said that Shelly's parents are taking care of her.

Eric said, "Katie, I can't even imagine the beatings you must have endured at the hands of Danny. I promise you, you'll always be safe with me."

I said, "I know I will. I used to be haunted by the memories of Danny's torment, but that was the past. Those nightmares are gone. Eric, you not only saved my life, but you saved my mind as well. I wish I could express what I'm feeling right now, but words cannot capture all my feelings for you. They go deeper than you'll ever know."

As time passed on, Danny's murder trial came and went. He couldn't worm his way out of this mess; not this time. He was convicted of pre-meditated, second-degree murder, carrying a life sentence. If Shelly's family has their way, he will never see daylight again. The judge gave him the maximum sentence with no chance of parole. Shelly's parents are raising Shelly's daughter, and are now trying to pick up the pieces of their lives.

As for Eric and I, we went on to live "happily ever after." I finished beauty school, and opened up my own hair salon. Three years later, we had our third child, a beautiful boy who looks just like Eric. We named him Eric Thomas Sommers. I thought we were blessed and complete until our fourth child arrived. She is just as beautiful as our other daughters are. We named her Ashley Taylor Sommers. Now our family was totally complete! We fulfilled our circle of life, and obtained the great American dream!

AFTERWORD

Life can be grand or it can be complicated. Whatever life holds for us, I have gratefully learned that we all have an enormous power within ourselves. It's called the "Human Spirit." It allows us to choose, and to follow our own destiny. That's the beauty of the one precious life that God gives us. So use it wisely, for when you least expect it, a twist of fate in your favor will help you……. **"Break out of the Darkness."**

About the Author

Linda lives in New York with her husband and four children. She has been a self-employed hair stylist for 20 years, yet she has always had a passion to write books. Currently writing children's books illustrated by her artistic children, this novel is her first, with many more to come!